KU-605-568

ACTRESS

BY THE SAME AUTHOR

FICTION

The Portable Virgin
The Wig My Father Wore
What Are You Like?
The Pleasure of Eliza Lynch
The Gathering
Taking Pictures
Yesterday's Weather
The Forgotten Waltz
The Green Road

NON-FICTION

Making Babies

ACTRESS

Anne Enright

JONATHAN CAPE
LONDON

1 3 5 7 9 10 8 6 4 2

Jonathan Cape, an imprint of Vintage,
20 Vauxhall Bridge Road,
London SW1V 2SA

Jonathan Cape is part of the Penguin Random House group of companies
whose addresses can be found at global.penguinrandomhouse.com.

Penguin
Random House
UK

Copyright © Anne Enright 2020

Anne Enright has asserted her right to be identified as the author of this
Work in accordance with the Copyright, Designs and Patents Act 1988

The lyrics from 'The Sea Around Us' are by Dominic Behan, used by
permission of Emerald Music (Ireland) Ltd.

First published by Jonathan Cape in 2020

penguin.co.uk/vintage

A CIP catalogue record for this book is available from the British Library

ISBN 9781787332065
ISBN 9781787332072 (export)

Typeset in 11/14 pt Stempel Garamond
by Integra Software Services Pvt. Ltd, Pondicherry

Printed and bound in Great Britain by Clays Ltd, Elcograf S.p.A.

Penguin Random House is committed to a sustainable future for our business,
our readers and our planet. This book is made from Forest Stewardship
Council® certified paper.

MIX
Paper from
responsible sources
FSC® C018179

'the more I applauded, the better, it seemed to me, did Berma act.'

In Search of Lost Time

PEOPLE ASK ME, 'What was she like?' and I try to figure out if they mean as a normal person: what was she like in her slippers, eating toast and marmalade, or what was she like as a mother, or what she was like as an actress – we did not use the word star. Mostly though, they mean what was she like before she went crazy, as though their own mother might turn overnight, like a bottle of milk left out of the fridge. Or they might, themselves, be secretly askew.

Something happens as they talk to me. I am used to it now. It works in them slowly; a growing wonder, as though recognising an old flame after many years.

'You have her eyes,' they say.

People loved her. Strangers, I mean. I saw them looking at her and nodding, though they failed to hear a single word she said.

And, yes, I have her eyes. At least, I have the same colour eyes as my mother; a hazel that, in her case, people liked to call green. Indeed, whole paragraphs were penned about bog and field, when journalists looked into my mother's eyes. And we have the same way of blinking, slow and fond, as though thinking of something very beautiful.

I know this because she taught me how to do it. 'Think about cherry blossom,' she said, 'drifting on the wind.' And sometimes, I do.

Such were the gifts I got from Katherine O'Dell, star of stage and screen.

'How are you, oh, mother of mine?'

'Never better,' she used to say, and the blossoms drifted by the tree-load, when she looked at me.

There was a man in the kitchen in Dartmouth Square (where everything important in my life seems to have happened), who knew someone who had slept with Marilyn, and 'Never washed,' he said. Some evening in my childhood I came down the stairs to hear this news, and he was such a nice old man, it stained me ever since. So when people ask, 'What was she like?' I have an urge to say, 'Pretty clean, actually,' and then to add, 'I mean, by the standards of the day.'

So all right. Here she is, Katherine O'Dell making her breakfast, requiring her breakfast from the fridge and the cupboards, some of which delight her and some of which let her down. Where is it, where is it, here it is! Yes! The marmalade. The sun is coming through the window, the smoke from her cigarette rises and twists in an elegant, double strand. What can I say? When she ate toast and marmalade she was like anyone else eating toast and marmalade, though the line between lip and skin, whatever that is called, is very precise, even when you are not seeing it on a cinema screen, twelve feet long.

So, here she is, eating toast. She works fast. She holds the slice of toast to her mouth, bites and chews, then bites again. Swallows. She does this maybe three or four times, sets the thing back on the plate. She takes it up for one more bite: leaves it down. After which, there is a little tug of love which the toast loses; a little wavy-over thing she

2

does with her hand, a shimmy of rejection or desire. No, she will not have any more toast.

She picks up the phone receiver and dials. Everything was 'marvellous!' when she was on this phone; a beige thing on the kitchen wall with a long clapped-out curly cord that you had to duck under as she paced and smoked, saying 'marvellous!' while giving me the wink, indicating her coffee, or a glass of wine that was out of reach, with a pointed finger and a rolling hand.

'Just marvellous,' she might say.

Or she talks to me, a girl of eight or nine sitting at the table in a pink cotton dress brought back from America. She involves the dog who waits under the table, like a dog in the movies, for scraps and crumbs. Mostly she speaks to the ceiling, at the place where it meets the wall. Her eyes rove along this line as though looking for ideas up there, or for justice. Yes, that is what she wants. She tucks her face down quickly to light another cigarette. She exhales.

The toast is now fully ignored. The toast is dead to her now. The chair is pushed back, the cigarette stubbed out on the actual plate. After which she gets up and walks away. Someone else will dispose of all that. Because I think I mentioned that my mother was a star. Not just on screen or on the stage, but at the breakfast table also, my mother Katherine O'Dell was a star.

An hour or so later she is back in the kitchen saying God dammit God dammit. She is banging dishes around. She might throw the toast out through the open window or crack the plate on the edge of the sink. Because Kitty is not around. Kitty is shopping for dinner, she is on a day off, nursing her cancerous sister. Kitty is never there when you want her, though she was there all the time. And when she arrives, laden or sad, the plate was an accident and

Kitty is a treasure who must be courted and spoiled. Our housekeeper, Kitty, had a daily in to clean, she had a fancy carpet sweeper and one of the first dishwashers in the country. It came in time for my twenty-first birthday, there was even a photograph: my mother opening the door in a shock of steam while Kitty, in the background, sticks to her own thoughts and to the big Belfast sink.

My mother put me into a dress for the occasion. We have moved on from the pink American cottons, through three-button pinafores and drop-waisted short dresses over skinny, raw knees. I am twenty-one. My arms are soft and mottled white: I am too tall. For my birthday, I sport a swamp-green and sickish pink thing with tulle pompoms on a long tulle skirt. My mother – there she is, holding the birthday cake high – wears black. In front of her is a crowd of people, and also me. There is something overdetermined about the faces in this second photograph. I look at them, over the years, their cheeks blotched, their eyes fixed, and I wonder what they feel.

Star struck.

You could look at those people for quite a while.

Their eyes watch her from behind a mask of delight, and it is not about attraction, this look, it is more about disaster. There is a painful stretch to some of the smiles that is envy about to happen. Especially the women. There is no denying this – my mother made women, especially, difficult to themselves.

In the middle of it all, is my own face at twenty-one, dreading the limelight and sweetened, at the same time, by her attention. The flames on the cake burn small and straight. I am held in my mother's gaze, while all around us are the fervent and the savage. Or maybe it is just the drink made them look that way. All around us are the faces of the crowd.

4

It was a terrible party. At least for me. I had graduated that summer and most of my college friends were already scattered. A couple of girls from school showed up too early in borrowed dresses, made uncertain, I thought, by all the junk in the house, but more probably by its size. They sat in the upstairs living room, a place furnished, one way or another, from the stages of Dublin, so you were always sitting in character, you were just not sure which one. A button back sofa in navy velvet, a carved wooden chair, fit for a Borgia, a little painted Scandinavian stool. We perched on these discarded stories and offered our own small tales of woe – unreliable boyfriends, back-stabbing girlfriends, mothers who were a complete nightmare. At least my schoolfriends talked about their mothers: I have always been, in this respect, properly shy. My efforts, that night, undone a little by the sound of her in the kitchen, Being Well-Known, as the whiskey sank and the noise level rose.

It was hard to find a tone.

A bunch of college drama types trailed in after ten, and sat around. Someone turned the lights down and the music up, and Melanie from school ended up snogging the president of DramSoc beside the bathroom door. Because that also happened in the late summer of 1973. You got waylaid. You went out to do your hair and ended up in a rummaging heap, stuck to the wall.

Some time towards midnight there were arrivals from the show at the Gate, who gathered around the upright piano, and the party settled down into singing and drinking like many another Saturday night in Dartmouth Square. My mother's crowd drifted up to the living room to be ignored by my own friends for being old. Or maybe all men were old in those days, with their baggy sports jackets and packets of fags, there was no difference between twenty-five and forty-five, everyone wore a tie.

5

Over the years, my mother entertained, in her big old kitchen, a shifting band of big, drinking men, all of them good company, some well known. They came to her for refuge, for conversation and carelessness, and the kind of approval that no thinking man, in those days, could expect in his own home. These were the men who charmed my childhood. They palmed me pound notes, recited Yeats before bed, sat me on their knees for teasing, or for various kinds of complicity. *Do you see that one over there, he sang for the Pope.* I loved some of them, and some of them – as a small revenge on my mother, perhaps – were truly fond of me.

But I didn't love them any more. I mean they did not excite me, at twenty-one. Perhaps they were not as glamorous a bunch as they used to be. Various *types*. A few ravenous wives. The girls who trailed along were either tourists – you could tell by the bawneen sweaters – or too clever and far too drunk. The men on whom they set their crocheted caps were theatre types, intellectuals, musicians, writers – they all wrote, one way or the other – and they were all, at least to themselves, quite important. There was talk of jobs in the *Irish Times* or 'out in' UCD. *Are you out in UCD?* A place that was exactly two miles down the road. Hughie Snell was 'out in Montrose' which meant he worked in television, and none of them, it goes without saying, were 'out' in any other way.

They took their cue from Niall Duggan, a courtly type who spoke in puns, inversions, mock-ee-yah Irish and *Sic transit*, sonorous, brief bursts of Latin, which always triggered heavy assent, *Carpe, yes, carpe indeed.* It was a high style of bullshit, quite formal, with no jokes about sex, no disrespecting women. Or no mentioning women, now I come to think about it. Except face to face, when he was often obscene.

Hard to explain.

Everything was a reference. Silent O'Boyle, for example, was named for the song by Thomas Moore and some incident at the urinals in the Palace Bar. *Silent O'Boyle be the ro-oar of thy wa-ters.* It was all both base and weirdly ennobled and even their lechery was over-styled. Silent O'Boyle talked to my right breast on the wonders of Baudelaire, before switching – in case it felt excluded, perhaps – to the left, for a teasing aperçu about the young Rimbaud. Then Duggan himself asking me, 'Would you ever get up on that character from Faulkner? What about Salinger? You would. You'd shag that miserable streak of ennui and the course of American letters, don't argue with me now, would be permanently changed. You'd save his life and wreck the book. That's the problem, you see? There's the perfidy.' When I was in first year, Duggan who was, of course, one of my lecturers out in UCD, promised me first-class honours in exchange for my virginity, and my mother said, 'She would never settle for less than all your worldly goods, Niall,' and then, 'Leave the child alone.'

They drank until their eyes set – like jelly, almost – blind to all of their impossibilities. At least that is how I thought of it, at twenty-one, when I did not drink because I did not like the taste, and these men could look at me any way they liked, because they were so old, and I was already in love with you.

At the given moment, her friend Hughie Snell sang, as he always did, in a high, trapped tenor.

'When other lips and other hearts
Their tales of love shall tell'

He sort of stooped over it; his mouth working around the vowel sounds, so they came out wonderfully squeezed.

'In such a mow-mint I bu-hut ask
Thot yoou'll re-memburr meee!'

It was an aria from *The Bohemian Girl* that was (and we were tired knowing this) a great favourite of the young Jimmy Joyce. Hughie claimed to be hopelessly in love with my mother, and people allowed him that, because he was so clearly homosexual. He put all this tormentedness into the song, which was a lovely thing, and his voice brought the vast night into the room.

Even the college types went still. I leant against the wall with tears in my eyes, and I thought about you, off Interrailing into the early autumn with your English Olivia. I wondered where you were: Pisa, or Verona, or Bratislava. You had left me, this time for good. Our love was impossible, you said. Or, no. You just needed a holiday, and Olivia was the perfect person for that. There was nothing wrong with Olivia.

You never did tell me how it all went. There were no anecdotes about squalid train carriages or Italian *pensions* with pink frilly lampshades. And you never told me what she was like in bed, though I did keep asking (I thought there was some trick to all that), you just smiled and said, 'Not like you.'

Hughie Snell pulled the last note through pursed lips, and lifted his eyebrows a little, as though surprised by the length of it. There was applause. After which, the piano player segued into a simple melody picked out on the high notes; a call that was answered by a voice on the stairs. We turned towards the door and saw a flurry of yellow light, followed by the bright flames of a birthday cake that was carried into the room by my mother. She walked towards me, her pace scooping and slow. She *processed.* And the song she had chosen to sing was that glorious old chestnut, 'Que Sera Sera'.

You must know that, by this time, she rarely sang, and certainly never on stage. 'I am too old,' she said, remembering,

8

perhaps, some unrepeatable perfection that brought the house to its feet in London, or New York, or Dublin town. But my goodness: my mother had a voice that arrived from everywhere. It slipped out of her mouth then came back to you from the far corner. Katherine O'Dell did not sing so much as pull the song out of the walls. She called it into being, and the air was charged with sound.

After which – Don't blow them out yet! – we leaned in for the photograph; an official snapper, brought by the social diarist from the *Evening Press*. Mama gave the lens her back, and a three-quarter profile. It was all staged. There is no doubt the cake was timed, the walk, the snap. I know that. And I also know my mother sang, that night, for me alone.

We all did 'Happy Birthday' then, and I blew the candles out. The cake was from the Tea Time Express and stuffed with cream.

Now that I look at the photograph, I see that my own dress is actually lovely; this fright of drab tulle. It made me look pale and interesting. And my mother's dress is a complete classic. Wide skirt, narrow bodice, three-quarter sleeves. It has a fold-over white satin boat neck that turned, as she angled herself away from the camera, into a reverse collar descending in two white puritan points down below her shoulder blades. Lots of bare skin. Early nineteen fifties, at a guess. Maybe Dior.

The headline reads, **Katherine O'Dell at Home**, and there is a second, smaller picture, of my mother with the new dishwasher, 'one of the first in Ireland, apparently!' with a bright look on her face that says, 'I have no idea how to work this thing.'

Katherine O'Dell enjoys her newly modernised kitchen, in Dublin's elegant Dartmouth Square.

I have so few clippings and, you know, I miss my mother every day. But I still can't read the damn things. They are unreadable. This one – which I treasure! – was written by a poisonous little soak you saw about town wearing a tuxedo and bow tie. He had a car and a driver, and middle-class women made actual squeaking sounds when he walked into their parties and occasions. Then he'd go back to Burgh Quay at three in the morning, and sit like Rodin's thinker before producing, for example, this:

Home from her latest triumph on Broadway, Katherine O'Dell took time this week to talk to our diarist Terry O'Sullivan about matters theatrical and domestic. She recently was in receipt of a dishwashing machine, 'The first in the country, at least I think it might be.' She got the idea in America, where such amenities are quite the norm, or so says the globe-trotting muse of writers as various as Samuel Beckett and Arthur Kopit. Does Hollywood call? More faintly, these days. 'There is nothing to compete, for me, with the thrill of the live stage.'

Beneath the cake picture he writes:

Coming of Age. A star-studded attendance for daughter Carmel's birthday party, including Christopher Cazenove, fresh from his performance at the Gate, fellow actor Hughie Snell, movie impresario Boyd O'Neill, architect Douglas Kelly, his wife Jenny and daughter Máire who has just graduated with honours from UCD. Máire now plans to work in the travel industry.

Máire is, of course, the prettiest girl there. She did not go into the travel industry. She got married and moved to Monkstown. The journalist also gets my name wrong, at my own birthday party. I am not called Carmel, wherever that came from. My name is Norah FitzMaurice.

I look at this clipping and wonder why it, of all possible things, should endure when so much else is lost and gone. The picture was such a fake, even at the time, but the years have made it somehow true: Katherine's bare back so elegant, the faces in front of her vivid, my own face (I am down at cake level – perhaps there was a chair) blinking up at her, faithful and bright. Her fine profile looking down at me.

The headline, the article, it all points to that thing, the actress and her overshadowed child. The picture adds to the lie that I am a poor copy of my mother, that she was timeless, and I am not – the iconic gives birth to the merely human. But that was not how it was between us. That is not how we felt about ourselves.

It was a great dress, the Maybe-Dior, I can see that now, but as I remember her that evening, she was wearing a hairpiece that left me mortified. She dyed her hair when other women did not dye their hair, or not so dark, and her face – according to herself – was gone. Katherine O'Dell was forty-five years old. She wasn't forty-five the way people do forty-five these days. She smoked thirty a day and she drank from 6 till whenever. My mother never ate a vegetable unless she was on a diet; she did not, I think, possess a pair of shoes without heels. She talked all day, and got bitter in the evening, when the wine made her face swell and her eyes very green.

Despite her posing, as though for *Life* magazine, with her new white goods, the truth is that Katherine O'Dell was, at forty-five, finished. Professionally, sexually. In those days, when a woman hit thirty she went home and shut the door.

So it is to her great credit that my mother refused to lie down and die. That she threw a party and put the money into an Ib Jorgensen dress for me and hunted through the old boxes and trunks for something she could still get into. One last time.

She was pregnant, the first whirl of the dress. I remember her telling me this as we got ready for the evening ahead. She plucked at the cloth below the high waist and said, 'Look. Room for two.'

There we were, standing in front of her bedroom mirror, me outside the dress as she remembered me inside the dress, inside her. She told me that, when she was expecting, she needed a few cheating inches, that was all. And a higher bust. Hoist up your bra straps and, Everything up! she said. Up, up, up! No one need ever know.

She did not say why such a thing should be hidden, and I did not ask. I knew I was her secret joy.

'Up! up! up!' she said, piling my hair up on top of my head.

I was the best thing ever.

'You're lovely,' she said, as I picked up a marsh-green pompom out of my lap, and let it fall.

I got my first-class honours, by the way. Not that it matters now. Not in the slightest. But late that night, maddened by the cake perhaps, Duggan said it was all because of my tits. I had really clever-looking tits.

'Fuck off, Niall,' I said.

And that is the other thing I can't explain, the fact that I was so drawn to him. He was the one I wanted to talk to, in any given room.

'Imagination is murder,' he said. 'But you know that, don't you. You know that in your bones.'

'Imagination is imagination,' I said.

'Who are you going to kill?' and he drew his hand back to indicate the crowd.

'How about you, Niall? I could kill you, if you like.'

'You already have, my darling. You already have.'

Indeed, the man sweated through skin so thick and white, he looked pretty much dead to me.

He was only forty-eight. Unbelievably. I had to look it up, to check. Niall Duggan drank and sobered up and drank again, he molested his students and snarled at his students, he shafted his colleagues and gave jobs to his friends, many of whom were mediocre. When I was twenty-one, I thought he was already finished, but he lived on – he kept spreading all that around – for another thirty years.

My mother died in 1986. I might as well get this fact over with. She was fifty-eight years old.

And on the night of my twenty-first birthday, as I recall, I could not bear to have her stand beside me. She bulged through the black dress in little rolls that threatened the seams at the waist and the whole rig smelt of the back of the wardrobe. This was the seventies, we were far too modern for black, and the word vintage was only used for cars. The dress was a costume, it made her look demented, I thought. So there you are. Did I already know she was crazy? Just the way all mothers are crazy to their daughters, all mothers are wrong.

There was a stage in the drinking, when faces went slow and the room filled with difficulty. People repeated themselves, or walked suddenly away. And just when it got too sticky – a fight in the corner, a woman crying on the landing – a different kind of music was struck up. If you went downstairs, you would find the party lodged in the kitchen; a few musicians around the table in from a late session in a local pub, the first sweetness of mandolin strings, little shivers and precursors of songs to come.

There was an amount of politics involved in an evening like this. It was a kind of rule of thumb that the later the arrival, the more sympathetic to the Republican Cause, and these particular musicians came last of all. A small group of men in suede jackets and wide ties, with differently patterned facial hair – as seen, indeed, on the cover of their first album, released later that year. There were sideburns, and long horseshoe moustaches; one of them had little wiggy things sprouting from either cheek. If you put it all together, I used to think, you would get the complete beard.

In the silence after a tune we waited – as though waiting was a solid thing – for Máire Rahilly, *Go on. You will.* A singer who made my mother look almost suburban; with a keening voice that cut right into you, she was grief in motion and pure wild. And the song Máire Rahilly sang, when she picked up her head to sing it, was in Irish. My college friends winced as they realised it, and looked around, as though for an excuse to go.

But nobody did go. Nobody ever left or was obliged to leave a night in Dartmouth Square. No one said goodbye, they just melted away. And though my mother always had a drink in her hand, she became, on those nights, more and more marvellously sober. The stories the next day were never about Katherine O'Dell who was Prospera in a tempest of drink and illusion. She was the hostess and enhancer, the one who stood back and let the badness roll.

I don't remember much by way of preparation, there was certainly no agonising over the guest list. She picked up the phone to ten or twelve people and sixty showed up, or a hundred and sixty, all of them known to each other, at least by reputation. Some sworn enemies – even of the hostess. I learned to rescue her early: my mother eye-rolling against a wall, cornered by an old schoolfriend, 'I never liked you, Katherine, not for years. I don't know why. I have tried to like you. I just can't.'

Dublin was a small town in those days, even the bullies were small, but the gossip was stupendous, and I know it wasn't healthy but I do miss it. We have all got very disconnected since, which is to say, sane.

And although he was there in the photograph, I have no strong recollection of Boyd O'Neill from that night. He was tall. He tended to drift through a crowd. Some time around the witching hour, you would see him in a corner disagreeing with his old sparring partner Niall Duggan. Two fighting cocks, the pair of them; O'Neill impressive and long in a turtleneck and jacket, Duggan a shambles in his stained suit. One a high curve, the other a low snarl, close to the ground. This is how I dream of them now, like a cartoon in *Dublin Opinion*, all vanity and comic violence, but they were dangerous too. I mean, they got inside you.

Of course you have to let them in. And I never gave Boyd O'Neill much room. He was, besides, too handsome for me. But I was drawn to Duggan, who had a rare ability to get into your head – those slightly bulbous grey eyes he had – it was as though he was fighting his way back out through your skin. I was a young woman, better looking than I knew, but I think that Niall Duggan did not want to possess me or to penetrate me, so much as to *be* me. Or to stop being me.

Is that a thing? As my daughter might say. Is that even a thing, now?

And I think it was all dreadful for him. Dreadful. That when he spoke to a clever woman of twenty-one, he could not hear himself think, there was such a clamour in his brain.

If you went back upstairs then, during the last rags of the evening, for someone's lost jacket or bag, you would see the reception rooms empty and disastrous, the furniture askew, and everywhere the silhouettes of bottles and glasses like a miniature cityscape, proliferating on tables and sideboards. Epic. Kitty would make her way through it the next day, ignoring broken glass as she worked the dustpan and brush, failing to see or judge the contents of the ashtray. My mother might pretend to be mortified, but I knew that Kitty felt no pain about our lives. The details did not interest her. She had enough troubles of her own.

But I am too far ahead of myself, here.

As is perhaps too well known, my mother was committed to the Central Mental Hospital in 1980 after an assault on that same Boyd O'Neill, a film producer more famous in Ireland than outside of it. She shot him in the foot – spawning in that moment a hundred Dublin punchlines. But it was all desperately upsetting, not least for O'Neill, who supported, at some risk to his reputation, a charge of attempted murder. My mother's performance, after she was arrested, gave hope to the defence – it was so badly done, we thought it must be real. She laughed at the wrong times, she crooned to herself and tugged at her hair. When the case finally came to trial, we found not one but two tame psychiatrists to declare her insane; she left the court in the same white van in which she had arrived. After three more years, she was released from the asylum, rattling with pills – a much reduced, soon to be terminally ill woman who was invisible, on the street, to those who passed her by.

O'Neill – and this is very important for me to say – endured in those same years repeated hospitalisations. He spent nearly as much time in various institutions as my mother. What was described in the papers as the loss of his big toe was, in fact, a messy and splintered wound that was stuck back together in five hours of surgery and subsequently refused to heal. There were four separate amputations, as they chased the problem up his afflicted right leg. He lived on antibiotics. He never worked again. The final, most successful, amputation ended just below the knee but he found the prosthesis unwearably difficult and could not sleep for phantom pains. My mad mother shot Boyd O'Neill in the foot, and the whole world thought that was sort of funny. But 'funny' is not the right word. Or it is only one word. For what happened there.

I was twenty-eight at the time of the assault. I struggled on for the next year or more, but there came a day when I could not make it in to work. I was writing a book, I said. And then that became true. I wrote, not one, but many books. But I never wrote the one I needed to write, the one that was shouting out to be written, the story of my mother and of Boyd O'Neill's wound.

SOME MONTHS AGO I got an email from someone called Holly Devane, requesting an interview about my mother, the kind of thing I would have turned down at one time, but I was getting nostalgic for interviews – it had been a while – and regretful, also, for my own long failure, as I thought, at that particular game. As a novelist, I mean. Not that it mattered a damn. The articles got written. Books got sold, more or less. It was a small agony, of the most banal kind.

So I invited Holly Devane out to the house in Bray, and I gave directions because it is not on any GPS, which is one of the many good things about this little town by the sea, that there are corners and cul-de-sacs known only to the people who live there, they are so old and tucked away.

In the morning before she came, I looked about my life a little and found it satisfactory. I straightened pictures, ran a cloth along the skirting boards. I mustered myself, that is, for whatever accusation was about to be levelled. Or none. Sometimes, they don't accuse you of anything. They don't try to prise anything out of you, or prise you out of anything – your shell, your complacency. Sometimes they don't bother disbelieving you (it must take so much energy,

I used to think), they just have a normal conversation, take notes, leave. After which they write something enormously wrong-headed, just to keep you on your toes.

But. You know. Not always.

Holly Devane arrived at the door on a blustery, cold day in spring. Her car was not parked so much as abandoned along the neighbour's wall. A child, it seemed to me: dark pea-coat, beanie, scarf, wispy blonde hair. She was, she told me twenty minutes later, 'Not really' when it came to the business of men. 'She wasn't really. She was actually.' Though she did like (men), she explained, and she sometimes dated (men), it wasn't, you know, in that hetero-normative way.

I was not sure how a conversation about my mother had turned into this, and so soon. I had a wood fire going in the grate, a cafetière ready to plunge on a tray that also contained oatmeal flapjacks that looked home-made. Holly had pulled up a stool and set a flat little video camera, or perhaps it was her phone, at a profoundly unflattering angle to film whatever she could coax me to say. Then she failed to turn it on. But she was terrific: kind and clever and gusting with enthusiasm; she would make a great English teacher, I thought. And she was well informed. She was writing her doctoral thesis about my mother, and this also made my heart jolt a little, in the hopes that Katherine O'Dell might, for once, be well served. So I looked at this girl quite keenly, while pretending not to look at her: the fit, restless little body, the flourishing intelligence that ran so close to stupidity. Her youth.

Holly did not yet have a title, but she hoped one day to turn her thesis into a published book. When I heard the word 'book' I shoved the plate of flapjacks at her but she declined. She asked a question, then another. I said, 'Oh well, that. You know that was just,' and it was twenty minutes or so later (sometime after the declaration about hetero-normativity) that I realised that 'Katherine O'Dell' was, as ever, about her, 'Holly Devane', and more crucially about her refusal of the hetero-normative, whatever that was: Adam and Eve in the Garden, and the forty thousand years of bullshit that ensued.

'What kind of a mother was she?'

'Well,' I said. 'She was mine.'

The child smelt around me, as people often do, for hints of maternal cruelty, narcissism, neglect and it was easy enough to let her down. I have had years of practice at this, and not just with journalists – my mother had been for so long beloved of a particular type of gay Irish man. But Holly's angle was new. She was interested in how my mother styled her femininity, by which she meant her sexual style, and this was not something I wanted to ponder for too long.

'She slept with men,' I said.

I did not know why I had let this girl into my house, suddenly. Here I was again, stuck in some other person's curiosity, conned into it by my own loneliness or, in this case, by my mother's loneliness – that gaping sense you get of the grave. She was so long dead. And I would give anything, even now, to bring her in from the cold.

Thinking all this, feeling the pang of it, distracted me from Holly Devane, who was telling me now that she was not interested in seeing my mother as a mirror, but as an act-or (she broke the word into two self-conscious syllables). She would portray my mother in all her radical subjectivity, by which she meant that she wanted to de-iconise her and show her as an agent in the world. Doing things.

'Shooting people,' I said.

'Yes. That too,' said Holly, and fell silent a moment.

I thought she was going to ask about politics, then. In the mid seventies, my mother liked to hang out with IRA men in New York and Boston – but mostly, I wanted to tell Holly Devane, in a hetero-normative way. It wasn't a shooting thing, or a terrorism thing, though it was a cause of some scandal in Dublin at the time. Or perhaps a better word is 'unease', because it was all very well singing rebel songs for nostalgic Irish Americans, but there was nothing nostalgic about an orthopaedic ward in Belfast after a kneecapping or a bomb. The romance went out of it very fast for most people, I mean, but not for my mother, who believed in a United Ireland, no matter what.

I took a breath to explain all this to Holly Devane, but it was too much to explain.

'I think they just used her for publicity purposes,' I said.

Holly blinked. She was too young to remember the Troubles, had no interest in Northern Ireland. She was not even interested in the IRA. Instead, she launched, with some wobbling along the runway, on a question that is, now, almost obligatory.

'I just wanted to ask you. I am sorry to ask this. But I thought it might be a, you know, a right question to ask. Do you ever wonder if she was abused as a child?'

'No, I don't,' I said. 'I really don't. I am glad you asked me that.'

I got rid of her, eventually. Fondness at the doorstep. Making promises I would not keep. An urge to shove her in the back, as she turned towards the gate, an urge to call after her, at the last minute. And a fight four hours later, when you said I should write the damn book myself.

We were in the kitchen, after dinner. A low sun was shining through my plants on the windowsill above the sink, where I had chilli in a yellow tin pot, and supermarket coriander. At a certain moment, the window behind them flared into a silvered scrim of dust and grime, so you could not see through the glass for the dirt of it.

I was really not in a great mood.

'Why don't you write it yourself?' you said.

And not – if you don't mind me pointing this out – in a nice way. Not in a long-suffering, husband-of-the-writer way. No. The tone you used was one of bottomless irritation, as though my failure to write this book was pretty much on a par with my failure to stack the dishwasher, which was what you were trying to do at the time.

So I was eating the last of the flapjacks and discussing the astonishing youth of Holly Devane, which made us both feel old. I was not stacking the dishes because the grief I hold for my mother made domestic labour briefly impossible, and you were a martyr to my incompetence in this and other matters. And besides, the damn casserole dish needed soaking, which was, in the circumstances (approaching old age, being in the business of dishwasher stacking utterly alone), a complete pain for you.

'Why don't you write it yourself?' you said.

'Like what?'

'Just saying.'

'Like, what do you want me to write?'

You raised both hands in the air.

Later, I woke in the night and you were also awake. I heard you swallow – a little glottal give-away in the darkness.

So there we were.

It was, perhaps, four o'clock in the morning. A bright night outside, the room was showing its dark shapes, against which I closed my eyes to sleep again. You were on your back, face to the ceiling. After a while, you swallowed again.

It used to be a sign of desire, back in the day. When we were nineteen or twenty and just starting out we would sit

22

side by side on the sofa and chat, and when we ran out of conversation, gaze ahead of us in a casual, musing way. We could do this for quite a while, looking up and about us, as though considering the curtains, until the pretence was broken by the bob and squelch of your swallow. So tiny and yet so loud. I knew exactly what it meant. Before too long, we would be naked – you were thinking about that, right now, and wondering how to make it happen. And before I could prevent it, I had swallowed too.

But it was four in the morning in Bray, County Wicklow, and we were no longer twenty years old. You were not thinking about sex, awake and alone in the middle of the night. It was not my presence that loomed for you in the darkness.

It was something else.

There should be a special word, you say, for trying to stay asleep even though you have to use the bathroom. This need to get up in the night is a recent development, it means you are middle-aged, or worse, so you hang on to sleep as if hanging on to youth itself. You do not want to wake up, even though you are already awake. You think if you stay completely still, you will never have to die.

'You awake?' I say.

'Uh, God.'

You heave yourself up and out. You stumble past the bedroom where our huge, teenaged son sleeps for ten hours at a stretch, past his sister's room, which is empty now, during the week. You run the flush and the tap. Water courses through the walls and it does not stop until until you are back under the warmth of the duvet, where you turn for the kiss that precedes sleep, and are asleep. Just like that. While I lie awake, thinking about this life we have made, how simple it has been and unexpected. And something else, now, rising in the darkness.

My book.

THE NEXT MORNING, I went online to book a cheap flight to London, Gatwick, and I paused a moment before selecting a date. The 23rd of April. I would fly on my mother's birthday (if a dead person can have a birthday) and I was flying to London because – there is no tactful way to say this – this is where she was from. Yes. Katherine O'Dell, the most Irish actress in the world, was technically British.

She was born in London and she spent her childhood there – never mind the red hair, the plaid shawl and the poetry. Never mind the rebel songs:

'The sea, oh the sea, it's the grá geal mo chroí

Long may it stay between England and me.'

A couple of weeks later, I looked from the plane at the distant, dappled skin of the Irish sea, slashed into a point, here and there, by the prow of a tiny boat.

'Thank God we're surrounded by water.'

No one knew where she was born, no one could ever know; it was a great and complicated secret. I wondered, as I crossed over this simple stretch of blue, why she went to so much trouble.

Of course she did not give her age, so that was one theory. If no one knew where she was born, then no one would know where to find her birth certificate. She was an actor, she was good at all that.

A lady never told, but I am telling now. Now that death has smashed the clock she was forever trying to turn back. And I hate to pin her down. I mean, it is with a real pang of betrayal I tell the world she was born in April 1928 in Herne Hill, a suburb of London. She was christened in the local church of Saints Philip and James and her given name was Katherine Anne FitzMaurice.

Later, she would take her mother's surname, Odell, for the stage and this was Irished to O'Dell in America, when she was twenty years old. At which point, her hair turned red with nostalgia for the old sod.

My mother was a great fake. She was also an artist, a rebel and a romantic – so you could call her anything you like, but you could not call her English, that would be a great insult. It would also, unfortunately, be true.

After the plane landed in Gatwick, I got a train to Victoria, then changed for a train out to Herne Hill, and England looked fine to me. Clicketty clack, clicketty clack on that lovely English public transport. More than fine. The tended back gardens, the rows of houses, mostly neat, the morning crowd of commuters, freshly washed and all polite. If mother was running away from this, then I did not know what she was running from.

I found the place very easily. Milkwood Road is a terrace of modest yellow-brick houses, five minutes' walk from the station. These days, it is separated from the railway line by the warehouses of the Mahatma Gandhi Industrial Estate but in 1928 there must have been a view of the trains as they went by. The house where Katherine was born is on the fork with Poplar Road. I walked to the point of the intersection and along the angled wall at the rear. There was no garden to speak of, either at the front of the little house or in the yard at the back. My mother was born in April. She had a lifelong fondness for magnolia, lived for the wisteria that blossomed each spring in Dartmouth Square, and I did not know if this yearning for blossom was affection or affectation until I made my sudden pilgrimage to Herne Hill, thinking, as I looked up at the two back windows with their dirty net curtains, that I was no further on.

Her parents were strolling players who moved from one set of rooms to another: the house they rented in 1928 was still, at a guess, rented out today. I walked back around to the front and, taking a breath, stepped through a gap in the low wall to knock at the door. Or to touch the door. The wood was warm, and when I felt the heat of it, I was grounded, as though ridding myself of static.

This was where she was born.

On the evening of the 23rd April, her father, Menton FitzMaurice, was onstage in Daly's, a theatre off Leicester Square. There had been a twinge, a pain or two. Fitz mentioned this to a neighbour on the way to the station but there was no sense of urgency and by the time the woman decided to check on her, my grandmother was crowning on the landing. This is what I was always told. That the front door was left open, a group of children gathered outside, while my grandmother, belly up, clung on to a spindle of the banister, making and suppressing a deep, animal noise. I see her like an illustration of the day: boot-heels jutting and the hat on her head (its absurd feather broken at an angle) all askew. Her skirts are in disarray, in this, the illustrated version of the tale, so whatever there is of water or blood is not on view. Nor is my mother's importunate head, the squeezed cone of her skull obliging its way through parting flesh, as my grandmother heaves or bumps down a step or two, the other hand flailing backwards, while the children stand solemn-eyed at the front gate below.

My grandfather, meanwhile, is playing Count Belovar in a delightful piece called *The Lady of the Eglantine*. He postures and declaims in a Hussar jacket and high-waisted slacks while my grandmother strains and moans. Fitz was undeniably gorgeous – that has to be said, somewhere, about my grandfather, and why not now, while his wife's feet find and lose purchase on a lower step, and my mother shoots down the stairs into the world. Backwards. My grandmother fishes about under her skirt and there is Katherine Anne – face up and already moving, to be caught by the neighbour who is kneeling on the stairs below. Out she comes. In an arc. Out and down. The neighbour shouts, 'Oh, Holy God. Hold on, hold on. Don't push,' but my grandmother does push and the placenta slops out on to a lower step, tethering the baby to the world. The neighbour lifts it higher. She turns to show the local midwife, who is making her way through the gathered children into the hall.

Look, a girl!

The Lady of the Eglantine is a musical comedy, the kind that is costumed in pastel colours, with soldiers that look like toy soldiers and ladies in summer crinolines. The plot is a happy reworking of the Bible story of Judith and Holofernes. In this version, instead of kissing the enemy (played by my grandfather) and then decapitating him, Judith kisses the handsome invader and lets the dagger drop. She has fallen in love. He has fallen in love. This is surely an altogether better way to end a war. I don't know what they do with the dagger in the end, perhaps they hang it over the marriage bed.

The critic at the *Spectator*, who loved everything about the production except my grandfather – who failed to mention him entirely – opines, 'Musical comedy is addressed to the great midriff of the British people; it is par excellence the bourgeois art form.' And though the show sounds too silly and the reviewer too clever, there is something reassuring about the jaunty modernity of her tone. Of course she doesn't chop off his head. It is 1928. These people are already like us, more or less: they know about class, they know about war, they know how to belt out a decent chorus of 'A Lady's "No!"' or 'Thinking and Dreaming of You'.

Later that year, the production went to New York where it opened under the title *The Lady of the Flowers*, and my grandfather followed on as a second cast. My mother was too young to remember this first trip to America. There is a picture of her, in a newfangled American pram set in front of some brownstone steps. Suitably grumpy, she is wearing a little cloche hat, like a baby flapper, with a lace *noisette* over one ear.

New York was, at that time, in the last hectic days of a boom. Prohibition was still in force, the town was permanently drunk, and such was the moral shock that my grandmother declined to call herself an actress and chose to stay at home instead. In later years, she remembered the terrible cold, and the heat, when it came, was hardly better. Her husband, she said, was seized by America, enraptured by it. There was talk of a part in a motion picture in California, but something happened to prevent it and the family returned to England, after four months, when the stage show closed in July.

The stock market crashed soon after, a fact ignored by my grandfather who continued to pine for his great, missed chance in America. It was the thing that turned him into a failed actor, the one from whom glory was snatched away. My mother, who had no interest in disappointment, described her father as the kind of hack who knew his own lines but not the rest of the play. And though she, in her turn, found fame on Broadway, she always immersed herself in the script as well as in the role. My mother sought the protection of her art, and was in that sense more modern than her father had been, but she inherited his beauty – they both had 'dramatic good looks', the ability to be over the top, just by standing still.

She certainly knew how to make an entrance.

Look, a girl!

Perhaps because of that first fall down the stairs in Herne Hill, my mother was always afraid of heights. She was afraid of the difference between the darkness of the wings and the light onstage, and when she stepped out, it was like falling, she said, or forgetting. She was ten years old when she made her actual debut under the name of Katherine Odell in the Royalton Theatre, London. She played a crocus, in a chorus of spring flowers. For this, she wore a petal skirt with saffron-coloured stockings and a green cap of which she was very proud, because of the fetching little stalk that came out of the top. That much, she remembered. All the rest of it – the script, the title of the play, the plot – these remained a mystery to the end of her days. There was a man who was a poet, she said, at least he was called 'The Poet', and a woman with bright lipstick, who was called 'A Tart' which made her laugh twice, once at the time and once ten years later, when she realised the name had nothing to do with food. But the experience of being a crocus was too intense for her to understand anything happening around her. It took everything she had to say, at just the right moment, 'And spring shall have her ding a ling a ling' or whatever the stupid line was, and then fall back off stage, as though wind-blown. She had no idea what words had just come out of her mouth, she said, and she also knew that nothing would feel so real again.

I used to do my homework at the kitchen table in Dartmouth Square while she romanced me with these tales of her youth. I almost pretended not to listen. I had my coloured markers organised in their plastic packet and I filled maps of Ireland with contour lines, or I illustrated my list of mountain lakes: paternoster, turlough, corrie. And I was sometimes a little affronted, as I put the lids on, and fanned the markers out by shade and hue – never mind all that *acting*, I was the most real thing in the room. I was right there.

I had been, all along.

Because, tucked inside her, on the day she shot out into the world, was the little egg of me. That was another thing she told me, as I scribbled bright blue water down the length of the River Shannon. She told me that I was nested inside her, from the day she was born, like a little Russian doll.

Twenty-four years later, I was pulled out of her in a nursing home in Brooklyn after a labour that was long and terrible, but bravely endured. It was late at night and my mother was out of her head on some drug, but she remembered the obstetrician very clearly, a man in a suit, who did not stop to undo his cufflinks before employing a *thing*, 'for all the world like a toilet plunger', to suck me out of her. It also sucked a rounded welt out of my skull. I came out battered, she said, and entirely alien. Then I opened my eyes, as though ready to go another round, and she knew that everything would be fine.

'Just fine.'

Which made perfect sense to me.

'And pity, like a naked newborn babe,' she said, striking a little pose. And she was very like a cherub, standing there in our kitchen holding an imaginary little trumpet; eyes rolled up, cheeks blown out, the boiling eggs chittering against each other and along the metal bottom of the pan.

Brava!

My mother could move in and out of character, right there in front of you. She would shift a shoulder, settle her mouth, change behind the eyes. And some deep, daughterly part of me was tickled pink by it.

Do it again, Mama! Do it again!

In the summer evenings, we would go into the small park at the centre of the square with a blanket and a wicker hamper. 'Let's take it into the Square,' she would say, and we would walk round to the gate and loll on the grass. The other residents were proud of the park, but they did not use it much, possibly because it felt so overlooked. This fact did not bother Katherine, who liked being the woman in the Square with her Foxford rug and her picnic, and her lovely daughter pouring invisible tea for her dolls. But her constant scene-setting made me uneasy, as did the blank façades to which we played. She did not need to pretend to be my mother, when she was my mother already. That was like double cream.

I much preferred our winter quarters in the basement kitchen, where we were more private. There was a big old range cooker down there, with a big easy chair beside it and a shelf above of old newspapers and forgotten ornaments, which included a china dog and a snow globe of New York, fogged over with cooking grease. The floor was chequered with black and red tiles, of which the red were a little more porous and worn so the bentwood chairs always had a wobble in them. I liked wriggling about on these chairs; getting up, re-setting, making good.

The other big room in the basement was Kitty's, and she scraped around in there in her leather slippers. Kitty did not move fast, and she rarely stopped moving. Her room was always a little dark and it had a smell that I found off-putting – I think she kept a chamber pot under the bed.

When it got truly cold, the kitchen was the only warm room in the house, so Kitty sorted and stacked and left us to it, while my mother sat reading or talking, the fags going, the wine glass set on the coolest part of the great stove. I think she rolled her tights down. It sounds a bit disgusting, but I think she sometimes sat there with her 'pantyhose', as she affected to call them, in a glinting, beige fog wreathed about her ankles. She could not take them off altogether, for some reason. Perhaps a lady never did.

The books she read were mostly hardbacks, memoir and biography, some of it funny. I liked the ones with illustrations: *My Hat Blew Off*, which was a series of comic newspaper columns by John D. Sheridan, *The Egg and I*, by Betty MacDonald. *For the Life of Me* was another title, but I can't (for the life of me), remember what it was about. She also liked sensational non-fiction: *The World's Most Wicked Women* – Elizabeth Báthory, Catherine the Great or Lizzie Borden with her axe. She favoured a female villain, especially an Irish one: *The Staining of the Green* had chapters on the murdering prostitute, Dorcas Kelly, the notorious abortionist, Mamie Cadden, and two robbing undertakers, Higgins and Flannagan.

I brooded, many years later, over her choice in gore.

She was most taken by Dorcas Kelly, a Dublin madame who killed five customers and was condemned to death in 1761. The execution happened in Baggot Street, which was only up the road from us. If we passed along that way, as we sometimes did, my mother would say, 'You know a woman was burned to death just over there. Just there, by the traffic lights.' On the day of Dorcas Kelly's execution, the prostitutes of Dublin rioted in Copper Alley. Perhaps they thought, my mother said, that she should have killed five more.

Katherine read constantly. She loved biographies of male dictators and enjoyed a long Stalin phase when she became obsessed, not by the Gulags or by the Yalta Conference, but by his wife's suicide, his taste for sweet Georgian wines, the way he made his ministers bark 'The Blue Danube' after dinner, like dogs. She quoted his daughter Svetlana, who said, 'He was a Sagittarius, you know, on the cusp with Capricorn.'

And I would sort my bag for the morning, my stacked copybooks, my textbooks, my markers – their colours a little too frank on the page but splendid in the soft, see-through plastic case. I worried about her tripping over her fallen tights as I left her to the last of the wine and went to bed.

Stalin was on the cusp. And forty million dead.

This was pretty much indelible, to me, tight-assed Virgo that I was, as an example of all that was infuriating about my mother.

She thought small ears were the sign of a serial killer and that yellow was the colour of insanity. 'Look at Van Gogh!' (I worried about my non-existent earlobes; it was a real concern. I tugged them in the mirror so I would grow up good). And although I was a down-the-line Virgo, she took comfort in my Libra rising, which meant that I was secretly creative. I might be a bit of a bore – as she liked to tell me when the drinking got too lonely – but I was also her rod and staff, her angel and best thing.

And indeed, I was a careful child. I liked facts, maps, arithmetic and science. Which was, perhaps, another reason for my sudden pilgrimage over to Herne Hill. I have always found reality very reassuring. It was an enormous comfort to touch the actual door behind which she was born, to feel how dense the wood was with being real, to sense, through the tips of my fingers, its exact temperature, the dark green paint on its surface scoured matt by years of weather.

This. This.

The day was overcast, and warm. A wheelie bin was jammed between the bay window and the low front wall and it smelt, sweetly, of rot. A white van nosed out of the industrial estate and I watched it go down Milkwood Road.

I turned back to the door and knocked, and I knew by the answering silence that the house was empty – perhaps it had been empty for some time. This was the opposite of a fairy-tale door. There was nothing behind it, just the shape of air made by the place that held her first; a banister slicing down into a narrow hall.

Once a year, the sun warmed the wood from the same angle as the day she was born. And although I really did not care where the planets were placed in that particular sky, I sensed, as I stood there, something immense about the precision of the earth in its vast round.

I was fifty-eight years old. In a few months I would turn fifty-nine, which was one birthday more than she had managed on this earth. I would spin beyond her, out into uncharted space. I was about to become older than my own mother.

A group of schoolboys went past, their shirts unmoored from grey school trousers, their ties yanked down. They were mock fighting and grabbing over some message on a phone screen. There was a scuffle and a chase, as they slung bags and trailing jackets at each other.

'You cant, Philips. You stupid cant.'

She lived in Herne Hill for seven months, then briefly in New York, and then back on other London streets, in unprepossessing small houses or sets of rooms in Hammersmith, Hackney, Notting Hill. She grew up wild, by her own account, superbly well loved by her own mother, adored by her father, chatty, mucky, hard to dress. And she was good, she said. She insisted on that fact. She was *such* a good child.

I wondered at the grain of her voice when she said this, because I was also a good child, and I did not know what the problem with that could be. But it seemed to make her sad – as though life had played a trick on her.

I listened from my place at the kitchen table or watched as she stepped out the back door to admire the fat sunsets we used to have in those foggy Dublin days, and when she came back in she told stories about her childhood to make my own childhood glow. The dog who nearly bit her, but didn't. The white mouse that got lost in the raspberry canes (or was it a rat?). The mean girl at school (where was she now?). The flasher. What her mother said about the flasher (You will live). Stories of survival, of dangers evaded and monsters slain. There were, when you thought about it, very few stories about being *good*.

She stole a go-kart when she was three. It belonged to a boy up the road. There was a little white plank to sit on and proper reins to pull the wheels either way, and it looked so lonely, sitting there, like it was just waiting for some nice person to give it a spin.

So she did. She paddled and pushed with her little fat legs until she was flying along. And when she turned, with much hauling and bumping, to face back the way she'd come, she realised that she did not know how to get home. It all looked the same.

'Are you lost, little girl?'

The man who stopped to speak to her was forty feet tall, with a low forehead, and a dark look. He had a big black umbrella and he poked at her with the handle of this umbrella until he had it hooked under the steering rope. Then he turned around and pulled. She had to stick her legs up and out (this story was often told with the help of a kitchen chair), she had to hang on to the edges of the box with her hands, as he dragged her along, until there was nothing else for it. She turned her face skywards. She looked up to the indifferent heavens and she howled.

Just like that, there were two women in the street beside her, one of them swatting at the man, 'Get away from that child!' and another grabbing the cart from under her, 'Get offa that thing this minute!' and it is her mother and the boy's mother. Her dark saviour takes great offence, unhooks the brolly and strides off up the road. The little bastard whose cart it is kicks her with his steel-capped boot, and her mother has her by the arm, hauling her inside saying, 'Never speak to strange men, do you hear me? Never, ever.' And it was so hard to tell if this was a story about a bad man or a bad little girl – I don't know how many times I heard it before the penny dropped.

'They didn't say that.'

She looks at me. I must have been a teenager by then. The doubting stage.

'They didn't have Irish accents.'

She thinks about it a moment. There is a small flash – perhaps of anger. She is shocked at herself, the way you are shocked when your memory goes.

'No. My God. That's true.'

They spoke in London accents. She has rewritten her childhood and lost the first draft.

Her Irish accent was a fake Irish accent, which turned into a symbolic Irish accent and then, in time, to one that sounded almost ordinary. I actually find it hard to remember what she sounded like – I mean to place her socially, or put her on some map. Even in private – especially in private – her voice was gorgeous. Like something you could eat.

By the time I was grown, I really think she spoke in standard south Dublin, the accent used by newsreaders and doctors, with the occasional profanity thrown in. I remember that when she was truly startled – when a chair collapsed or the milk boiled over – there was something a bit cockney in the way she said 'Fahck!'

So I reclaim it a little: the English childhood that she abandoned or denied. I walk along an ordinary street in Herne Hill and gather it in: the red postbox waiting for the postman in his red van, the Belisha beacon and the zebra crossing, the sweetshop on the corner with a sign saying Wall's ice-cream. All of them discarded by her, to be replaced with other childhood furniture; an Irish country town, perhaps, a wild evening sky, a bit of cloth to wrap the babby in, and a neighbour with big, laundry-scrubbing forearms to say, 'Oh, Holy God, Oh, Holy God' (of course she did) as my mother shot out into this world. Inhaled the air of it.

'The stage chose me, you know.'

And earned her first round of applause.

HER FATHER, MENTON FitzMaurice, was born in 1899. He was the son of an Irish Captain in the British army who was stationed in Fermoy, County Cork, and of a local woman called O'Brien. It is possible they were not married, though this did not matter for long – Captain John FitzMaurice died in the Second Boer War when his son was two years old.

There must have been some provision made. The boy was sent to minor public schools in both Ireland and England and he would, when he was grown, play soldiers all his days.

In Ireland he was posh, in England he was uneasy. My grandfather was a small man who looked larger in a uniform. He could screw in a monocle and bark with the best of them, but he could also play Irish, as required. Especially when he was in London; he bandied his legs and capered about. He stuck out his elbows, and picked at his lapels, and whistled Toor-Aye-Ay.

Fitz was a mongrel, as actors often are, but he kept his mother's faith all through his life and he never let it go. My grandfather was a Catholic and this mattered to him enormously. Wherever he was, in whatever town he found himself, London, or New York, or Castlebar, he attended Sunday Mass. He maintained his religious practice as you would a secret nobility, if you were an orphaned boy.

This upstanding piety was a great asset when Fitz toured Ireland with the fit-ups, as he did during both world wars. These theatrical troupes brought Shakespeare and melodrama around the Irish countryside, causing all kinds of stirrings and excitement in Irish country hearts. They came rolling into town: first the principals in the 'royal car', then the rest of the company in a big, honking lorry, from which they scattered to find half-decent digs, returning as soon as they could to 'fit up' for that night's show. They did two shows a day, and never the same show twice. *Othello*, *Trilby*, *Oedipus*: jealousy, incest, blood and desire. The fit-ups were not popular with the local clergy, on whom they relied for school and parish halls, so as soon as they were billeted, Fitz was dispatched to attend Mass. He was sent off to pray.

Which he did, impeccably. Fitz made a quiet entrance, a small but serious genuflection. With his well-cut overcoat and modest air, you might not notice him, or pretend not to notice him, until the singing, when he came into his own.

'Fay-haith OF our Fa-ha-the-errs, HOL-y Faith,' Fitz had a voice of great purity, to shame and uplift the entire, straggle-tongued congregation. And every woman who heard him considered the sixpence at the bottom of the sewing basket, the shilling they had hidden on top of the dresser, the price of a ticket for that night's show.

His wife, Margaret Odell, was also small and pretty in a matching, slightly unconvincing way. By my mother's account she was a gentle, low-voiced woman with a trace of a Yorkshire accent. I have no memory of her, though she lived with us for a while, and in later years I often asked what she was like. My mother said that she was lovely, and when I asked what kind of lovely, she said, 'Just. You know.'

There is a photograph of her holding me as a baby, wearing a close-printed floral blouse in dark purple and dark green. I am wearing a kiss curl and a perfect, gummy replica of my mother's 'get me out of here' smile.

Apart from her ability to tilt her head for the camera, just so, I have no idea what style of a person my grandmother was. For some reason, I could not make her into a memory.

'Was she nice?'

'Of course!'

But what way was she nice? I thought it might involve cake.

'Did she make jokes?'

'Oh yes,' said my mother, whose sense of humour was wicked to the point of abandon. 'She could be quite …'

'Mean?'

'No. No.'

'But funny?'

'Oh yes. She had a way of, you know,' and she gave a little happy shrug of sorrow, a shilly-shally of the shoulders, as if to say, 'Hey, hey, rain or shine.' My grandmother was, in all of these recovered gestures, like a sweet-natured, slightly sad child. And I do not know if this was just the fashion, or if it is something essential to the person she was. The twirl of a parasol, a little skip and a hop. A sigh.

Hey nonny no.

She played milkmaids, abandoned sweethearts. Her Ophelia, a critic wrote, 'appeared as though she had forgotten to take the dinner off the hob'. In a stage photograph I found online she wears a kimono and a tasselled hat that looks like a lampshade out of a Shanghai bordello; her small teeth showing under it in a sweet, posed smile.

In some dream sense, there is a knife tucked into that wide sleeve: she is just keeping things nice for a while. In reality, of course, she kept things nice for ever. Her later career was spent singing Gilbert and Sullivan in jewelled slippers that curled up at the tip, an ample-bosomed woman dressed as a Chinese boy. Surely I would remember that cleavage, so mighty and milky white? She died when I was five.

And, What was she like? I said. What was she like? I whined. What was she like?

'She was lovely,' my mother said in her sad voice. And there is no evidence that I can find to the contrary.

Nor do I remember any cake.

I do remember sitting in my grandfather's lap for two minutes, before wriggling off it, and I remember how he adored me. I knew by the shake of his hand as he picked in his fob pocket for a coin, or got down on hands and knees to annoy me with his old head. There is a quick little watercolour of us by Tisdall, who was a friend of my mother's. It turned up a few years ago in an exhibition in the National Gallery in Dublin's Merrion Square. Very easy and exquisite; my grandfather sits in the sunlight with his eyes closed, while I use him like an armchair, a good place to read a book.

I still come across him on TV, on Sunday afternoons or late at night when I am flicking away from shopping channels in hotel bedrooms. Jet-lagged or disconnected, I hit on a British film of the fifties in which Fitz is about to make an entrance, usually in uniform. He is playing the bluff old general, or the pipe-considering RAF colonel who crosses out lost planes on a chalkboard. He is the coward, the liar, the one who makes the wrong decision and walks off screen contented. It is something about the mouth, perhaps. Fitz spoke like a fake, and you might think this was acting, but he spoke like the same fake in every role.

Even then, in middle age, he carried his handsome like an unwanted gift – one he offered to the world, but could never quite give away.

Some of the men in those films had fought in the real Battle of Britain but not Fitz. He was on stage in Tuam in September 1939, on the day that war was declared. By the end of October, the London furniture was in storage. His wife and daughter had travelled to join him in peaceful Ireland and Katherine was enrolled in an Irish school – Kylemore Abbey in County Galway – where she boarded for the next five years.

Katherine's early education had been, at best, haphazard. There were various prep schools in Hammersmith and Notting Hill. She spent a year in St Teresa's, a Catholic boarding school in Surrey, and attended the De Leon theatre school in Greenwich for a time. Suddenly, at the age of eleven, she was transported to a castle on a lake in the far west of Ireland. The school at Kylemore looked like something off a biscuit box. If you climbed the mountain behind it you could see the wilds of Connemara under a huge, wind-blown Irish sky. In the shelter of convent walls below was an oasis of herb gardens and fern walks, where the insect nuns walked in a pattern of slow squares, reading their hours. This austere school proved a still point for the daughter of touring players and, by the age of sixteen, young Katherine Anne was rapt with love of the nuns.

During the summers, she worked with the fit-ups.

One of my mother's most repeated stories was about the time when she arrived in a small, nameless town in the middle of Ireland, to find that there was no one to meet her. She had no idea where she was supposed to go. She was twelve years old. This is the abiding image I have of her childhood: a girl standing on a station platform with one of those brown suitcases carried by refugee children – from which, if the movies are to be believed, many different print dresses, cardigans, coats, straw hats and galoshes would subsequently emerge. She holds the case in both hands as the train empties around her: a woman with a flapping chicken tucked under her arm, an old man with a white clay pipe, a pair of sweethearts. After which, no one.

The girl climbs a clanging iron footbridge and pauses at the top to take in a view. On one side of the tracks is a patchwork of small fields bounded by a river and, beyond the glittering river, miles of bog. And though the land is poor, it looks so rich: the dark gold of gorse set against the chocolate of opened earth, the brown scrub made purple by distance, as it rises into a set of low hills.

On the other side of the bridge are the roofs of an Irish country town; thatch and corrugated iron, and black slate drying to blue after rain. She goes towards these roofs, and descends the metal steps. As she walks through the station archway, a horse and dray rattles past, and she stands looking after it. There is still no one to meet her. A dog roots in the open gutter. An oily chugging announces the grocer's van, and then it is gone.

The girl casts about her until she sees something posted on the station wall. She goes back to it and her earnest young face tilts up to read.

Tonight, for one night only
Ireland's Greatest Actor
Anew McMaster
Plays Othello

with an astounding cast including
Menton FitzMaurice as Iago
The beautiful
Pleasance McMaster
Lillian MacVeigh and many others
no effects spared
At
The Confraternity Hall
8pm

The point of the story was not that she was lost in Ireland, but that she was never lost in Ireland, because her parents were up there on the wall. They were always easy to find.

Anew McMaster, whose company it was on the poster, was an English actor-manager in the grand old style. He believed in dark velvet curtains with spangles on them: music, thrills, poetry, tears. Mac gave it everything, or an approximation of everything (he had little respect for an actor who had to learn his lines) and he liked to have a strong cast around him, especially if they were on the short side. Mac himself was impressively tall.

And Fitz was really quite short, so they were a perfect match. Fitz was a useful actor and an easy companion and he became, for many seasons, Mac's second fiddle and sidekick. My grandfather was one of those performers who love the road because they are, anyway, always a little adrift. Mild-mannered and fastidious, his eyes were described variously as 'liquid' or 'limpid', or once as 'beseeching'. He could also be a little silly. In a satirical column by 'Lycurgus', published in *Dublin Opinion* in 1945, 'FitzBorris' is an actor so vain of his figure he 'ever tended towards the front of the stage' with disastrous conse-quences in Boyle, County Roscommon, where he edges 'crabwise all the way into the pit'.

The same piece gives us a picture of McMaster (here thinly veiled as 'McNamara') at the height of his powers.

McNamara played the Moor in gleaming blackface, stripped to the waist, his powerful upper arm encased in a gold band, his ageing girth likewise encircled in a belt of gold-painted tin, with a hoop in his ear and a fiery flashing in his eye. His hand left a black mark on her white flesh very like a bruise, as he flung the young Desdemona across the floor with a fearsome 'Have you prayed tonight?' that had one lachiko attempt the stage, only to be hauled back into an increasingly riotous crowd, the gallants towards the front, matrons and spinsters pressed trembling against the back wall. 'Shame!' came the call, and was echoed round, 'Shame, shame,' and 'No!' cried a lone voice into the silence that descended, when her form went limp beneath the pillow he held over her pitiful, sweet face. 'God and His holy mother have mercy on us all!'

Mac's daughter Pleasance played Desdemona to his Othello, Portia to his Shylock and Trilby to her father's Svengali. She was not a great actress, but she would do. Pleasance was fine-skinned and blonde with good cheekbones – the kind of girl who could look very plain one minute and beautiful the next. Mac called her his 'little Saxon'. He liked her with her hair loose, in medieval green, perhaps, and carrying a garland or an archer's bow. But the truth was that she was a gentle person. The best of her was sweet and slightly hurt, the worst tearful and vague.

My mother loved Pleasance, who was a year older than she was and very kind. The girls sometimes stayed together in the cottage Mac rented on Howth Head, outside Dublin, and it is more than possible that Pleasance was with her,

45

in her famous railway station scene. The wonder of it is, that they arrived in the right town. In 1940, for example, the company managed Ballina, Sligo, Tuam, Ballyshannon, Dundalk, Mullingar, Athlone, Clonmel, Cloughjordan, Limerick, Bandon, Charleville, Cork Opera House, the Theatre Royal, Waterford and Dublin. They presented three Shakespeares: *Hamlet, Othello* and *The Merchant of Venice* and three melodramas: *Little Lord Fauntleroy, Laburnum Grove* and *Trilby.*

Trilby, which is set in Paris, was staged just after that city was occupied by the Nazis, so the programming feels timely, but not in a good way. This blitheness was perhaps typical of some twist in Ireland's attitude during a war, in which they claimed to be neutral. Mac played the part of Svengali with a fake beard, staring eyes and a bump of putty added to the bridge of his nose – a portrayal more anti-Semitic, even, than his Shylock. Of course, no one knew, at that stage, who was going to win the damn war. They might have been testing their options, getting ready to jump either way.

Ireland, meanwhile, was a good place to be for the duration. There was fresh food to be found in the countryside, though a lack of petrol meant that Mac and his wife had to abandon the royal car and travel squashed into the cab of the truck with the female players. Timber, which was increasingly scarce, was sourced from the town undertaker and sold back to him at the end of the run (a poetical way to be planted, Fitz said, with the scenery painted on the inside). Salaries were suspended, with everyone put on shares. For Fitz and his wife, Margaret Odell, this amounted to less than four pounds a week each, while their daughter would be lucky to get two.

She was put to work at the box office, the props table, and also onstage, where she played serving-maids, messengers and various boys. Katherine Odell was a useful girl. She had no choice. If the actor needed a prop, then you handed them the prop. If a line had to be said, then you said the line. As a daughter in *Oedipus Rex*, she shuffled miserably on to watch her father, played by Mac, reel around, bleeding from his eye sockets. She learned the early art of 'looking like a gawm', because that was all that child actors did onstage, she said, or serving-maids: it was all about dropping the tray.

Come on. See something terrible.

'Don't MOVE YOUR FACE!' Mac would scream. 'Drop the tray!'

'I don't have a tray, Mr McMaster.'

'Exactly, darling. My point, exactly.'

Mac sometimes broke out of role, mid performance, to attend to the set, which was not always rock solid, or he took a bow at the end of a big scene ('Provinces only, dear') so the audience might show their appreciation. He liked to strip down, to show the pulse and suck of his diaphragm under the massive ribcage, the marvellous workings of his lungs. Mac believed that the Irish were especially responsive to the spoken word and he did not speak the line so much as thrill to it, switching from basso profundo to baritone on either side of a breath. His was a highly technical style, and all done at speed. There were whole weeks when he acted outside himself and did not know what he was doing wrong, and then there were nights when the cast gathered in the wings to watch because Mac was on form. Fitz, who shared the stage with him was, on these occasions, 'stupefied', the actors were 'dazzled', the audience 'enraptured'. It was, as my mother described it, a mutual possession of actor and character. They went down in flames.

'Unforgettable.'

Then she would sigh and say, 'Oh, that is all long out of fashion, now.'

These summers were the happiest of Katherine's life. She never tired speaking of it all: the beauty of the open road, moving from one poor set of lodgings to the next, going out to a privy at night and finding a bull tied to a ring on the wall. She described sleeping in a big bed in County Galway with her mother on one side of her and Lillian MacVeigh on the other, all of them in long cotton nightdresses, and then later finding out that Lillian had once lost a little baby girl who would have been her age had she lived – so that was what she felt when she woke so warm in the morning, she felt that lost and impossible love.

Mac liked the country audiences because they did not know how a play would end. ('Oh, give her a good shake!' a woman in Ballyshannon shouted when Romeo discovered Juliet, apparently dead, in the tomb.) But my mother had no interest in laughing at the good people of St John's Hall in Tralee or The Boathouse in Cappoquin, she was a great believer in the nobility of the crowd. In later years she came to envy them, she said, because they were seeing these works for the first time. The Irish audience was like a sea, in the swirling rush of its attention. They just got it, she said.

They were given a note as they left Sligo. A messenger arrived in the pelting rain with a piece of paper that he handed up to the cab of the lorry. He said it was from their landlady, and when Katherine's mother opened it, she read, 'The weather is terrible for God's sake mind yourself.' And that is what it was like to play an Irish country town.

One day when Katherine was just thirteen, Mac's daughter Pleasance fell ill with scarlet fever and she had to take over, at three hours notice, the role of Trilby O'Ferrall. This is the little Irish *grisette*, or artist's model, who is hypnotised by Svengali to become a great singer (though when she is awake, she can not sing at all).

The lines were not that hard to learn, she had seen the play many times. The trance was easy, but she found it hard to do Trilby unhypnotised. There was a certain peasant heartiness to the character, that my mother found hard to catch.

'Just put your hands on your hips and swing about a bit,' said Mac.

The costume helped. She penned in the eyebrows and the blue eyeshadow, put her hair in a double bun, rouged her cheeks, then slapped her cheeks. She flashed her eyes at the eyes in the mirror, and despaired. She was not made for fresh-air parts.

And then it was time. Katherine trembled in the wings, as the hall started to fill. There was a hole to peep through to check the audience, a deliberate small rip in the blacks, but she did not stand on tiptoe to see how many were in. You could almost tell from the thickness of the air, by the way it soaked up the sound. The place smelt of farm work. A cough here or there, the sound of boiled sweets passed around in paper bags. And one lady at least who liked to comment on the action to the lady sitting beside her.

'Oh, she's in for it now.'

There was always one.

And there was always someone odd in the front row, because odd people like to sit up front to get a clear view – and why wouldn't they. This odd person was called a God-help-us and he was harmless. That was the thing you had to get used to – the fact that you would be safe, on stage. The audience would not touch you, not ever. They liked sitting in the darkness, forgetting who they were. It was all about suspense, they were not watching so much as anticipating what would happen next. That is what Mac meant when he said, 'the play is the thing,' he meant the story itself would keep you from harm.

And what happened after the play?

Lots of things.

But nothing *really*. A man doffed his hat, a woman took you by the hands in a flurry of admiration. People passed you in the street, and knew.

She stood in the wings and sensed them all out there in the scrapey chairs of Ballinasloe town hall; the drunk in the third row, the priest in the back of the hall, the young girl in love, the old man remembering love, the mother forgetting her children as she recalled some deeper sorrow.

The play, as seen from the side, seemed to have little to do with her. She watched it, the way you watch an oncoming train, wondering if it will stop at a far platform – and suddenly you realise it is coming straight at you. There was no avoiding this thing. She would have to step into it, a kind of collision in time. The play was alive. It was made of air, with rules of iron. It was a marvel, and when it was over you were also Marvellous, Darling.

Because even if you could not remember the line, you opened your mouth and the line came out of you. It was like a gap in your mind, that opened and filled itself at the same time. The words she spoke would fit it precisely. They would be the right words. Everything would happen in the future the way it had been rehearsed in the past, but it would be much better this time. It would be for real.

Meanwhile, her hands felt too large for her body, she did not know whether to hold them in front of her or let them dangle by her thighs. She picked up the sides of her skirt, and dropped them again, sensing the outline of herself there in the small space, the tip of her nose, the bulge of her lips, that were so dry, she had to wet them with her tongue. She felt the audience as a dark anticipation, a few feet away, unseen. She heard her cue and she picked up her skirts.

And went on.

She did not know how she did it. How she put one foot in front of the other, how she turned and spoke, what she said, what the other actors said in reply. Anything at all might have come out of her. But it was a triumph. Whatever it was. She could not remember what she had done, but it was perfect, apparently. It was just marvellous.

After this, her friend Pleasance tried to get Katherine to play the part full-time, because she was fourteen and fed up doing weird scenes with her father. Mac, however, refused to swap out his Trilbys, or lose his blonde and pathetic Desdemona. Instead, he tried Katherine in the role of Portia and taught her how to deliver a Shakespearean line.

> 'The quality of mercy is not strained,
> It droppeth as the gentle rain from heaven
> Upon the place beneath. It is twice bless'd'

He closed his eyes as she spoke and he let it shiver through him. Then he opened his eyes and smiled.

She had to dress as a boy, hold her lapel in one hand, gesture with the other, speak, wave a piece of paper, wear a floppy hat under which she stuffed her long brown hair. She had no chest to disguise.

And was she not afraid?

I asked her that a lot.

The whole thing appalled me. Even the words she used – the way people 'died' on stage or started 'corpsing'. There were so many anecdotes of cheap disaster: an actor went on with no sword and he used a shoe instead. An actor forgot his lines. Or his pants. An actor fell down a hole.

He was obliged to drink soap in his tea. And he kept going, that actor with no pants or no wig or no line or no sword, heroically, foolishly, he did not stop spouting this stuff, not for an instant.

An actor is really stabbed in a fake fight and the audience gasps and breaks into applause. Or an actor comes on drunk, and there is nothing worse. In Borrisokane, an actor dies on stage, he really dies, he rolls his eyes up into the back of his head and he says, 'I am dying,' in a helpful tone of voice, and the actors keep going until belief drains out of them. They stall, the lines dribble out of their mouths, and still no one moves. Then they run to shield the man's actual and real dying from public view.

But mostly, nothing happened. Mostly it was fine.

No matter how often she did it, there was no getting over that moment when she stepped out into the light. The play was waiting for her, just over that line. It was in the gestures and declamations, it was in the words as they rolled. Her real and destined self was right there, a space she could step into, or that stepped into her. Each time. Or nearly every time.

Were you not afraid? I said.

Oh. Terrified.

Really?

Not that she ever let on.

It was all very well being good, she said, but you had to be smart too. And quiet. You must be like the theatre mouse – did I know about the mouse? The mouse who survives by nibbling greasepaint. She sleeps curled up in a high wig, eats through the fly ropes, knows the words to all the plays. This mouse was called Josephine and, in later variations, she could sing. And Josephine the singing mouse kept my mother company in all those cold dressing rooms, in all the towns when she was a girl. Josephine listened to her line runs, the way I did now, and she squeaked the occasional prompt from under the boards. When all was finished and the audience gone, Josephine sang her little song. And the other mice found her to be a little stuck-up, it had to be said, but they loved her talent, which was prodigious, for a mouse.

Katherine Anne Fitzmaurice knew it could never get better than this. Great plays, great performances that were sometimes also awful. They ran on belief alone (Ballina, Sligo, Tuam, Ballyshannon, Dundalk, Mullingar, Clonmel and Athlone). It was all built out of cardboard, greasepaint and panic. Bad acoustics, bad corsets and the wrong shoes; that heap of junk they drove, night after night, over an Irish country moon.

For her second summer on the road the McMaster tour was joined by a young Boyd O'Neill, the man she would come to shoot, some forty years later. Not, I think, that they noticed each other much. She was fourteen and still playing messengers and maids. At twenty-five he had just set up the Cloondara Players, a group who would later become responsible for one of the biggest amateur drama festivals in the country. He was also, in those early days, a schoolteacher and a sometime poet, an enthusiastic speaker of the Gaelic language with a Pioneer pin on his lapel.

Mac clearly took him on for no pay – one of his favourite things to do – and this may have caused resentment among the rest of the company. These people were proud players: they sang and recited and fell on their backsides, as though their lives depended on it, for under four quid a week. Boyd had a job to go to at summer's end so financially, and perhaps creatively, he was like a well-dressed man in a room full of people who were naked. Hard to know who would feel, in the circumstances, more of a fool.

When I thought about Boyd – and after the incident, I thought about the man a lot – I remembered how many of her friends dismissed him, over the years. There was something 'beige' about him, according to Snell. Lillian MacVeigh said that he was shy.

He did not drink.

Also he could not act. As criticism went, I always found this one hilarious. Lots of them couldn't act, and it didn't stop them. I think what they meant was that he found it hard to let himself go.

Boyd worked slowly towards a goal the others did not see and he became, in time, a powerful man. This was not, clearly, his fault. But he was never 'talented', whatever that word meant. He did not like performing – I suspect he could not bear it. He preferred to watch people and to move them around in his mind. Which is what producers do. The man was a natural strategist. This was harder to see in his early days, when he was also a great believer – in the Irish language, in the possibilities for a truly Irish theatre and, later, in a broadcasting culture that would reflect and define the nation state. ('Tweed knickers' – that is what Hughie Snell called him.) And all this might seem a bit self-important, now, but these were matters of real and proper concern. (The contempt he showed Snell was complete, he never did forgive him, not as he rose high and poor Snell sank increasingly low. And when they carried Snell out in a box, a year after my mother died, he sat at the top of the church, as though to get a better view.)

In any case, Boyd did well. And though he bruised a number of egos on his way up, he probably meant well, by which I mean he was idealistic, or he thought of himself as an idealist – especially in his thirties and forties, when whatever he did to advance his own career was also, somehow, done for the common good.

In 1961 he left the Cloondara Players and joined RTÉ, Ireland's new national television station, where he produced some of their live Playhouse series, which went out on a Saturday night. Those early studio tapes were all reused and the original recordings wiped and lost, so it is hard to say what the broadcasts were actually like. Some surviving scraps show work that is, by modern standards, bizarrely slow. At first it feels like suspense: every shot of a cup of tea being carefully poured seems to invite an axe murderer in through the window – then it turns out to be just a cup of tea.

'Do you take sugar in that?' says the woman with the pot.

But the series galvanised the country week after week. It was a terrific opportunity for Boyd, who had a keen eye for talent, perhaps because he had no specific talent of his own.

'I am glad I got the job,' he was famous for saying, when he bagged the prized and pensionable post of Deputy Head of Drama, 'because there's an awful lot of charlatans out there.'

It is hard to admire people who are so busy admiring themselves, but what of it? Boyd had a certain personal style. There was nothing in all this that might make you, twenty years later, reach for your gun.

I have a vivid memory of singing into a tape recorder for him when I was four or five. Some men liked to make a fuss of me in order to somehow ignore my mother, but Boyd really did love children, I think. They gave him the chance to be a nice man.

Which he was. He was also that. Boyd was a tender-hearted man.

He set his big reel-to-reel machine on a low coffee table in the living room and I sang 'Getting to Know You' into his blunt silver microphone while he listened to his earphones and watched the floor. Or he looked right at me, his mouth stuck in an open smile, willing me along. And he was so painfully fond of me, in that moment. Although there was nothing sexual in his attention, it was still too much attention. He loved me, as he harvested my young voice, even though I was not his to love. It stayed with me a long time after: the excitement of the new tape machine, my plain, sweet singing, and the melancholy of Boyd, hunkered there. I wonder if he knew, by that time, that he would never have children of his own.

Famously, this lifelong abstainer took to the drink just when others were starting to dry out. Boyd soured in middle age. He had suffered the death of some ideal, perhaps, or of his mother. He had always been competitive but, in his late forties and early fifties, his ambition became keener and more personal. Perhaps he had risen as far as he could in Ireland, a place that seemed to disappoint him, more and more. No one knew when he started but, by the time I was of an age to notice such things, Boyd was on the brandy, which suited him for being a slightly superior tipple. It was hard to tell if he was drunk, but I suspect he really was drunk, quite a lot of the time.

And then, when he was fifty-six years old, a wild Irish-American director arrived in town and life opened up again for Boyd. In 1973, he was briefly, gloriously, credited as producer on a major international feature film. This was a co-production with RTÉ shot in the west of Ireland called *My Dark Rosaleen* and starring – not my mother, as you will have guessed, but a raven-haired American beauty called Maura Herlihy.

Very few big shoots happened in Ireland in those days, and the glamour of it was off the scale. The Bishop of Elphin came to bless the camera, he couldn't be stopped. Every hotel from Limerick to Sligo was occupied, there were catering trucks and limousines. Maura Herlihy's skin cream had to be mixed fresh each morning in refrigerated conditions. Oliver Reed started a bar fight in the local pub, which subsequently put up a plaque. The completed movie brought Boyd to European festivals, to the red carpets of New York and LA. He personally flew the print to Sydney, Australia, where the Irish ambassador met him off the plane.

The next year, Boyd left the national broadcaster to set up an independent film company which he called Cast A Cold Eye Productions, renting a small office in Wicklow Street in the centre of Dublin. It was a grand move, made in middle age, and it was one he may have come to regret. An amount of swagger must have been required for the next five years, which were spent in that purgatory called 'development'. Boyd spent his time juggling scripts, courting international finance, writing fantasy casts on the backs of envelopes for his once-hot director, now down-and-out in LA.

As the next big movie failed to materialise, Boyd found other projects to occupy his time. He put his name to six beautiful half-hour programmes by Liam MacMathúna called *Lámh, Lámh Eile*, about crafts on the Aran Islands. This was followed by a series of hagiographical television documentaries called *Talking to Giants,* in which he himself sat in to discuss matters of the age with intellectual and artistic figures such as Freddie Ayer, Isaiah Berlin, the Irish poet Austin Clarke and the Catholic theologian Hans Küng. He kept his image high.

He came to supper, at least once. When I think about it, she must have been courting him, because these theatre suppers were slightly frantic. They were catered by Kitty's niece and involved the big fish kettle, for a full poached salmon of falling-apart pink, with transparent slices of cucumber ruched along the sides. Boyd was a reluctant guest. I see him leaning back from the gathering, tall and thin, snidely in control of himself. Drinking almost invisibly, as though from a permanent straw. At some stage in the evening he insulted someone with a high-pitched, slightly nasal remark, but once the fight was started, he declined to join in.

I have a sharp memory of him standing in the living room with his head tipped back against the wall. The rooms on the first floor were papered in a very pale damask pattern, in that washed-out blue you see near the horizon when the sun is setting. He looked, as he stood there, as though he had been painted some centuries ago; in his face, the kind of indifference you get from powerful men, when they are tired.

As far as sex was concerned, it was hard to tell what he got up to. Boyd had no children, which was in those days seen as a great sorrow, but his wife was perfectly nice and she seemed dedicated to him. Or perhaps my memory of her is coloured by guilt, sitting in court number nine and seeing the two of them there, solid in their respectability, a couple, worn in together by familiarity and time, she loving him, he accepting of her love and care. My mother, by contrast, horribly mad and alone.

He did not come to her funeral. I was grateful for that.

Boyd O'Neill died, eleven difficult years after the assault, at the age of seventy-four. His retirement was spent hobbling about various committees and boards, the Gate Theatre, and the Société Européenne de Producteurs Télévisueles. He drank at home or, occasionally, at the Shelbourne's Horseshoe Bar. I passed him once in the foyer there, on a winter's day. It was coming up to Christmas; he was sitting in an armchair just beyond the revolving door and, by an accident of timing, we looked each other a long, held moment, eye to eye. After which I dreamed about him for a year or more, asking me to shoot him again – there was, at that moment, something so supplicatory about the man.

But in the summer of 1942 he was twenty-six and my mother was fourteen and it is doubtful they ever had a conversation. She ran about with Pleasance and was ignored, apart from the occasional annoyance: like the actor who stuck his hands down her blouse, crowing, 'Annyting yit?' and he was so gorgeous she wanted to 'die, just die'. There was the usual range of badness, but certainly none from Boyd, who was a 'bit of a prieshteen', meaning a pious, celibate type.

There is a photograph of him taken the previous autumn with the Cloondara Players when he was twenty-four years old. Boyd sits surrounded by the cast of Lady Gregory's one-act play *Spreading the News:* the women are in plaid shawls, the men crouching forward in Paddy caps and dented hats. A tall policeman stands at the back, his cheeks emblazoned with circles of rouge, and the young Boyd O'Neill sits at the front with a silver trophy on his knee. He has a face so open you would call it foolish, were it not for his calm eyes. He is, in his own way, perfect – some mother's best-loved son.

But my mother did not love him, or not especially. Besides, the story of that summer's tour (Tuam, Swinford, Westport, Castlebar, Kiltimagh, Cavan, Kells, Doneraile, Tipperary, Mitchelstown, Fethard and Fermoy) was not about boring old Boyd O'Neill but about Katherine Odell, soon to be famous star of stage and screen. The question was never, 'What was he like at twenty-six?' It was, 'What was she like at fourteen?' Did she already know what destiny held in store?

'I was just a littlest mouse,' she said. 'I scurried around, and when no one was there to notice me, I sang my little mouse song.'

No one, that I can discover, spoke about her at all until three years later when, at the age of seventeen, she featured in a letter from Anew McMaster to a casting director at the Gate Theatre, in which various actresses are described and dismissed by him as, 'too fey', 'tubercular', or 'terribly dim'. McMaster seems to rate the young Katherine FitzMaurice, however. He describes her, perhaps a little archly, as his 'young ward out in Howth, who is staying with the girls while her parents drub out the last few weeks of this tour. She is a toy breed, after Fitz. Beautiful in the same way, but in its female incarnation. Odd and moving, that. She can speak the verse. Not sure how young.'

As for Boyd, looking for an early glimpse of the man brought me to his schoolfriend from Coláiste Mhuire, Dermod Mulherne, who was later to become Bishop of Clonfert. After Boyd's death in 1991 he wrote a considered tribute for the school magazine, first in Irish and then translated into English on the facing page. In it, he described Boyd as quietly unstoppable. 'We did not always agree,' he wrote, adding that he thought of his friend as a great soul but one 'who made his own spiritual path in life …' This is a considerable understatement. Boyd's signal success as a television producer was a play about a young priest called *Ecce Homo* which was the cause of some controversy at the time. The play may have been about homosexuality, or heterosexuality, or it may just have been about loneliness. It was certainly about a young curate who flees, after a difficult day, from the kindness of a busty, frilly-bloused, female parishioner. The role was played by an Englishman because, rumour had it, no Irish actor would take it on.

The studio tape is long since wiped but a single exterior scene survives. Shot on film in St Stephen's Green, it shows a handsome, sad priest watching some carefree children as they throw bread to the ducks. Sitting in an archive booth as the tape rolled on, I could not believe what I had uncovered. I checked the date: 1966. This surely was Ireland's first ever public reference to the sexual abuse of children by a priest – or perhaps by anyone. But like the sitcom cup of tea that remains a cup of tea, the scene with the ducks turns out to be, endlessly, just about ducks.

The Bishop ignores all this scandalous lack of subtext, to sail regally on:

'He was in his habits, supremely modest, even as a boy. Self-sufficient to the point of frugality, generous to those who did not share his intellectual gifts, gentle with the gentler sex, generous with the needy, an advocate for the poor. He considered a vocation for a while and was a great loss to the Church, as evidenced by his later career. Quietly, however, I had my doubts. If I am accusing him of pride, it was a spiritual pride and not a temporal one. Boyd considered himself an outsider, even when working at the heart of power. This put him in a false position and, in later days, he fancied himself beset by enemies, intellectual and artistic, who were not there.'

Or who were very much there. As my mother was to demonstrate on the morning in May 1980 when she walked up the narrow stairs to his office on Wicklow Street with a prop gun that turned out to be a real gun, and walked back down again, fully mad.

'Beset' is a good word for a man who 'went and got himself shot', as Dublin likes to phrase these things – the way you could get yourself robbed or, especially, raped. We lived in the passive tense in those more difficult – certainly more tactful – times. Embarrassment was everywhere. You could also 'get yourself' murdered or 'find yourself' in dire straits. Many of my mother's actorly friends sometimes 'found' themselves, for example, behind with the rent.

Boyd came out from his office to greet my mother in the anteroom where his personal assistant Mary Bohan had her desk. He was not in the habit of greeting people in the outer office, he said, but in this case he made an exception. This was partly a courtesy for a well-known and respected actress; it was also a way to keep the meeting brief. He opened his door and went towards her so that she could kiss him on either cheek and this was not his personal custom either, he said, but he knew it was what actresses like to do.

She started to walk towards him, lifting both arms, and immediately jolted backwards. The shot was like a misfire. Badly timed, hardly aimed. It was as though she did not know what the thing in her hand was. From the shocked expression on her face, he thought that she had been hurt and that he, for some strange reason, was feeling the pain of it. He found he was clutching the door frame. He looked down at his shoe.

Even then, he said, he expected her to hand him the gun. She had come to give him something, that is what she said at the door, 'I have something to give him.' She had rung beforehand to say the same thing: she had something for him, or maybe she said that she had something 'for him to see'. He had expected a script, as sometimes happens with actresses, who are always on the lookout for a star vehicle, a story in which they could play a leading role. She had brought him such material in the past and, though he did not welcome these interruptions, it was hard to turn a woman like Katherine O'Dell from his door.

The defence argued, a little sweatily, that the gun was indeed intended as a gift for Boyd, that it continued to be a prop gun despite the accidental split second when it became a real gun. But they did not fool me. My mother wore, for the occasion, an old-fashioned suit of aqua summer tweed: round collar, metal buttons like plaited rope, probably Chanel. She was dressed for a shooting, and for the six o'clock news.

She let the gun drop – it was the clunk of it hitting the floor that made Mary Bohan scream and reach for the phone. Or, it wasn't a scream, she said, in court. It came out funny, as if there was a bird caught in her throat.

When she heard this strangulated sound, my mother turned to her with a flicker of curiosity ('so cold,' Mary said) as though making a note of it. Then she turned and walked back down the stairs, out on to Wicklow Street, down to Grafton Street and into Bewley's Café which was about three hundred yards distant. There was a waitress there called Tattens who always made a great fuss of her: very grand and queenly, with white hair and excellent skin. She crooned as usual over her charge, as she served my mother's milky coffee and cinnamon bun. They spoke about the weather, 'Yes, very mild,' the coffee, 'Thank you so much, thank you,' my mother's work prospects, which were, if Tattens only knew it, suddenly much worse, 'And when can we expect to see you back on stage?' They ignored the fuss of ambulance and police sirens stuck in the traffic outside.

'We talked about Jimmy O'Dea,' said Tattens, referring to a much loved Dublin actor, many years dead. 'And the glory days of the Queen's.'

After her post-shooting cup of coffee, Katherine walked up Dawson Street to get a taxi outside the Shelbourne and she came home to Dartmouth Square where she was apprehended within the hour. There was no fuss. A uniformed Garda came to the door, and knocked. She took his elbow as they walked down the front steps and he gave a sharp salute as she sat into the backseat of the waiting car. Or perhaps the salute is the stuff of legend – I do not know.

When I rang Pearse Street Garda Station, I was told she was helping police with their inquiries. Also that she did not seem to have any shoes.

Of course, everyone in Dublin thought she had been sleeping with him, much to Boyd's helpless irritation. There was a letter sent to the papers, pre-empting libel. 'My client did not have sexual relations with his attacker, nor attempt to have sexual relations with his attacker, nor did she ever attempt to have contact of a sexual or romantic nature with him.'

No one believed him – except, at a guess, his wife. But I also believed him. I did not think she shot him for love.

He really was a pill. By the time I knew Boyd, and I did not know him well, his youthful lack of talent had turned into something else. I got the impression he was indeed 'beset' – by fools, whippersnappers and by looseness of various kinds. Perhaps it was the brandy made him sarcastic. Nothing was right. He disapproved of things. He was in a mild and semi-permanent state of pain.

My mother, meanwhile, permitted anything, so long as it was glorious. So long as Proust was invoked, or Yeats. So long as you quoted the Bard himself, you could drink all night, you could fall over, swear, thump the wife. And if you had just come from Paris then all the better, because of course you would have news of Samuel Beckett (*he just talked about the cricket!*). Above all you could – not to put too fine a point on it – fuck who you liked. Many of these men were too drunk or covertly Catholic, too fretful or secretly monogamous to get up to much, but others were not. Dick Maguire, who was an alright poet, liked rich American women, though he never seemed to land one, and when he wasn't chasing Mellons and Carnegies he liked fourteen-year-old boys. Especially, as he liked to ruefully admit, if they were a nice shade of brown.

'Oh stop it, Dick,' my mother said.

Outside, Catholic Ireland raged on.

I sit down and write a long email to Holly Devane, who wanted to know about my mother's 'sexual style' (these phrases burn into you slowly, I find). I want to say that some people are closed, and some are open. These are, suddenly, the two sides of an argument I have been having all my life, and I find I have a large amount to say to Ms Devane about the artist who is completely open, who is just Give Give Give, and the audience who takes, and takes, and then likes to criticise.

That is the essential difference: there are those who watch, judge and collect. There are those who scatter, flame and die.

Then I delete it all, for being more of my mother's *dramatics.*

No one asked her to do it.

Katherine O'Dell thought she was offering something to the crowd, of joy or of pain. In later years, she considered herself some sort of sacrifice – set aflame, perhaps, by the glare of their attention. But, you know, maybe she was just standing up there, emoting in the light.

At least, that is what Boyd seemed to imply, when he turned her down for the big Irish movie, *My Dark Rosaleen.*

He went to the trouble of inviting her to a screen test in Ardmore Studios. He did not even send a car.

She did the lines perfectly, she said.

Boyd was sitting with the producers behind the big camera and when she was finished, he didn't say she was marvellous, actually. He leaned across to the wild American director – who was clearly his friend, now – and, under his breath, he said:

'You see what I mean?'

MY MOTHER'S FIRST true love, she once said, was Pleasance McNamara, who was a girl as nice as her name. There was a picture of the pair of them as they walked through Dublin, snapped by the street photographer on O'Connell Bridge. Both in durable tweed, nipped in at the waist, my mother's hair is drawn up on either side of her face like a set of curtains, with a pair of unlikely looking bunches dangling down. They are in high good spirits – Pleasance pitching forward slightly, my mother, in profile, is eye-rolling and daft with the fact of the camera there. She looks, as she would say, 'like Mary Hick'.

They laughed all day, she said. Anything at all could set them off. A woman with her hat on the wrong way. They would have to hang on to each other. A fingered drawing in the condensation on the window of the bus, the conductor himself, standing in front of you, waiting for his coin, it was enough to send you into fits. The boy they met on Thormanby Road and counting white horses – after the seventh one, he would appear.

'Will you link me?' she might say, thirty years later, offering me an elbow as we walked down the street, and

I loved to do just that: it was always a sign of adventure in the air.

The girls shared a bed in the McMasters' cottage on Howth Head, or they took opposite chairs at the hearth with their books. When they looked out the window, Dublin Bay was spread below them; the sea in all its moods any time you lifted your head. There was a submarine lurking under the skin of the water, maybe, a smuggler's skiff chugging quietly out of Howth. As the tide of war turned, the bay became more busy: a tracery of cattle boats and fishing trawlers, fancy sailboats and the North Wall packet. They left the curtains open to see the city surface in the darkness; a net of lights slung carelessly towards the hills.

Once a day, the big mailboat left Dún Laoghaire, stuffed with workers for the munitions factories in Coventry and Leeds. Mac had a telescope you could look through to see the black line of people standing by the rails, some of them waving as they watched the coastline recede. Off to England, though you did not call it that; in those days people just 'went over the other side'.

And when the war ended, there was no stopping them. The two girls got on the mailboat and they were in London in time for the great Victory Parade. From the way she told it, you would think they docked in the middle of the Mall. There were tanks and bagpipes, soldiers and horses, fireworks over the Thames and the royal barge floating down. Drunks bumped into each other in the darkness or spread blankets on park benches to sleep and she was pulled into a rough kiss by a Canadian officer. The feel of his hand lingered in the small of her back and they were not sure, suddenly, what accent to use – some remarks passed by Land Girls in uniform: very common, very prejudiced remarks about the Irish sitting out the war.

By the autumn of 1946, the girls had established them-selves in digs in Notting Hill. This was a single room with a gas ring and a privy on the landing. There was a curtain to draw around the wash-basin and one, exceptionally creaky bed, where they slept top to toe. Together, they enrolled in a Pitman course in shorthand and typing. Pleasance, who had bookkeeping, was taken on by the box office at the Aldwych in time for the Christmas revue. Katherine, meanwhile, found work as a receptionist for George (Nobby) Clark, a theatre impresario whose repu-tation as a womaniser was made during the divorce case of a well-known actress, when she was accused in open court of having sexual relations with him in his rooms on the Strand.

'I never even noticed,' my mother said. 'Though I have to say she was in there an awfully long time.'

Nobby was a round, bald little man. She used to sit at a desk outside his office door, and this door had a bubbled glass pane, just as you might imagine, with his name written across it in gold leaf outlined in black.

George Clark
Theatrical Agent

And in they came. In those days they all wore hats, high and forward – Tudor style or hunting style – they pulled the silk of their blouse out from under a tweed cuff, checked the seams of their fabulous post-war stockings, before opening the door to say, 'Nobby! Darling!' with their hands outstretched. Sometimes, in the winter, there was a muff. Twenty minutes later, out they came again.

Innocence, she liked to tell me, is a great protection.

Not that I needed protecting much, in those days. I stuck to the books.

'You stick to the books!' my mother said, looking at me across the kitchen table, as though I had done something wrong, or was just about to.

Which I certainly was not.

I stacked them beside me each night: Irish Maths French History Geography English Biology. Clearly a very adhesive business, the books. Besides, if I pretended not to be listening there was the chance that I would hear some more, so it was back to xylem and phloem, stalagmites and stalactites, the mouse goes up the ballerina's leg and her tights come down.

I always felt safe on the page.

In the summer of 1946, London was bombed out and the rubble a haze of purple weed, with sudden gaps in ordinary streets where absent houses loomed as the autumn fogs rolled in. The girls queued and queued. They bartered on the street and ran the curtains through the sewing machine for a grand night out at the Savoy, because the war was won and it was all marvellous. The town was full of men. Pleasance wore diamanté bracelets over white evening gloves and kept her cigarette holder angled high. Hunger kept them slim.

In January 1947 the water froze, not just in the pipes, but in the jug on their nightstand, in the cistern and even in the toilet bowl. She recalled waking one morning with Pleasance, fully dressed the pair of them, the ceiling bright with reflected snow, ice flowers on the window's inside and something you could not identify missing from the world, not just the sounds of footfall, or of cars, but a new absence.

Pleasance opening her clear eyes wide, saying, 'What is it?'

It was the silence of water, waiting to flow.

People jammed into the theatres to keep warm, Mac sent a goose marvellously wrapped in brown paper with a stamp on its rump, and Fitz returned to London with a suitcase full of butter, the proceeds of which he put towards a flat in Soho, over Jimmy's in Frith Street. It is possible that for those months he was more smuggler than actor, he often travelled over and back to Ireland. He had a card that read, *dealer in fine books*, an occupation that got harder as the weather warmed up and the books oozed, golden, out of his suitcase and on to the boat-train floor. My grandmother, meanwhile, switched to vaudeville, donning her curly-toed slippers for the 'Chinese geisha' (*sic*) Choo Chin Chan.

('It is amazing,' my mother would later remark, 'just how many whores your grandmother played, sweet woman that she was. Whore after whore after whore. Her own morals were impeccable, you know, she was married at seventeen.')

Fitz, meanwhile, suggested his young daughter to a director he knew for the role of Talitha in *The Awoken*, which was then casting for a run in the West End. At least that was one version of the story; the other was that the director came to see a queue of young hopefuls at Nobby Clark's and picked the girl who brought his tea.

'What about her?'

'Who, the girl?'

'What's your name, dear?'

'Oh, no,' she said.

Who, me?

She had to be dragged onstage. No, really.

'The stage chose me, you know,' is what she liked to say, her hand wavering at her breastbone – as though all she ever wanted was a four-bed in Finchley and a man in a wrinkle-proof tie. She might have been in the suburbs somewhere, baking scones. Two blond children, a gingham apron and a dog – the shadow of this beautiful, lost life fell over every subsequent success. It was one of the most infuriating things about my mother, the way she insisted that she might have been happy instead.

The truth was that, beautiful though she was, Katherine Odell would never be snapped up by a Cambridge man and introduced to his mother over afternoon tea. Finchley did not want her. And if I sound a little too forensic about her expectations, it is because I hated it so much – I hated how close her talent ran to shame.

'The stage chose me, you know.'

Whatever she wanted at nineteen, or pretended to want, young Katherine Odell was perfectly suited to the role of Talitha, which was thrust upon her by Nobby Clark in the late spring of 1947. Rehearsals went on for an expansive four weeks, the play opened in The Criterion at the beginning of June. After ten years' experience of working on stage, she finally made her debut.

A new play by Jack Ashburnham, *The Awoken*, concerns a girl who wakes from a coma and slowly recovers her memory, along with her ability to walk and speak. As she does so, she recalls the identity of the man whose attempted seduction laid her low (it was not so much a coma, perhaps, as a prolonged swoon) and this man has been – you guessed it – by her bedside, all along. The part of Talitha had so few lines you might call it mute, and Katherine Odell was, by all accounts, brilliant as one of those spooked-out revenants, neither child nor woman, who wander around such stories in their white cotton shifts. 'Luminous' was a key word. One leading critic wrote, 'If called upon to swear, I would say that her small feet never touched the ground.'

The Awoken ran for six packed-out months in the West End and her performance remained 'magical'. She was photographed for *Harper's Bazaar* and *Illustrated* magazine. Orson Welles came to check her out for a role in a film that would not, in fact, get made.

'I wasn't asking and he wasn't shooting,' she used to say, 'but he still showed up to turn me down.' Welles sat in her dressing room, planted a silver-topped cane in front of himself even though he was not old enough for a cane. His cigar was huge, his face was big as a serving-platter. She chatted about the usual things, but it was all wrong, apparently, because his face snapped shut suddenly, and he cracked the cane on the ground and was gone. It was like watching your future walk out of the room, she said. This rejection, though it felt both devastating and odd, was actually a sign of the heat she was generating just then. Katherine Odell was the last person in London to know it: she was a star.

It happened instantly. Perhaps there is no other way. A star is born not made, because stars are not actors – some of them, indeed, are very bad actors, at least that is what my mother used to say. Whatever a star has, they had it all along and, at nineteen, Katherine Odell had it in spades. Offstage, you could hardly see her, onstage you could not look away.

My mother said it was about stillness. This is what the poet Stephen Spender told her when he came backstage and bent to kiss her hand. He said she was so still that, when she played a winter scene, he could see her breath fog the air in front of her young mouth. That is how good she was.

Or perhaps, it was all down to Mac's great instruction: DROP THE TRAY!!

Indeed, she had a habit of holding her hands out in front of her, late into her career. She said it was a more dynamic posture than letting them dangle like cabbages down by your side. Which led one critic to say that she looked on the brink of rushing towards something, at all times.

She was at the theatre at six every evening for a play in which she had exactly five lines. She warmed her throat, stretched her face about, picked a peck of pickled pepper. The routine never changed. Katherine sat quietly for half an hour before approaching the mirror, and another half hour when her make-up was done. On her five-minute call, she stood up, walked out of her dressing room and went to her place in the wings. She pulled it out, as they say, every single night and she slept until three in the afternoon. Fitz, who was now permanently settled in his rooms in Frith Street, worked with Nobby on the contract so that there was money for everyone, even for her.

It must have been a tender time. She did not speak much about the public aspects of success as they are usually portrayed: applause, flashbulbs popping, stage-door john-nies and white flowers scenting her dressing room. Instead, she spoke about the mighty and heroic sleeping she did in her beautiful new sheets of imported American cotton. After another month of packed houses there was a whole new bed, another two weeks and it was time to leave Notting Hill for 'an' hotel (as she always styled it) in Berkeley Square, where room service knocked on the door with scrambled eggs in the middle of the afternoon. These were done with crème fraîche and chives, and she had never eaten anything so good, she just wolfed them down. Later, they put her name on the menu, they called the whole thing after her: Eggs O'Dell.

She also spoke, a little painfully, about Pleasance McMaster who became, in those months, so hard to please. Pleasance said that she, Katherine, had changed, though she was the same person she had always been. And anyway, she didn't have time to change. She barely had time to buy clothes to wear for the things expected of her now – where would she get the time to change?

Whatever that meant.

For my mother, people were always and essentially them-selves. Women, especially, remained constant: through love and tragedy, joy and sorrow. Which meant she could not figure out what was wrong with Pleasance, who was sworn *always* to be her friend.

One evening the girls went along to Ivor Novello's – an old rival of Mac's from way back. Some people said it was because of Novello that Mac had run away to Ireland, others that they remained close friends. Whatever the truth of it, Ivor took the girls on when they got started in London – he made sure they met people and had a good time. And one evening, 'How could I not have known?' my mother said.

'The look on her face.'

It was as though Pleasance was in pain. Like a little shard of something was sticking into her, a sliver of metal or glass. Ivor sat in to the piano and everyone sang. There was an awful lot to drink. Then Ivor took my mother's shoe and proposed a toast to the room. Hard to believe anyone drank champagne from a shoe still warm from a human foot, but it really was a thing back then, and Novello liked to do it, or at least pretend to do it. Of course, the girl had to dance on the table first, or somewhere up high, so the man could just peel it off her, you didn't go hopping around on one foot, undoing your buckles and straps.

(*Really?* I said nothing, I stuck to the books, *the mice run up the ballerina's legs and the tights come down*).

In this case, it wasn't a table, it was the top of a baby grand, as he thumped and trilled through the accompani-ment and she sang, 'Waltz of my Heart'. It was just Ivor.

He poured the champagne from way up high, and he raised the shoe – it was a little satin thing with a diamanté bow. My mother now sitting on top of the piano, her bare feet pointed sweetly down at the keys, and a crazy, drinking,

75

cheering group around them, among them Pleasance McMaster, who smiled and smiled.

'To Talitha, arise!' said Ivor. He put the shoe to his lips and pretended to sip.

'Arise!' they all said, and Pleasance lifted her glass, and my mother would never forget the look on her friend's face – as though something inside her was being strangled, very slowly.

'Arise!'

How could I not have known.

'Arise!'

They were still living together in Notting Hill and when they got home, Pleasance said that she, Katherine, had no time for her any more. Pleasance was a little emotional. She said that Katherine was always gone, these days. Even though they had just been together at Ivor's, and come back home together, and were now taking off their make-up together, Pleasance looked straight at her and said, 'I don't see you any more'.

What am I? Transparent?

She was right there.

There was something in this that made Katherine shiver, like the feel of moonlight on your skin. She had to turn and check the mirror, because she did not know what it was that Pleasance saw, she looked at her so strangely. But the image in the glass was just Katherine – a little flushed from the success of the evening, but otherwise herself.

They went to bed as ever, top to toe, and Pleasance turned and fell asleep while my mother lay blinking at the ceiling, extra awake. It was so unfair.

It was just *work*, she said. What was she supposed to do, fall over and forget her lines so Pleasance could sympathise, the way she liked to do? 'Oh poor Katherine. Poor darling. Oh poor you.' Though she really could do with some sympathy because Orson Welles was not the only pig who turned up to her dressing room, just to check her out and walk away. Some of the men were terribly – really oddly – rude and unpleasant. As though she was taking something away from them. It was all very confusing, and it was wicked of Pleasance to see it any other way.

After that, there was no more fun.

'Of course there was oodles of fun,' she said, but not with Pleasance. There was no more laughing on the tram. No more secret tickling at the back of your knee, when you were trying to hold a proper conversation. There was no more *always*.

A few years later, Pleasance married the actor Bernard Forbes, who would be one of the first directors of the Granada television soap, *Coronation Street*. She embarked upon the life that Katherine failed to acquire: first of all in a small flat with babies and the smell of nappies drying, and then, later, a house in Purley, Surrey. She reared three children, sent them off to university in Nottingham, Durham and Dublin. One of them, as my mother frequently told me, is a doctor now.

Pleasance came to my mother's funeral. She brought her husband and her Dublin daughter, who lives on Howth Head as her grandparents once did. Though the house is less good than the one they used to rent – poor players that they were – all those years ago.

It took me a moment to think who she was, this middle-aged woman occupying a forward pew. She was not an actress, clearly. She was the kind of woman an actress would imitate but never be: ash-blonde hair, stiff with spray, a good camel coat, black patents with two-inch block heels. She took me in her arms.

'Oh poor you.' The voice that came out of her was girlish and light. It was Pleasance, of course it was.

'Poor baby.' She was wearing White Linen perfume by Estée Lauder, and under the soft coat she was firm, round, girdled about.

'I am so sorry.'

I pulled back to look at her.

'She is in a better place,' I said, though I did not believe my mother was anywhere but dead. The last years had been so rough, it was the simplest thing to say – as opposed to, I don't know, 'Thank goodness, eh? Glad that's over.'

Bernard, the husband, hung back in the church porch with a wounded look to him, waiting for her to be done. Later I imagined how it was for them now – the tough times when the children were young all sentimentalised, Bernard's drinking years put behind them, his eye for an actress forgiven, or so it seemed. He wanted nothing but Pleasance, he was jealous of her time. No wonder she looked so radiant and soft. She had come into her own.

She searched my face with her faded blue eyes and it was one of those roving looks that is both specific and large.

'How are you?'

'I am fine,' I said. 'I am fine.'

'You will be, my darling. Give it time.'

My mother's best friend.

Loyalty would not let them part. They swore to each other and to the world that they were close, even when it was down to Christmas cards. They did articles for the newspapers about friendship: 'How we met.' My mother cursing afterwards, flinging the paper away from her, saying, 'God, that woman is such hard work. Such. Hard. Work.' Because there was no pleasing Pleasance, not any more.

The day I went to my mother's birthplace in Herne Hill, I also called in to see Pleasance who still lives in Surrey, in a supervised apartment block in a place called Waddon Ponds. She opened the door herself, with no need of a cane. At eighty-three, Pleasance was still lovely – perhaps even more so – that ditzy quality she had was made more sweet by the vagueness of age.

'Oh my dear, how are you?'

Her wood-pigeon voice still cooed commiseration, and it was a while before I realised she was more or less demented. She remembered very little, and what she did recall was rinsed in saccharine. Though the occasional glimpse stole through.

'She had terrific pipes. My father always called it your pipes, and hers were very open and true, she would lie down with her head on a book, for hours. We knew a man could swallow a goldfish and bring it back up still flapping and she thought about him a lot, how you open that, what is the word? The swallowing bit, how you open it all up. She just opened her mouth and there it was. Perfect pitch. Like pressing the key on a piano. Not fish, of course. He could swallow all kinds of things. Keys. Razor blades. It was awful to watch. He played Blackpool, Grimsby, places like that. Poor boy, he learned it in an institution, you know.'

I stayed as long as I could and kept her company before heading off for my plane. I thought about the years since my mother had died – how ordinary they might have been: full of gossip, hair appointments, chats on the phone. Grandchildren. She never saw her grandchildren.

I took out the picture I carry of my two children, Pamela and Max, and her finger wavered over each of them, tipping the surface of the photograph with an old fingernail.

'Oh yes. Oh lovely.'

I asked her not to get out of her chair as I said goodbye, but she pushed up anyway, then made a small grab at my coat sleeve to steady herself. She gave me that sweet, searching look and, 'Take care of yourself,' she said.

'You too.' I looked at her fondly and she shivered, on a deep inhale – some hurt so distant and ancient, it was gone before she knew it was there.

'You have her eyes,' she said.

'Yes.'

'I suppose people tell you that all the time.'

IN MAY 1948, Katherine Odell brought *The Awoken* to Broadway. She boarded the *Queen Mary* at Southhampton and her appearance at the rails was captured by Pathé News.

She was booked into a room at the Waldorf Astoria for a planned six-week run, that turned into twenty-three. At first she was left to enjoy the city alone, but something happened when the show caught on. Dinners were held. Nobby made a deal with an American agency and a series of New York hostesses took her under their wing for theatre suppers and gallery visits, shopping in the morning, coffee in the afternoon.

She found these rich women very confusing at first: Fanny and Lindsay and Jill, with their whims and shifts, their sudden changes of plan. She heard confidences about their lives and did not know how to respond. They were so melancholy and then so dismissive. It was as though the wealthy did not believe in having problems, at least, not for long; as though they found problems, which had been meat and drink to Pleasance, to be a bit of a bore. And this, Katherine realised one day – with a great lightening of the heart – was not such a bad way to proceed.

So it was soon marvellous to go about with these opaque women, who swapped her amongst themselves like a new thing. They steered her around New York and introduced her to 'everyone', whoever that was: famous doctors and famous flower arrangers, a dancer whose brother had won the Nobel Prize in Chemistry, Clifford Odets, who ignored her, a woman whose father owned a whole newspaper, an artist who whispered into her ear the filthiest thing she had ever heard – she would take it to her grave with her, there was no point whatsoever asking what it was he said.

She spent a morning crossing from Saks to Barneys, and the bills – when Fanny or Lindsay waved a hand, something happened, so my mother almost thought it was free – but the bill was delivered to her agency and deducted directly from her payslip, enough money to buy a house in Ireland, the dollar was so high back then, she had no idea what had just happened, or how to stop it happening again. She was so upset she was shaking, but her agent just took her by the shoulders and said, 'You really don't know what is coming for you, do you?' This man was the famous Eddie Malk of the William Morris west-coast office. He was generally known to be in love with Ruth Roman and was then in the middle of a spectacular divorce, which did not seem to take up much of his time. Eddie Malk knew everyone. He had vision.

They went to Sardi's on the opening night and stayed up for the reviews which were only moderately good. The one in the *Tribune* contained a typo – an extra apostrophe in Katherine's name, rendering her O'Dell and this made her laugh.

'I quite like it,' she said to Eddie, wrapping an imaginary shawl about her and throwing her head back to declare, 'I've lost him, surely. I've lost the only Playboy of the Western World.' The next day he was in her hotel room going through her wardrobe, rifling through the hangers, throwing the outfits on one chair or another. My mother, her quilt about her chin, sat watching him from the bed.

'From now on,' he said, 'you wear any colour you like, so long as it is green.' By this he meant anything from teal to emerald, all forty shades of it. The hotel hairdresser arrived, pulled my mother's head gently back into the sink and two hours later she was a flaming redhead.

'Auburn,' said Eddie.

Katherine looked in the mirror and saw ginger, a shade so derided by the girls at school in Connemara, it would make you weep. You would die rather than be ginger. She was not sure why. It was something to do with living in a ditch and also with incest, it was more than just dirty, it was epic, and though she did think it suited her pale skin, she still cried and cried.

'Auburn,' said Eddie again, then he gave her the America speech.

'You are in America, now,' he said. 'You can be anything you want to be.'

And when she said that she did not want to be this, he said, 'You can be whatever you miss most. What do you miss most?'

She missed Connemara. She missed the small towns, the view from the top of the footbridge of bog and gorse, the woman in Sligo who sent them a note to say, 'The weather is terrible for God's sake mind yourself.'

'Ireland,' she said.

She was playing eight shows a week and now, in the afternoon, there was more work: Eddie making her speak into a microphone, a man who did things with her feet; a woman who plucked her eyebrows into a thin line.

She could never remember where she was taken after the show came down.

'I should have kept a diary.'

There was Chicken Kiev in the Russian Tea Rooms, and a gilt cave of a room behind a bar on 43rd Street with a man she thought was Mafia until she saw him up on the altar of St Patrick's Cathedral, she was sure it was the same one. One evening, a man sent over a bottle of champagne and Eddie said, 'Go ahead, you can drink it if you want,' and after that she never did more than dab the rim of a glass against her lips. She was twenty years old. She had a new feeling around Eddie, it tugged at her insides, the way they understood each other. It wasn't romantic, though she could see how it might also be that. If she had to put a word on it, she would call it ambition.

Eddie sending her to an audition that turned out to be a card game in a back room.

'Be nice,' said Eddie and then, 'Not too nice!'

One of those days, she walked down Fifth Avenue with her new hair, her new corset, her new heels, and something happened to the people who passed her by. Heads turned. She was like a pebble dropped into a pool of their attention. And she sank deliciously, into it, delighted by the way she could hide now, in plain view.

(Because they did not know her at all, and that was the great joke of it.)

Then it was August and everyone was out of town. Eddie disappeared, came back with a pale indent where he used to wear a ring. She went boating with college types on the lake in Central Park, a young man with a number at the end of his name, something like George Meredith the third. The trees were turning a hundred shades of rust and gold and there was a maple on the bank the same colour as her new hair. She dipped her fingertips into the dull city water and she was as lonely as it is possible for a woman in New York to be.

It got harder to come down after the high of the show, now that the show was old. The hotel, realising her habit of walking the corridors at night, allocated a bellhop to keep her silent company, and this boy stood by the lift with a crystal ashtray in both hands. She smoked one Chesterfield after another, loosely packed cigarettes that she sucked the innards out of in huge, crackling inhalations. She loved smoking alone. Like drinking or eating, it was something a lady did not relish in public unless she was common – as, she was discovering, many of the women hanging around Broadway were. 'It was less glamorous than you might think,' she used to say. It was fine going about if you had a man's arm to hold, a car at the door, but things turned easily. You went to powder your nose and came back to a different room, the feeling that it was time to go.

She was supposed to be accompanied by her co-star, Philip Greenfield, who played the young doctor hero in *The Awoken*. But though Philip was a gallant escort he clearly had other inclinations. She was not sure what it was he liked, but she was pretty sure he liked it a lot. Philip was so easily distracted, she thought maybe prostitutes, something terribly dark and dangerous. Or maybe he was taking pills. It was some time before she realised that it was other men he was after – at the age of twenty, she did not know that such a thing was possible. Of course she *knew*, but she did not think it happened to a man if he was handsome, and Philip was very handsome. Philip was dreamy. They had the best time. Philip said, 'It is all in the eyes,' just before they entered a room. He was such a good dancer, he made it feel like a waltz, as you made your way around the party and then off out the door. They were often photographed laughing together, but when the taxicab dropped her at the Astoria, he climbed back in and was gone.

She persuaded the silent bellhop into the street one night after rain, she just did it with a smile. They walked together all the way to the East River, another time up to Central Park. She was always looking for the edges of things. One night they made it down to the Battery and the waves were high and wild in the moonlight. The water went all the way to Ireland, she said.

Although she was young, the bellhop was even younger, a blushing boy with blue eyes. He was from Fermanagh. A Protestant, he told her. He said he had never spoken to a Catholic girl before he met her. He said that she was very nice and this fact seemed to surprise him. It was a formal announcement he made, as though he was speaking on behalf of all Protestants, everywhere. And when she laughed and said he must talk to Catholics all the time here in the big city, he said, 'I mean from home.'

His name was James Nixon, and he had the loveliest Northern accent. Walking those streets with him was like strolling down a country lane. Shapes in dark alleyways, shouts and altercations on a distant street, and the sound of his voice was hawthorn in the hedgerows, turning the city smells to meadowsweet. He carried a hotel umbrella to protect her, but when she walked with Jim Nixon, she did not mind when it rained.

On the night they stood looking to sea, with Liberty out there in the darkness, James Nixon said his sister had scarlet fever on the crossing and was locked away from them, for quarantine. She was buried at night, when she died. They just slid her off a plank. That is the story he told, when they looked out over the waters that stretched, in the moonlight, all the way home.

And a part of her wondered if he had not made it up – it was all so opportune. And she felt so guilty for wondering this. It was such a terrible story, if it was true.

Then, for no reason, he was gone. The next night, a different bellhop in the same uniform held the door open for her, and he said, 'Shall I call you a cab, Miss Odell?' But she did not want a cab. She walked three blocks of the city night before turning back to the safety of her room.

For the next week or more she wanted to ask what had happened to James Nixon, but she sensed that she could not. She thought about handing a note for him in at the concierge desk – or would that be, somehow, undiplomatic? She never saw him again.

She slept all morning, every morning. One rare afternoon when she had nothing to do, she went over to Saks to see what she might buy for Pleasance who she pined for even though her letters were so thin and few. She touched the cashmere and the silk but it was all too extravagant for Pleasance and the cheaper stuff did not please her, Katherine, any more. Her tastes had changed, and there was no going back, apparently – this journey was a one-way street. In the end she got nothing, sent a long letter, or wrote a long letter and did not send it, or just felt hopeless instead.

In October, the weather came down hard, and she really might have gone home, if she knew how to go home. Later, when she wondered about this, she decided that she did not know how else to feel but good. Every night she stepped out in front of the stage-lights she felt destined, but it was the same destiny, repeated. It was the same lines in the same show, and this went on for many consecutive nights, until the city itself became unreal.

While she felt stuck in some kind of loop, the machinery of her life continued to move on without her. In September her agent, Eddie Malk, found the opportunity he had been waiting for. He persuaded the producers of an upcoming show into a sweet Irish accent and by the autumn, Katherine was in rehearsal for what proved to be her defining role.

A Prayer Before Morning by Sheldon Cox opened in November 1948 in the Adelphi on 54th Street. Now better known by its movie title, *Mulligan's Holy War,* this was the hit that would, in time, bring her to Hollywood and to lasting fame.

Set during the Allied invasion of France a (newly punctuated) Katherine O'Dell plays a feisty Irish nursing sister called Sister Mary Felicitas who labours in a field hospital in Normandy, tending to the wounded behind the lines. Her makeshift ward is sheltered by the bombed out remains of an old church. The original stage set showed moonlight coming through stained-glass windows, a line of beds and a small oratory to one side. There is the constant drone of aircraft, the far-off sound of big guns. Sometimes we hear the wail of a blues harmonica played by a wounded soldier from Mississippi, or the mutterings of a blinded boy called Jimmy, dreaming he can see.

Sister Mary, a spirited young thing from the West of Ireland, tangles with an American-Irish captain called Mulligan when he comes searching for an enemy soldier suspected of Nazi war crimes. The man is found among her patients, bandaged and barely conscious, and the nun protests he is not well enough to stand trial. The captain insists, she resists, and over the course of a few days' argument they fall in love. It is Mulligan who dies in the end; shot by the malingering Nazi after a long and impossible night, some of which the lovers spend in prayer. This reversal – the sacrifice of the male rather than the female love interest – was remarkable, and it turned Sister Mary Felicitas into a sensation. The lovers' first kiss, which is also their last, is the kind of thing to make a bishop blush.

Captain Mulligan falls back from Sister Mary's lips to die in her lap, as she sits in the rubble of the bombed-out altar steps. His dead body is awkward and long, and this clumsy Pièta seems to say something new and accurate about death, belief and war.

'He is gone from me now,' she says. 'He has taken the moon with him and the sun too. He has taken what's before me and what is behind me, and great is my fear that he has taken my God from me.'

Of course he hasn't taken God away from her; the blues-playing American soldier slides out the opening bars of 'Amazing Grace' and two orderlies come to lift the body away. As she stands, Sister Mary's face is illuminated by the dappled light of the rose window. It is dawn. The blinded boy shouts in agony, 'The sun, the sun!' and Sister Mary Felicitas is back by his side, saying, 'Yes, Jimmy, oh yes, Jimmy, you can see it, you can see the sun!'

Blackout.

Audiences in New York wept, jumped to their feet, shouted their admiration and applause. They showered her – literally – they threw flowers and objects on to the stage. A man in the front row pulled his silk handkerchief out of his front pocket and sent it fluttering high, so she thought he had pelted her with a live bird. It was all a little alarming, she said.

Her lingering, luvvie curtain call never changed – that clearing of her gaze as though realising the audience had been there – *oh my goodness!* – all along. The first of it was a slight flinching. There is so much noise and she is still between things, she is coming back to herself, seeing that she is dressed, for some reason, in nun's clothes.

It is all so very surprising, *Oh, there you are*, a hand to the crowd. And, *Yes! Here I am*, the same hand at her breast. It looks quite fake, but I think it was entirely real.

89

I mean, I think there was a moment between acting the nun and acting the actress that my mother was herself. There was a slice of time between those two points when she was lost – when she did not exist, almost – and then she found herself, or was handed back to herself by the crowd.

Such gratitude. From her. From them.

It's only me. Bowing. Sweeping back. Sweeping forward to bow again. *I could not do it without you, you have been so wonderful. Yes, I love you too.*

Taking off her veil.

It was exhausting, we all knew it. It took everything she had, this business of getting into character, and then being in character, and then, painfully, coming out of character. It was such a long journey back to the real world. No one knew why it should be so tiring or what the true alchemy of it was, but it was the difference between a real perfor-mance and just going through the motions, it was the difference between losing the audience and having them in the palm of your hand.

By the time the stage show opened in November, she was renting an apartment on Washington Square and, although I hope she had a lover by now, it is also possible she was as innocent as her publicity photographs showed her still to be. She was only twenty-one. She worked all the time. Katherine O'Dell was built for work, it was what she knew. But she was also just a girl – what was the word she used? 'It was a gas,' she said, with a slight American tinge to it. 'It was the cat's miaow.'

She was still seen in the papers out and about with Philip Greenfield and the following year they would, at the behest of the studio, get married in LA. They lived together as a couple for eighteen heady months, first in the Hollywood Hills and then on San Remo Drive in Brentwood, where they had a large house with two Austrian maids and a pool. During this time, there were many managed photo opportunities depicting the kind of life my mother always mourned for – domestic events, picnics, encounters with children. But Philip's career failed to ignite on the west coast and it did not take long for rumours to circulate of fights behind closed doors.

My mother's husband, Philip Greenfield, was another self-invented man. Dark haired and charming, he was born in Willesden, and graduated from London's Slade School of Art. When they moved to San Remo Drive he converted the pool house into a sculptor's studio, where he also liked to entertain during the hot afternoons. I suspect Philip taught my mother how to drink, though it is likely she would have learned that all by herself. He also took sleeping tablets and Quaaludes, a habit she would, in later life, fail to control. But I do not blame Philip for robbing her of sleep, either (she never stopped blaming Pleasance who 'just rolled over and did it' as though wrapping herself in my mother's peace of mind).

The marriage seemed like a good idea. She and Philip had some wonderful times in LA, at least they had some wonderful weekends. And when there was a break in the filming of *Mulligan* (or of her next movie, the mostly forgotten *Wings Over the Valley*) she might take a car and meet him for a swim and dinner at the house of a new friend. They drank spirits, and some champagne. It was martinis at lunch, martinis before dinner, whiskey late at night, and in the morning a vodka fixer. Philip had a recipe for a Bloody Mary with paprika and an egg that she swore by for a hangover, all her days. She used to press it on people, calling it 'my husband's Bloody Mary', though Philip was long dead, and a husband only ever in name.

Magazine gossip would tell you that she found out about his male lovers slowly and experienced that as some kind of betrayal, but that is not what she said to me. Drunk or sober, maudlin or sweetly confiding, she never, within my hearing, implied that she cared about his sexual style. There was no bitterness. If Philip's name cropped up, she might pause and think about him, as some sorrow that could not be undone.

'Oh yes, Philip,' she said, or even, 'Poor Philip,' and when the rumours of his sexuality became publicly confirmed (a process which took many decades), she just said Philip was marvellous, they were so happy for a time, and she would always love him for himself. She was utterly loyal to his name.

They were troupers. They had the same job, which was to keep up appearances, not for their own sake but for the sake of the paying public, because you could not let your audience down. My mother had a great regard for the dreams of the paying public, who were, as she pointed out, often very poor. Unfortunately, over time, Philip became less good at all this. In January 1951, he was picked up, confused and bleeding from the head, on the beach in Santa Monica. A few weeks later, he crashed his car just before dawn, right on Hollywood Boulevard. The studio managed to keep it quiet, but the press picked up a DUI charge in March. She filed for divorce in May after a difficult year, and Greenfield moved out, leaving his sculptures (a series of coloured metal discs on upright black rods) scattered around the property. Philip went up to Monterey. He died as a result of a fall in his kitchen in 1961, when I was nine years old.

But in New York, back in the day, he was still the best dancer in town. He took the part of a cockney soldier in *Prayer before Morning*, to keep Katherine company during the long Broadway run, all 358 exhausting iterations of it. They spoke on the phone every day, or took an acting class together in the afternoon. Six months into the ten-month run, her father Fitz – who never took an acting class in his life – made the trip across the pond and he lingered a little too long in New York. Her mother, who may have been suffering from medical problems that year, stayed at home.

Katherine O'Dell was twenty years old when the studio married her off to her best friend. It happened so soon after she signed her contract, I wondered why it was not written down along with the clauses about her hair, her weight and the length of her fingernails. (There was also a morality clause, which is a bit of a joke considering what we know of the town in those years.) The studio owned her 'image', if such a thing could be legally owned. What this meant was that Katherine O'Dell's private life would be subject to the guidance and scrutiny of the publicity department, her personal choices monitored and sold by them as content to the press.

'My Irish Katherine.'

'Katherine O'Dell's recipe for home-made soda bread.'

'Whatever happened to Tall, Dark and Handsome? Katherine O'Dell says that mysterious men are hard to find, these days.'

'Katherine to wed her British beau.'

Her wedding was indeed a fairy tale. She wore a simple dress in white chiffon with a little Peter Pan collar. Philip played the Englishman in a morning suit, and though the black-and-white of the photographs can not show the exact hue, in his buttonhole was a lilac-coloured rose.

They look untouchably happy.

(How does an actor say, 'I do,' up there in front of the congregation? This was something I worried about as a child – how does an actor *mean* things?) But although she played romantic roles, my mother was not personally romantic. I mean, she was not self-deluded. I do not think she wanted, or ever attempted to have, a sexual relationship with Philip Greenfield.

I made the mistake of telling someone the truth of all of this once, I took the risk. Actually with Melanie, my friend from school. I told her my mother's marriage was just for show and she was astounded.

'What do you mean?'

I don't think our relationship survived the confidence. At fifteen, Melanie did not know what a homosexual was, really, or what he might to do for pleasure, and I was suddenly mortified. I was deeply ashamed of my mother for marrying a man she loved, but not in that way.

She was ambitious, I told myself later. She was unprotected.

And also, Why not?

But of course the reason she married Philip is that the studio told her to marry Philip. It was part of the job, and Katherine O'Dell did not, for a second, consider turning the job down. No one did. You could not walk away from fame, it would be like walking away from destiny, which is to say from your future, inevitable self. The real you, revealed at last.

Mr and Mrs Greenfield lived in a Spanish-style bungalow in Beachwood Canyon, from which Katherine was picked up every morning at seven to go down to the lot. She was given acting lessons, much to her annoyance, because they were so old-fashioned (DROP THE TRAY!!) compared to the ones she had taken in New York. She was schooled in answering questions from journalists. She also learned to dance the foxtrot, how to faint, how to stick her arm up straight and waggle her hand when the script said 'wave'.

She was told to stay out of the sun and then dragged right into it, for swimming lessons, tennis, archery and horse-riding. The fine hair by her ears was painfully plucked back in order to made her expression more 'open'. Her face was taped back at the sides to train her in smooth, unmoving reactions and she learned how to cry without grimacing while someone blew menthol in her eye.

Mulligan's Holy War was shot in the autumn of 1950 and put on general release in the New Year. In it, Katherine O'Dell is, for the first time, recognisable as the actress she would become. We find it hard to think of her any other way, indeed, but it wasn't a given. Before they took a chance with *Mulligan*, the studio tried her out in a thriller called *The Spiral*. I look at the tape of it and imagine other futures for her, ones that were not so Irish after all.

The Spiral is a harmless thriller, set in the bright hills above LA. In it, Katherine plays the murdered woman's unreliable sister, who smokes with trembling fingers and keeps schtum.

'Was your sister seeing someone?'

The gumshoe leans in to light her cigarette. She looks up at him. When she opens her mouth, an unfamiliar woman hops out of it.

'I am not sure what you mean.'

Each time I see this movie, I want to yelp and point. It is as though my mother had been possessed – or at the least overdubbed. She speaks with the elocution accent actors used in those days; a transatlantic, upper-class imagining, so crystalline as to be transparent.

'I wish I could help you, Detective, I really do.'

This voice has no nationality and it expresses no emotion, though the words are crisped at the edges with something like contempt. Because what else should a beautiful woman be, but contemptuous?

'My sister was not a happy woman, Detective, I think you might have guessed that by now.'

There is something else in this first recorded performance, something that drags contrary to the disdainful voice. The sister manages to look somehow unwashed, there is a sag in the seat of her little wool suit, her hands are often at her face or neck, and her red hair seems more whorish than Irish, more bordello than bog. This slight dilapidation shows a real relationship between the actress and cinematographer – as though she understood from shot to shot how her face would play in the light. My mother worked the lens. She knew how to make the viewer wait, because she controlled the frame, and this kind of knowledge was, famously, not something you could either teach or learn. She stole every scene.

The man behind the camera was the great Laslo Molnár who came to America from Hungary in 1938. Many of the people she and Philip met that first year were European emigrés, the conversations around their dinner tables, as she recalled them, as likely to be about the rise of fascism as of Mickey Mouse. Feminism, not so much, judging by the slightly soiled sexuality of *The Spiral*. But it is easy to see how she and Philip might fit in.

After this first modest success, she continued to prepare for *Mulligan*, with costume and make-up tests, ballet classes and voice coaching. She was not permitted to get her hair wet and slept in oiled cotton gloves to preserve her white, prayerful hands. On the first day of shooting, she threw all their hard work in the pan.

'I threw it in the pan!' she liked to declare.

Sister Mary Felicitas can not be contained by her nun's habit, nor even by the frame of the screen. She is irrepressible. Her voice is lilting, her beauty heedless and unadorned. Katherine makes an utterly convincing Irish virgin, being both roguish and pure. There is no doubt it was the look in her eye – what Kael called 'the twinkle in the wimple' – rather than the hokum script, that made the movie sing.

It was a very physical performance – Hollywood always loved a running nun and she dashed about, making her heavy skirts fly. But the real joy of it was in the accent, as Sister Felicitas brought the untameable sweetness of Connemara to the war-torn darkness of northern France.

After my mother left the movies, this Irishness would grow more poetic and controlled. Over time, it became a kind of national statement, or national lullaby. Her mature stage voice was highly achieved and very beautiful; deliberately, almost wilfully melodic, with consonants both soft and slender; she worked in tiny dragging delays, and each word or running phrase was inflected for wildness or ironic effect. All this happened off the beat, so though it was a mannered style, you fell into it. 'Always surprising,' the critics said. 'Delightful.' She was, as she said herself, a bit of a tart.

As was Sister Mary Felicitas, in her day. A complete flirt.

'Oh, I'm an awful girl!' she exclaims, running around with a bit of business over an escaped canary. 'Oh, stop it, I am so thick.'

At her (or her agent, Eddie's) request they brought the same cinematographer from *Spiral*, Laslo Molnár, and again, unfailingly, she hit her mark, found her light, saw herself as she was seen through the lens, and gave, with every take, some new or useful variation on the last. She also knew her lines.

So good was their rapport that for some years I thought Laslo might be my father, even though the timelines refused to line up. By 1951, he was working in Europe again, and though he was over and back for the next few years, the rise of McCarthyism made him feel less welcome in America and he finally settled in Italy, which is where I went to meet him when I was thirty-five years old.

It was the summer after we sold Dartmouth Square. My mother had been dead for more than a year, and we were still living in our big shabby flat by the Pepper Canister Church, trying to disentangle the snarl of her debts. I thought having a baby might give me a sense of purpose so we were in that unloosed moment when sex is about the future, and this thrown focus stole some of our pleasure, I think. I had a couple of late periods but nothing seemed to take and, secretly, I did not think I was capable of having a baby. I could not align my wanting. If I could just want the right thing, I thought, and at the right time, then my body would give in and want it too.

I woke up one spring morning with a sudden urge to discover my DNA before I tried to pass it along. This was the missing thing. This was the rope I needed to haul my baby out of the universe and into my body. I needed to find out who I 'was'.

Or maybe it was permission I was seeking – that is also something we use fathers for.

Laslo lived in Genoa on Via al Capo de Santa Chiara, a hillside road overlooking the sea. The taxi-man raised his eyebrows at the address and left me outside a substantial house with narrow arched windows, possibly Renaissance, very old.

Molnár opened the door himself, and drew me into the hallway where it took me a moment to adjust to the dimness of the interior. He was slight but not frail, a barely physical presence in his old age.

Though it was more than a year since her death, he spoke his condolences to me, there in the hall. Laslo had black eyes that were nothing like my eyes, intelligent hands touching my questing hand. I had guessed, by the ease of his invitation, that his relationship with Katherine was not a complicated one. I knew it with a sinking of the blood: this man was not my father. He took my elbow and used it to steer me in to a reception room, then disappeared briefly to organise some tea.

The room was dark and cool. A trio of small, bright windows were bisected by the horizon line, dividing blue sea from blue sky. Overhead was a dark, coffered ceiling and there were blood-brown tiles in a herringbone pattern on the floor. I had forgotten what it was like to live in a beautiful house. There were pictures on the walls that I wanted to look at, and furniture that was suffered rather than sat in; a lot of old brocade rendered pink by age.

He shuffled back in and settled a tray on a heavy black sideboard that was deeply carved with medallions of Medusa heads. Molnár wore a double-breasted jacket of summer houndstooth, a rust-coloured cravat. His neck, as it emerged from this impeccable rig, was stringy and brown and his face marked in deep folds, but his eyes were easy and very dark. He seemed profoundly satisfied by the visual world: everywhere he looked was settled and improved by his gaze. I wanted him to see me, and when he did I felt grateful, as though I had been – but beautifully – understood.

When the pleasantries were done, I had no difficulty asking him.

'I am looking for my father,' I said. 'I wonder if you knew him.'

He checked my face so that I was crossed and recrossed from eye to eye, forehead to chin, then back again. He shook his head.

'I wish I could help you.'

'No?'

He turned away, reminded of something, then he circled a helpless hand, as though to say, 'What can you do?' Some encompassing truth. Later I would remember this gesture with a sharp sense of grievance, but in the moment it made sense. Indeed, what can you do? Children are conceived. There is no other way for us to come into the world, that we know.

'Do you mind so much?'

I blushed, I don't know why. Perhaps because he had guessed the unnatural truth – that having a mother was almost enough for me.

'It comes and goes.'

Your mother was marvellous, he said. He talked about her for some time, about her combination of instinct and intelligence, but his mind was turning on other matters. It was not an easy town, he said.

'As you know.'

'Yes.'

It may have been hard for her, for a time. It must have been Eddie Malk, her agent in New York, who protected her when I came along. She was divorced. Philip was drunk. The studio could only offer an abortion, or insist on an abortion, which was entirely usual, though illegal at the time. She was alone. She was in dispute about her next big film, *My Name is Legion*, which was already shooting without her. The script was terrible, the role an oddly pathetic sexual dominatrix, a blend of Dietrich's *Blue Angel* and Blanche du Bois, entirely unsuited to her innocent Irish appeal. It may be that the role was simply too perverse for anyone. The director, Theodor von Braun, was in the throes of an opium addiction, and the part was subsequently bounced from actress to actress before the project was finally shelved on the grounds of indecency. It was one of those movies where people wonder, after the fact, how on earth things got that far.

It was during the chaos of *My Name is Legion* that she left the house in the Palisades and flew to New York, where she simply seemed to disappear. Laslo, briefly back in town, called to give her a book, and found the house proceeding without her: the Austrian maids in uniform, the dog sleeping on the sofa in the open-plan living room, the pool still and clear.

She was gone. And this fact was also not remarkable. People travelled. Women were allowed to leave, and when they came back their faces were changed. Not a bad quality to have in a face, but yes, yes, none of it was fair, and it was all difficult. At a guess, she went to Eddie in New York because Eddie did not care what people thought. He had the right kind of carelessness for such matters. Eddie was a proper human being.

As for the father: definitely not von Braun; he was impotent, absolutely and documented. Sadly not Philip. Definitely not Eddie Malk, that was not geographically possible. And besides, Eddie would have loved a daughter. No, definitely not Eddie. Beyond that, he could not say.

'Such things happen.'

'You think?'

'Not bad, some of them. Not everything that happened was bad.'

I thought he was lying, suddenly.

'Really?'

'You are the evidence of that.'

Molnár smiled at me, this man who was not my father. Even though he would have been such a fantastic father to have had.

I felt the shame of myself very keenly, at that moment. I felt as I used to feel when my mother was weeping in her room in Dartmouth Square, or weeping in the kitchen, when she pulled the phone out of the wall or when she waved some newspaper around, ripped it up, or shoved it in the bin. What was wrong with my mother? Me. I was the wrong thing. I was more than inconvenient. I was a disaster. I felt utterly unwanted and small. Laslo's face flickered as he saw all this, but he did not look away.

We spoke till dinner time and, as we did, I felt a slow sense of restitution. The sea, the room, Laslo's careful attention, all these things gave something back to me. In the course of that afternoon, my life began to feel less unfair.

At one stage, a door, which was of a piece with the ancient wallpapered wall, opened and a woman came through it. A young woman, Italian blonde, her hair bleached by the sun. She was barefoot and carried a baby in her arms, and there was a peasant look to her flowered skirt which was very lovely and may have cost anything at all. She was quite the apparition, backlit in the dark room. I saw, through the gathered blouse of thin cotton voile, that she was naked underneath it – as though we were in the sixties still (we were not in the sixties). She bent her head to nuzzle the baby which was, I think, also naked, though I can not be sure. There was, in any case, a velvet little back, softly muscled, that she stroked as she walked towards a matching door on the other side of the room, smiling a little at Laslo as she passed. A sidelong smile. She did not acknowledge me, though she certainly knew I was there. The hippy granddaughter as village idiot, perhaps. But so beautiful and glowing in the light from the small windows, the shadow of her nipples dark against the cloth of her blouse. It was enough to watch her, which we did. Laslo practising some kind of forbearance as she passed and then left, closing the door at her own chosen speed.

He turned to smile an apology for this beautiful intrusion and I felt that emptiness when you think yourself interesting to a man and are suddenly disabused. Though he likes you well enough, the women in his bed are something else again. And this seems a little impolite, this weakness he has for women who are, in many other ways, not so interesting as you. It is a cause of some regret.

And yet, although this old man had just turned me down twice – first as a daughter and then as a lover – the scene moved me in ways I could not quantify. For years after, I wanted the room, the sea, the Madonna too. She was a form of poetry, I understood that; a living image this old man was always losing, could never quite possess. The best he could do was keep her for a while. For this, he would endure her small cruelties, her unhappiness. He would forbear.

The child with the velvety back grew up to be a catwalk model who made the celebrity magazines, now and then. He died of a heroin overdose at the age of twenty-four and when I read about his death, I realised I had not thought about Laslo Molnár for a long time. I also realised the blonde woman was not a poem, or a Madonna, but an actual woman – not a very nice one – and that Laslo Molnár, the father I had wanted to be mine, was a bit of a creep.

It's funny how you change.

Every few years I consider a trip to LA so I can sit in traffic and imagine my mother there, maybe take one of the bus tours, the ones that stop at the houses of the stars. I could look at the palms on Roxbury Drive, the huge ficus trees along Rodeo, go on the lot, move through air that has been filmed, printed, cut and distributed thousands of times. Re-blasted, diffused through other, distant air. Turned into money and also loss. I am supposed to dream the rehashed dream, like drinking water out of the common tap: every glass has been through five sets of kidneys before it gets to you and it still tastes real good.

I rang one of the bus tours, don't ask me when, and I spoke my mother's name. The woman at the other end of the line went away to check the houses in Beachwood Canyon, the ones on San Remo Drive, said she was not on their list. I said it was two doors up from Thomas Mann, and she said he was also not on their list, and she asked me to spell the names one more time.

IT WAS ALWAYS publicly assumed, if anything was assumed, that I was the daughter of Philip Greenfield. Privately, my mother did not encourage an idea which would not survive scrutiny. The father she described to me was, in some ways, like Philip, because of his great good manners, but he was not, in fact, Philip. He was called Don.

She always said he was lovely, that he was an artist in his way and one of the most perceptive people you could ever meet. He died in a car crash out by Big Sur in the spring, just one of those stupid things, and then she discovered she was pregnant with me. That was the first version, and it did for years. My father was lean and eager, played tennis in baggy whites, he had an Underwood typewriter and smoked a pipe in an office on the lot – one of those writers' bungalows that was painted sunset pink. On the day that he died the ocean was very blue and the car roof down as they wound about the hairpin bends. Sometimes, when I thought about it, there was a woman in the front seat beside him. This woman was there to startle at the sight of the oncoming truck and fend it away with her lifted hands, before we saw, from a great distance, the car jolting down the rocky slope, her chiffon scarf drifting high. I played the scene over in my mind many times. His death was a chance to cut away from difficulty into silence. It was so tiny, like a bullet hole in the sky.

My father was funny, I knew that. A sense of his gallantry never left me, of quiet glamour and kindness – that was the other word Katherine insisted on, my father was 'kind'. It made me feel very important to have a father who was both dead and kind. He must have been so young. I felt his youthfulness on summer days. It settled in the silences and rose in the yearnings of the years to come, when, in my adolescence, I was struck or smitten by some brown-eyed man. My father was a lover and a dancer, he wore tennis ducks (whatever they were) and swam every day. Though it was surprisingly hard to keep him so. It was hard work keeping my dead Daddy *good*.

Other versions slipped into my head, many of them also from the movies. He was, for a few sharp seconds, the handsome man who is the wrong man. He was the cold-hearted killer, the sadist and rapist, the snarling drunk or the sneering aristocrat; he was all the bad men as well as the good man I wanted and adored. And he was, in all of this, never naked, my dead father, neither on screen nor in my head. Not ever. He was a bit rumpled, rarely less than gorgeous. He drank – but only whiskey – and he never ate, except, on occasion, a few, rueful bar-counter nuts.

I was around twelve, I think, when I started to query the phrase my mother used about this guy who went over a cliff in Big Sur (but what cliff? and when?).

'It was not to be,' she said.

Or, sometimes, with an added sigh, 'Ah. Yes. It was not to be.'

When she said this she was not referring to his incon-venient dying. She was talking about their love, which had been impossible. And it was impossible not because they were mismatched (she was too flighty, he was too stern, she was a star, he was a lowly mechanic in the movies' dream machine) but because he was *already taken*. They were having an affair. My father, or let us call him 'the man', already had a wife.

It was not to be.

She must have had some terrible power over him, this wife. She was an invalid or she drank, she blackmailed him emotionally or she blackmailed him actually with notes made from clipped-out newsprint and magazines. She was mean to his dog. And she was rich, of course she was. She owned the car with the high fins and the shiny chrome trim, and they were fighting – probably about my mother, whom he loved so desperately. She grabbed the wheel, this wife person, and it was her chiffon scarf that streamed vertical as the car bounced and rolled down the steep hillside.

Afterwards, she clawed her way out of there to collapse on the rocky slope, a few yards further up, as he bled and died.

And the car radio played on.

It was not to be.

A part of me loved killing my already-dead father, because it also killed my suspicion that he was actually not dead, but having a great time somewhere far away. That he hated my mother for getting pregnant, and he hated me for being her pregnancy. He hated me for existing, because my existence spoiled their love. The best I could muster some days, when I could not kill my father properly on a cliff road in Big Sur (his head slumped against the steering wheel, his unconscious cheek stuck to the horn) was that he was, whoever he was, serenely unaware.

They were ships that passed in the night.

My serenely unaware father the airline pilot flicks the switches on the cockpit console, he eases back the throttles, looks at the clouds as the plane lifts into them, and is serenely unaware that the smile on his face is repeated on my face, as I change gears on my bicycle in a city far away. My father finishes an equation on a paper tablecloth, says, 'Get me the control centre, it's going to blow!' and is serenely unaware of the flourish I make at the end of my homework when x is definitively and properly multiplied by y. My fine, careless father pulls the paper out of his typewriter. I pull the paper out of the typewriter. He scrunches it into a ball, throws it at the wastepaper bin. I throw it into the wastepaper bin, he misses, I miss, it feels OK.

I took to watching myself as I did normal things: the way I hopped putting on one side of my pants, my impatience with shoelaces, my inability to close a door – how uncanny! – these were, in fact, secret echoes of a man who was serenely unaware of my existence. What a joyous surprise it would be, when we finally put on our shoes, or flew our planes together. Unless he did not want to do that. Unless he already knew all about me and had run the hell away.

This was too hurtful to contemplate – I had to kill him all over again. Sometimes I killed him six times a day.

When I learned how babies are actually made, biologically, I started to put the word 'father' into inverted commas, because he was not a real person, or a special person, he was just an excuse. He was the necessary thing. We could, my mother and I, discard him when we were done. Used. Emptied. Gone.

They were ships that pass in the night.

A phrase I never understood – these night-passing ships never touched each other. One ship never grazed the belly of the other ship, there was no connection – how could there be? It was too dark for semaphore. Perhaps if they used those big, shuttered searchlights to blink out some message, but that would hardly conjure a mood of melancholy passion. Ships that passed in the night always stayed ships, in my child's mind. A gazillion spermatozoa (yuck) and then me.

One day, the man, in all his versions, was gone. I had not even seen him leave. By the time I was fourteen and mad for boys, my 'father' was a non-subject. I don't know how people do this with their children – I never managed with mine – how they put some idea so far beyond discussion it learns how to disappear.

My teenage energies were spent running away from my mother or back to her, and there was, between us, enough love and trouble to keep us busy, with no need for any 'father' to distract or intervene. We got on so very well without him. Or, more properly, without any of them: the good man, the bad man, the lover, monster, vampire, knight in shining armour, the many different men my father's absence spawned.

But it stayed with me, the whispered childhood knowledge that he was lovely, he was glamorous, he was a little bit unreal. And the boys I fell for were also lovely – slightly too lovely, some of them, too well mannered, or too witty; a couple of them were too handsome, and all of them, it turned out, were mad about my mother.

(Sometimes, their mothers were also mad about my mother, and this was especially galling.

'You have her eyes. Did anyone ever say that to you?'

'Oh, thank you.')

The summer I left school I had, in quick succession, two gay boyfriends called Michael. The first was Michael Farrelly: very arch and ferociously funny, he became, in time, a notorious barrister with a blonde and perfect wife followed, in late middle age, by a surprisingly nondescript husband. The second was Michael Hone who made me feel, as I kissed him, that I could fall off the table on which I was perched, so balanced and deft was the tip of his weightless tongue. Michael Hone, who kissed me until I did not know which way was up, moved to America in his early twenties and we lost touch: there is no record of him that I can find now, online.

Back in 1970, in that long summer between school and college, I went to the cinema and ate banana splits with one Michael after another and they both spent a lot of time talking about Katherine O'Dell, who was, they seemed to imply, very much past her prime. Michael Farrelly threw his head back and said, 'He is gone from me now,' quoting *Mulligan's Holy War*, an imitation that was so precise and insulting, I found I could not breathe. Once he'd started, he couldn't stop, and I couldn't stop listening to him and telling him not to. We had so much fun, I was worried that he might do it to her face, if he ever met her. And then he did meet her.

'Oh. Hello,' she said, wandering into the living room one afternoon, when I thought she was not at home.

'This is Michael,' I said.

'How do you do?' she said.

And he lost the plot.

'Oh. Never better,' he said, and there was a little breathiness in there, a sigh of air. My mother blanked a moment and then she gave a smart, thin smile.

'Well, I'll leave you two to get on, so,' she said, and promptly walked back out again, leaving Mick Farrelly bereft.

'What did you expect?' I said.

We split up soon after that. I told him the line between admiration and malice was so thin with some people, it was almost the same thing.

I thought I would do better by Michael Hone until I took him home to Dartmouth Square and turned to see him crush one of her scarves, briefly, to his face.

It is possible that I came to enjoy the power. She was mine to bestow or withhold. The glorious kissing session on the edge of the dining-room table happened in the afterglow of one evening's adventure, when I finally opened her bedroom door and let Michael Hone step inside.

Even when my mother was away, Kitty was scrupulous about this room, which was the best in the house, with two windows overlooking the park, swagged about with heavy curtains. There was a dressing table with a sharp fan of mirrors angled to catch the light. And it all seemed the height of elegance to me, as it clearly also did to Michael Hone, who ran his hand over the dark paper on the wall, as though in wonder at the size of the floral design. The carpet was pigeon grey, with a deep pile that left the marks of the Hoover in it like a mowed lawn; silvery as it went one way, and violet the other. The quilt on her bed was a deep, rich purple. She had more pillows than Irish people had on their beds in those days, and a few of them were also dark purple and satin shiny. A pair of wardrobes in the same pale wood as the dressing table stood in the alcoves on either side of the fireplace, which was white.

Michael turned to me and said, 'It's so nice.'

And I said, 'Yes.'

When I was a girl, I liked to come in here before Kitty got to it, when Katherine's things were still scattered across the carpet, the lids were off the pots and tubes on her dresser and her book, still warm, splayed on the bed. On the nightstand was a lamp with a lilac shade and a picture of me in a silver frame. This was taken when I was six, a black-and-white studio shot of a girl in a gingham dress with the bottomless gaze of a child. If my mother was on her travels, this photograph was gone from the table – she had packed it into her luggage – and I felt its absence keenly. Then it was back, or I was back on the dressing table, which meant that she was home.

Now and then there was a morning when, for some reason, the photograph was laid face-down on the little table, and I would set it up again, pulling the triangular stand out at the back. I liked doing this. The stand was held at its limit by its own string, and everything on the secret side of the frame was covered in soft grey velveteen.

Of course she had lovers. Some part of me knew this was why she turned me face-down on the nightstand. It was just hard to tell who these lovers might be. She had so many friends, not to mention doctors, therapists, voice coaches, and briefly while in London, a guru. There was a woman called Heidi who came to massage and exercise her; she wore a white coat and looked, I thought, really quite butch. This is when I was nine or ten and every time she turned around ('Every time I turn around,' she said) I was right there.

I was very quiet. There was a wine merchant who lingered all afternoon, urging her to try this year or that. There was Niall Duggan, lecturer and critic, who sat and talked, as the contents of the cocktail cabinet disappeared, and there was a tame priest called Father Des, a man who said my mother's acting made the audience believe in God. One afternoon there was a very smarmy fellow who asked did we have a spare towel, by any chance. He turned out to be a chiropodist. When I came back into the living room he was on one knee with my mother's bare foot in his hand.

'She puts her cigarette out on the side of the plate, apparently.'

I think he was talking about Princess Margaret.

'Really,' said my mother, reaching down to slip off the other shoe.

I hated them all. Slyly.

I moithered about. If she turned to check, I was always there, leaving dirty marks on the windowpane or suck marks on the top of my own arm, wreaking some tiny, harmless destruction.

'What are you doing, Norah?'

'Nothing.'

I don't know if she was actually busy, in the romantic sense, or if I was just endlessly suspicious. Her accountant was, I decided, fully in love with her. A self-deleting man, tactful in the extreme, he considered himself a knight in shining armour as he saved her from financial foolishness and misadventure. He came twice a year, the papers spread over the dining-room table. I could hear his soothing murmur through the wood of the door, her voice, by comparison helpless, petulant, completely unstaged.

The pet priest came every Thursday afternoon, and they spoke together in full sentences. Father Des was handsome like a wax doll, a young Jesuit who read everything and went to the theatre every week. He was enormously useful to have around. Father Des would marry people that other priests would turn down for some canonical reason, of which there were many. If one of the parties was Protestant, or unbaptised, or had a foreign divorce, or if they were cohabiting and unrepentant. This was a nightmare for theatre people, the girls especially, because it was all very well falling in love, but no wedding meant you were stuck with a man who was far too interesting for his own good. Father Des could fix all that. He had access to a chapel – a little Gothic thing beside an old Dominican convent on the Northside. He gave informal, sitting-room confessions, his funeral sermons were tactful and brief. He would also, and sometimes surreptitiously, baptise an awkwardly conceived child.

So he was not your usual priest but he was still a priest, as he liked to remind people with a gentle smile. Father Des had a kindly air I did not trust, for being universally applied. He made me feel like a potted plant. It was always lovely when he was in the room, and yet no one had a good time.

She was very low-voiced and musical with Father Des; she asked serious questions and listened to his answers and she kept her own, often scandalous, opinions to herself. I was not sure about this version of Katherine O'Dell – a woman who wore white gloves in summer and was always looking for absolution from some helpless, sweet sin. This was her Graceful Penitent – she modelled the look on Grace Kelly, of course – and the sin was hard to identify. It was the sin of making men want her, perhaps.

My mother was a Catholic, as her father, Fitz, had been before her. She was not the habitual type, so Masses were missed and rosaries left unsaid and this meant she was a very bad Catholic, which in those days was mostly a question of turning up and droning on. Katherine managed to be both bohemian and believer. We never passed a church without going in to light a candle – to Joan of Arc in Notre-Dame, Saint Dymphna in Sligo and, when in Venice, the eyeless Santa Lucia in the church of that name. She sprinkled things with holy water, including me and, in a drawer of her art deco dressing table, she had a wooden box containing a relic of a terrifying man called Padre Pio who was not yet a saint, he was not even dead. The Padre was photographed in a brown cowl, under which was a rolling, wild eye that seemed to say, 'Look!' And when you did look there was blood oozing out of his hands, back and front. The bloody relic was a tiny scrap of spotted cloth, held under a bubble of glass and set into a medal, with the words 'ex sanguine' around it. And this was the most precious object in the house. It was, she said mysteriously, 'a guarantee'.

This animist approach to the higher mysteries was the source of some condescension from Father Des, who also seemed to like it. He often brought a couple of hardbacks for my mother which she read or abandoned, and one afternoon I found him in the living room reading alone. We talked about Darwin, as I recall. He knew about dinosaurs and about Peking Man – both subjects of profound interest to me – and he also spoke about the evolution of the soul. I was, at the age of nine, considering a career in chemistry ('Not *the chemist's*,' as I liked to explain to people, who assumed I wanted to sell lipsticks and nappy cream) so I found this talk of 'the soul' a bit of a reach, at least in evolutionary terms. I did not point this out to him. The book in his hand was called *The Seven Stages of Suffering*, and even this small fact seemed to root me to the floor. I stood by his knee, feeling itchy, until Kitty found me and dragged me off for my tea.

But there was no lover, or not that I knew at the time. No actual sex. I never saw anything, met anyone. I never bumped into a strange man in the house – except for once, I think, when I was really quite young, a terrible rustling, and after that, never again.

Despite the Father in his name, I did not confuse Father Des with my father and I did not confuse God the Father with my father, even though, like God, he was both absent and amazing. The worst you could say about my father problem is that I found it hard to settle down. I liked my men brown-eyed and easygoing and this was incredibly lucky – that I did not fall in love with death, even though my father was dead, or probably dead; at least I never did for long.

Though I did, as a kind of revenge, go to bed with Niall Duggan. Which was the worst of it, really. It happened a few years out of college, when I was busy being a Girl About Town; a phase which involved getting drunk with, and then shagging, various people, including Niall Duggan, who made me feel so clever – or the drink made me feel clever – I do seem to remember feeling clever at the time. I did not consider it revenge on my absent father (or my foolish mother, indeed), I thought of it as a mistake I wanted to make. A secret awfulness that, afterwards, made me secretly, sourly happy. Yes, I slept with Niall Duggan.

'The Fucker', as we used to call him at college. Duggan the Fucker.

I slipped away as soon as he was unconscious, and I wanted to shout my escape into the street, to tell the world that I had done it, and had been victorious. Ding Dong, the bastard's dead.

I did not have a Daddy Thing after all.

I sent him crashing through that rail near Big Sur. The car sailed overheard, a dark slab of undercarriage, the chiffon scarf trailing after it in the ghost of a scream, and *crunch, boink, boink, thud,* my father died, one more time. There was no connection between Niall Duggan and such a man, who would be forever young and suave.

Anyhoo, apart from two gay boyfriends and one old fucker, and a few wonderful, or wonderfully wrong-headed, encounters, experienced in drink, apart from all my various and different mistakes, many of them lovely, I did not have a Daddy problem. I think that much is clear.

Because they loved each other, my mother and father; it was just not to be.

116

Dear Holly Devane,

My mother belonged to that special category of Irish celebrity who was allowed to have lovers without public recrimination. Even so, she kept herself more or less neat and her love life out of the public eye.

Katherine O'Dell was a star. Her 'sexual style', so called, was to be the centre of something. Or the centre of a whole lot of nothing. That is why Ireland allowed her privacy – in those days, such matters were understood.

I think it is possible that my conception was arbitrary, that the relationship was fleeting, that I was what is sometimes called a mistake, whether happy, or unhappy. I think this is her information to keep or divulge, not mine. My mother never said I was 'a mistake', she said I was 'a miracle'. Make of that what you will.

Personally I don't care, and this might be hard for you to understand. He was just a guy. It happens. I would swap all the information in the world for her happiness, and she was never happy. She was eaten alive by people like you, Holly Devane. She was never happy. Though she put on a damn fine show.

AMONG THE IMAGES of my mother that exist online is a black-and-white photograph of me, watching her from the wings. I am four or five years of age and sitting on a stool, in a little matinee coat and a bowl haircut. Beyond me, Katherine O'Dell performs to the unseen crowd. She is dressed in a glittering dark gown, you can not see the edges of her or the shape her figure makes, just the slice of cheekbone, the line of her chin. Her hands are uplifted.

I don't remember the photograph being taken, but I do remember the occasion. It was at the Gaiety Theatre in Dublin and my mother was part of a gala evening, in which she sang a medley of Irish songs, things like 'Kitty of Coleraine' or 'Galway Bay.'

'If you ever go across the sea to Ireland,' she sang – even though she was actually in Ireland at the time. No one seemed to care about that. After Hollywood she was all about emigrant nostalgia: she could miss the old sod while standing in her own kitchen, she used to say. And indeed, she often did.

The shiver of delight I felt on hearing my mother sing was always close to embarrassment and the sight of her on a real, public stage stilled me absolutely. I was transfixed. Watching her made me feel so lucky and so alone.

But I was in the wings which is the best place, because the song can not get you there. From the side, the stage shows its gaffer tape and the unpainted backs of things; the discovery of this makeshift reality was more magical to me than anything I saw while sitting out front. Though in the photograph, it is true, my mother, in her sparkly dress, looks very magical indeed.

'They might as well go chasing after moonbeams,
Or light a penny candle from a star.'

And though the picture is in black and white, I remember my clothes in Kodachrome red and dark green, a little silk dress and a wool coat with its velvet collar, and I remember the fuss of that evening, going out before Christmas to see my Mama sing. I don't know whether I went back to the dressing room, who took me there or brought me home, but I do remember – and vividly – the wind of her coming off stage.

She swept past me, her hand reaching blind into the darkness, then she stopped and turned.

'Oh, there you are.' She bent over to kiss me, and it lifted from her like fresh air after a walk, a mix of nervous sweat and electricity. She was crackling with the attention of the crowd.

And still they clapped.

'How was that?' she said. 'Was it all right?'

'Yes.'

I would like to note here that a grown woman asked a five-year-old girl to tell her that her performance was not a disaster, to reassure her and to praise. I know this is true, because she always did it. And I said (famously),

'I thought you were an angel. I thought I was dead and gone to heaven.'

She loved this, of course, and told the story often. Though she left out the bit about my being dead.

The sparkles on her gown were, in fact, plastic bits stuck on flesh-coloured net that creased, as she bent over me, like a second, loose skin. The cut of the dress exposed interesting parts of her body, like the sinewy underarm, that shifted from hollow to mound when she went back out there and waved. Then she returned from the light, back to me.

But if there is a moment I loved more than any other, it was those steps we took together into the darkness and complication of backstage, the hum of the audience thinning behind us as the hall emptied and the crowd splintered into the various bright faces of people who came around the long way, to kiss and exclaim that she had been Marvellous, Darling.

It was a place of secret corridors and blind ends. There was a sudden or hidden door, which revealed, when you opened it, your own reflection in the full-length mirror on the opposite wall. This room had a bicycle in the corner, a double sink, bunches of flowers stuffed into jars, a long counter, where a woman sat fixing a fan of green feathers into her hair. Or sometimes it was not a woman, it was a girl with a pot tummy in white tights and tutu, it was a man who said, 'Don't mind me, ladies, coming through.' At the end of this room, behind another door, my mother's street shoes were primly stacked and waiting beneath her bentwood chair. Backstage was the best place, where everyone was mixed up and undone.

It was just such a hidden path Katherine took when she came to Ireland in 1952 with a fat American baby in her arms. She travelled incognito. There were no photographs, on this trip, of Katherine O'Dell waving from the rails. Her mother came to meet the boat at Liverpool docks and, together, they boarded the packet to Dun Laoghaire where they were met by Lillian MacVeigh who had rented, at my mother's request, a house for them all in the nearby village of Dalkey.

Lillian was so nice. She was like a second grandmother to me, a second mother to Katherine, who had a choice of women to help lift me in the night. I have never tried to discover where this house was, though the area is familiar to me, with its narrow streets and unexpected glimpses of the sea. From the outside, it would look too small, I think, because when it surrounded me, the place was vast. The green of the garden trembled outside the French windows, and the light was never the same twice. It was autumn when we arrived and we stayed until the spring, by which time the studio had dragged Katherine O'Dell back to America, in order to destroy her career.

At least, that is how she described it.

This was not my fault, although I knew that by having a private baby she had done something that actresses were not supposed to do. I was a clandestine treasure. I was her desperation! We had six months, seven? We had enough, it seemed.

I knew how to be loved. I lay easy in my frilled bassinet, sat steady in my twin grandmothers' arms, while my mother sailed away to fight dragons, answer riddles and weep in wastelands alone. At least that is how I imagined it. Later, she told me it was like fighting a fog. She had returned to a different town. Something was lost, or changed, and she could not say what it was.

In her absence we moved to Dartmouth Square, a house she may have secured before leaving for America. She was gone a long time. I was walking through the park, my baby feet discovering grass, when she decided the studio was trying to kill her career – and back she came, in a rush, to me.

These things happen to every actor. I know this now. You could say that not having a job is one of the most important parts of the job. But at the time, Katherine could not explain – even to herself – what was going on. It was so hard to get a fix on things. There weren't that many Irish parts, after all, and there were too many girls with red hair. She wanted to do Shakespeare, they did not do Shakespeare. She persuaded someone into a screenplay of *Hedda Gabler*, which was not a runner, the same with *A Doll's House*. She wanted another nurse movie or a nun movie, but the war was too long over for that.

The role she settled on was the Princess of Cleves, set in Hollywood's idea of medieval France. The costumes weighed half as much as she did, and left her with a recurring problem in the small muscles between her ribs. *The French Princess* was an adultery story with a pious twist; in it, she plays a noblewoman in love with a man who is not her husband. When this husband dies, she is free to follow her heart, but she decides – for reasons that seem to need no explanation – to enter a convent instead. So the story was a bit like *Mulligan*, but much worse. The thing was supposed to be yearning and pure but it ended up stilted and sexless, and it was completely overshadowed, on release, by Jean Simmons as Queen Elizabeth I, a role that should have been hers, my mother said, as though she had a monopoly on spirited virgins, or on redheads, or on European queens. This was the first, but not the sharpest, of these regrets. The actor's sad cry of, 'Mine! Mine!' It was the beginning of being robbed.

'You were robbed,' her friend Hughie Snell liked to reassure her about Amelia Earhart or St Bernadette, about the Oscar, the Tony, the ribbon, the gong, the headline review.

'You were robbed.'

When I was young, I thought this was an actual event. It happened during the night. My mother had been burgled – her bedroom rifled, her dressing table all ransacked – though when I woke, the house looked identical to the way it had been before.

It seemed to me that there was no need to rob my mother, when she was so busy losing all she had. By the end of 1954 she had abandoned her American contract and was back on the stage in London, playing Tatyana in *Eugene Onegin*, and entirely happy. It took some years for her – or her accountant – to realise the truth of this move. She would never be so famous again.

By 1958, when I was six years old, the house in Brentwood was gone, the things inside it lost and dispersed, the first of many such scatterings. In years to come she would remember these objects, as though they had never really belonged to her: Philip's rod sculptures, the huge terracotta vases that marched down to the pool, a coffee table in a great, raw hunk of walnut, a pair of white kid gloves, the right hand signed by Charles Laughton, 'To my darling O'Dell: Applause.'

The movies she made in the years after I was born did not do well. Best among them was the British drama *When Angels Weep* (1955) in which she played the mother of small children whose father is a troubled artist – played by Kenneth More in splattered overalls. The next year she travelled to New Mexico to film *Devil's Horn Ranch*, a long, cruel shoot with a script that was rewritten from day to day, and from which she was slowly erased. Both movies performed poorly at the box office and left her no further on.

It was not just things that seemed to drift away from her. Men were also lost. In London, she lost a lovely man called Pearse MacNeil who was so handsome and fine. An Oxford don and nature poet, Pearse was the gentlest person – but he suffered terribly after the death of his father General Pearse Andrew McNeil and was committed, possibly while my mother and he were lovers, to an asylum in the South of France, where he would stay for many years.

'Really, Mother. *Really*?'

Of course he was mad in France, as opposed to, say, Coulsdon – and not just France but the lavender-scented *South* of France. Hard to know if she had lost a man or gained a story. Though she did keep losing things. Her keys. Her car. Pleasance, of course. That little watercolour of her father with me on his knee. My passport. Her passport. Her poet. Her sculptor. Her might-have-been.

She lost a whole house once, a little place on the side of a mountain in the Italian Alps, north of Lucca. Dirt cheap. She bought it from a friend of Benjamin Britten's. Then she forgot the name of the town.

In the first decade of my life, my mother discarded her past and mislaid any number of possible futures. She did it recklessly. She lost her favourite director, Guy Fellowes, to a terrible late-night falling-out in the middle of a London street. She lost Eddie Malk to cancer, shortly after I started school. The next year, she lost her own mother, an event so astonishing it wiped my memory of my grandmother entirely, though I remember with great clarity the nun who let me hold her hand at the top of the school line around this time, a woman whose cheek was covered in a haze of soft white down.

She never lost me. I was right there.

I was a climbing child, sturdy and round. I got up on to the table, I scaled the kitchen cupboard where the sugar was stored. I climbed into the lilac bush and broke it. Best of all was a big friendly tree in the little park, one that was not near the railings, because I did not want to fall down and get myself impaled. I rode my tricycle on the footpath around the square, and this was a great trick, because you had to cross the road to get to it, but once you were on the inside edge, you could go round it all day, north-east-south-west, or vice versa, clockwise or the bad way round, and no matter how far you travelled you always came back to the house again.

Homecomings were astounding, joyous affairs, with dancing and presents. She and Kitty would stand me on the dining-room table to dress me in all she had brought back, the suitcases were opened and the contents spilled out on the floor. As the years went by, these reunions became less frequent, and the departures (always silent, always unmarked) also more rare.

There were still wonderful career moments in this decade of decline. An indelible production of *Lovers' Meeting* at the Abbey Theatre in Dublin, Catherine in *Wuthering Heights*, in London, and eight months on Broadway as a convincing, if slightly over-aged, Pegeen Mike. You would think that nothing was wrong, if you looked at all this from the outside.

When I was thirteen, Fitz died.

My grandfather doted on us both, but especially on his daughter. He believed her to be wonderful, and so she was. But he was always on the scrounge, Fitz. His interest in my mother's business affairs was not entirely wholesome and his drinking became problematic as he aged. Perhaps this was the reason I found her descriptions of him a little too disapproving – many of them were delivered with a wave of her own glass. But the man died from cirrhosis of the liver, so who can say what degradations she witnessed in his last years.

He lived alone in the Soho flat, after the death of his wife. My mother saw him whenever she was working in London or she would go over to check on him, from time to time. She came back fuming. There was always a situation, it always involved money. The mad landlady kept climbing into his bed. Or it was another woman – one of his many other women – all of them unsuitable, neurotic, sometimes aristocratic. They all wanted to sleep with him, if my mother was to be believed. All these dreadful women wanted to sleep with this poor old man, who was annoying for other reasons, but never for *that* reason. Who was mostly just *silly*, just *hopeless*, endlessly prey to unscrupulous, formerly glamorous harpies who wanted him – of course they did – because he was Fitz, and he made such a marvellous ruin, still impeccable in his old age.

He turned them all down. Thank goodness.

Meanwhile, standards slipped. Bones were broken. People got thrown down the stairs. The blackouts got worse and his stomach was destroyed. A female friend of Peter O'Toole's told her that Fitz soiled himself one long night in the Gay Hussar, and he kept saying, 'Who farted?', looking over his shoulder like a schoolboy.

('My God,' said my mother. 'Who tells you that about your own father?')

And then he died.

She broke the news to me like a good mother. She stood beside me where I sat in my usual spot at the end of the kitchen table and she smoothed my hair with her hand. Afterwards, she asked me was I all right and I said I was fine. Privately, I did not know why she was checking up on me. The man was old, and old people die. But I knew he was my grandfather and that I was supposed to be sad, so I sighed. She bent to kiss me.

'Poor darling,' she said.

She did it all so perfectly, and I did it so perfectly. I did not think, for a single second, that she might adore him the way that I adored her.

'Are you all right?' she said.

'Yes. Yes, I am fine.'

A couple of weeks later she came home and there were no presents (to my shame this is what I remember most) and it took me a moment to realise that she had gone over to London for the funeral. She did not talk for a while. She sat at the kitchen table.

'Oh yes, thank you, Kitty,' she said and then sat and looked at her food. At one point she keeled forward and laid her cheek along her cigarette arm, which was stuck out straight across the tabletop. She was weeping. If such a thing can be said of someone who was making no sound and shedding no tears. Then she straightened up, pushed the palm of her hand up across her cheek and resumed her cigarette, ate through exhaled smoke, and poured herself some red wine.

A few glasses in, she started to tell us about it all: the ghastly women who came, the men who failed to show. He had a High Mass, a little to her surprise, it was all done by his queer Monseigneur friend, so this priest and that priest came to concelebrate. There were candles and altar boys, and a curate who swung the thurible and intoned. It was like a bad matinee in Bognor, she said – the hall was empty and the stage was full. A boy soprano in ruff and smock did 'Panis Angelicus' and, while the box was sent back down the aisle, an attempt at 'Faith of Our Fathers', which was a hymn she subsequently took to singing while doing her leg exercises, up and down the stairs.

Fay-haith OF our Fa-ha-the-errs, HOL-y Faith.

The old hoor, she called him. And guess what he did next? *The old hewer.*

I came home from school sometime after he died, and I heard a record playing in the living room. I did not know what it was, but the sound crept under my uniform, somehow, and settled on my skin. When I pushed open the door, I saw my mother sitting on the sofa with a record sleeve in her hand, *Favourite Irish Poems.* The reader was my grandfather. The sound of him filled the air between us.

She saw me in the doorway, and smiled.

The voice was marvellous – you would never think, from the rich sonorous sweep of it, that the man was five foot four. And there was something else that we both heard, as we listened to the way he did it. We heard his craft.

He was reciting Yeats. The accent was Irish, in a mode now gone out of fashion. Each syllable sounded separate as a teacher reading with a pointy stick.

'I will arise and go now, and go to Inisfree
And a small cabin build there, of clay and wattles
    made:
Nine bean-rows will I have there, a hive for the
    honey-bee,
And live alone in the bee-loud glade.'

Fitz caught the fragility of the old man; the way Yeats sounded testy when he read his work, as though obliged to expose his yearning to the crowd.

'And I shall have some peace there, for peace comes
    dropping slow.'

And there was no need to ask if Fitz knew Yeats – of course he did. They met in London at some gala and the poet mistook him for Bunny Garnett, a friend of Lady Ottoline Morell. This was a story much told, because Bunny, apart from everything else, was a great queer, which made it all the more hilarious.

These are the kinds of detail that linger for me now, when I think, *Was he?* and sometimes, *Were they all?* Were these men, my grandfather, his great friend McMaster, were they gay, more or less? *Was that all it was?*

But there are other details that are harder to dislodge. Once, when I was grown, my mother told me Fitz had suffered, in his old age, 'a thinning of the soul'. It was a few months before her own final illness, and we were sitting outside a cafe in off-season Nerja, a little southern Spanish town. She stubbed out her cigarette in the breeze-blown ashtray, and there was a great flatness to the way she said it, as though there was not much of her father left, when the time came for him to go.

But she hated London, when Fitz was no longer in it. She hated the way they sneered at an Irish accent, the racism, she said, was awful. *No Blacks No Dogs No Irish* that was the sign you saw still around the place. As far as the English were concerned we were all just dirty-lazy-drunk-and-stupid. You have no idea what it is like, sitting next to someone at dinner who thinks they are superior to you, that they have been superior to you for centuries, no matter what you achieve and they fail to achieve, not just in the world but in their own horrible little hearts. Some stunted failure of a human being, looking down his nose at you, because he is English.

And I took all this in. I mean, I listened to all this. And I did not pause to say, 'But you are English too.'

One of Ireland's first television programmes featured Katherine O' Dell singing 'Down by the Salley Gardens', a well-known musical setting of the poem by Yeats. It was broadcast on RTÉ's opening night in 1961. Of all the lost or wiped recordings, this is the one I miss most. It was better than the moon landings. A television set was bought for the occasion and placed beside the living-room window, so a cable could be run up to an aerial on the roof. The room was full of people. Afterwards they all said, 'Yaroo!' and 'Beir Bua!' and grown men had tears in their eyes. The next day at school, Jackie Gogarty, who was the most beautiful girl in the class, came up and picked dreamily at the sleeve of my jumper.

'Was that your mother?' she said.

Katherine O'Dell's connection with Yeats continued after Fitz died, in both Ireland and America. It was prestige work for the most part: a recital at Lincoln Center, another at Stanford University. She played Cathleen ní Houlihán at the Kennedy Center in Washington for an audience of politicians and ambassadors, but she was not averse to 'swinging the old shillelagh', as she put it, among the American Irish of Boston and New York. We needed the money, certainly, but the work was rewarding in other ways. People came up to her after she left the stage and they told her their stories of exile and loss. These tales started badly and they ended worse – brothers were found hanged from the rafters, daughters were whipped out the door, and their little babies snatched from their arms by the nuns.

There were so many tears to shed. She counted the weepers from her vantage point in the wings: well-dressed women with handkerchiefs, worn old men with tears glistening in the darkness. They wept at happy songs as well as sad, at poetry as well as the dancing. They were not all poor. They were not, indeed, all of them Irish (whisper it who dared) so my mother fitted right in. They were the audience of her childhood, from Ballyshannon, Fethard, Dromineer and Fermoy, now transplanted, and they filled her, she said, with the same noble fire.

The emigrant circuit also brought her into contact with Irish Republicans: men whose difficulty – whose wound – would become her wound, over time. The country they had left when they got on the boat to America was not even their country, so long as the North of it still belonged to the British. First it was broken and then it was lost. If it was a song you could sing it. And indeed she often did.

'At Boolavogue', 'The West's Awake' and 'Only Our Rivers Run Free'.

She came back from these American trips exhausted, but also satisfied, you might even say vindicated. As though the sense of injustice unleashed in her by middle age had found somewhere real to land.

If Katherine O'Dell was Irish for love, she was also Irish for money, because we really needed the money. Hollywood was a brothel, she said, London was impossible now, and where else was she to go? Fitz left nothing but debts. I know this because she refused to pay the undertakers for a very long time. I was of an age to notice such practical matters and, once I started noticing, I never stopped. It was, in some ways, the end of my childhood. I knew, at thirteen, that she had an account in Coutts on the Strand and that there wasn't much money in it. After my grandfather died, I would spend much of my life sorting things out for my mother.

I also started seeing her from the outside. It happened when she reached across the tabletop, not weeping, with her arm outstretched and the fag still going at the end of it. I began to see how she was, in the world.

*

Now that I look back, I think she may have had a romance going in New York or Boston. I also think it is possible she was involved with a 'sympathiser' or even with an actual member of the IRA. But there are many different kinds of Irish in America and a hundred reasons for a woman like Katherine O'Dell to keep her private life out of the public eye.

I am just not sure that her love affairs form the answer to any proper question. It seemed to me, growing up, that she spent a lot of time in despair about all of that and a very few moments happy. She was a bohemian. For Katherine O'Dell, sex was just one aspect of the great problem she sometimes called Love, and other times Art. It came and went. Celibacy was as difficult as unemployment, and a lover nearly as good as a role: both were a kind of performance, she was, by them, 'possessed'. By being in love. By not being in love. Forsaking love.

I thought it was all complete malarkey. There were letters she tore up, and others left unopened. There were phone calls that dived into a whisper when I walked in the room. There certainly were proposals of marriage. One man asked her to marry him on his birthday, every year – enormously rich – if it had been her own birthday, she liked to say, she might not have turned him down. There were declarations and reunions, and one discreet relationship, I would later discover, that lasted for almost a decade. I suspect that, in all this drama, there was not much by way of actual sex. I may be wrong.

In this, as in so many things, I am the opposite of my mother.

And I pause to think about this for a while, as I listen out for the sounds of your coming home, the clink of the gate handle, the creak of the metal hinge. I think about our long marriage, having what Niall Duggan used to call 'housewife sex' – as though men were always importunate, and women long-suffering. But that is a funny lie, I mean it is an interesting lie to tell, and I don't know why it is the one that Niall Duggan chose. I suppose women in those days were afraid of getting pregnant. But it was common enough when I was growing up, the idea that women did not like sex. So common that, when the time came to lose my virginity, I expected some blunt, awful event, like getting yourself stabbed.

Who told me this (apart from everyone?) – that a man takes his pleasure and gives only pain. That sex is a kind of punishment, and this punishment is perfect because it fits the crime so well. Here. This is what you get, for *wanting*.

Imagine my surprise.

Then.

Imagine my surprise, when it came to it – my second year in college, when we were still eyeing each other across the Belfield bar. You were in an uncertain relationship with a girl who had a real, live car, and we were going to be lovers, there was no doubt in anyone's mind about that, the way we did not speak to each other after a sudden discussion about French Cinema, when we disbelieved each other immediately. It was November 1971. You were walking around, freezing, in a corduroy jacket with a leather waistcoat underneath it and I was just disgusted with you, I was about to expose you as a fraud – yes, to the world, but more importantly and essentially to yourself. I would hold the mirror up to your fraudulence, after which you would shriek and dissolve in your own fake reflection and I would not have to sleep with you after all.

Job done.

Meanwhile there was the onerous business of my virginity to be managed, because if I was going to sleep with you it would have to be as an equal and not as a pierced possession, I would not give you that satisfaction, goddammit, you would not have my blood or my pain.

It was 1971 and condoms were hard to come by in Dublin. Except, of course, in the bathroom in Dartmouth Square, where my mother had left some in the mirrored cabinet after a trip abroad when I was seventeen years of age, causing me to shout about something else ('Why is this place such a mess?') while not mentioning them or touching them for the next two years. 'With reservoir,' promised the box, disgustingly, every time I looked in there for witch hazel or Nivea cream, then shut the door to see my worried reflection slice into view. There was an expiry date on the pack which read like my own expiry date, so inured was I to the idea that women 'go off' if they have to wait too long. Two years later, the gently petrifying condoms in their sad packets were like my gently petrifying hymen – if I had a hymen: this was another question whose answer was not entirely clear.

There was another fight, this time in Hartigan's pub, about *A Clockwork Orange*, a film you admired and I did not, despite the fact that neither of us had seen it (nor would see it, as it wasn't screened in Dublin). Nor had you read the book. It was this last fact, revealed after two hours of solid spoof, that I found most infuriating. You had, by being so completely arrogant and stupid, put me in a position of having to sleep with someone else, as soon as possible.

By this time, I was going out with an engineering student called Shay Vincent, who had a bedsit on Harcourt Street – so called, he said, because there was nowhere to sit except the bed. So it was on the bed we kissed and rolled about, crackling with static from his nylon quilt. My hair stuck flat to the fabric, as though fastening me there by a thousand tiny points, and Shay stroked it with the flat of a tablespoon – in order to ground me, he said. He meant, in an electrical way. The spoon was cold from the drawer and Shay fell silent as he drew it across my eyebrow and down along the orbital bone. I was very happy when he did this. I wanted him to slip the thing between my lips a moment, to see how that felt.

Sexually speaking, Shay was very keen to take it to the next level. His father was a vet in County Carlow and this gave him a certain understanding of the mechanics involved – or perhaps he should say 'hydraulics'. He had a way of swallowing a joke, with a little bobbing lift of his chin, as though agreeing with himself while tossing down a peanut. This was somewhere between irritating and endearing (the whole sexual question was making me very cranky with men). When he managed to stop talking, Shay was a great kisser, if a little over-articulate there too. And he was lovely. He still is. I saw him a few years ago when he was home from America, as I do every five years or so, and we are quite shy with each other, but we shared a look as we remembered – different things, at a guess, but also the same thing – how it changed our lives.

With hindsight, the foreplay lasted for many weeks and this is why there was no pain. This first surprise was quickly lost in a larger astonishment, that such a thing could happen inside you – a place I had not properly considered – it felt like he was going up into my head, right into my mind. Afterwards, he asked me was I OK, and I said, 'Yes.' A little later, he asked me what did I think of that. I said it was like being a plane all your life and not knowing you could fly.

He was an engineering student. I did not tell him it was like a baby taking a first step, realising what feet were really for. I said it was the fulfilment of design.

Shay's window frames were stuffed with newspaper against draughts, and he left the Superser heater on all evening so we could be naked, which was another new thing now – after years of sly fumblings and slapping away, there we were, truthful and right. We looked so epic in the light of the gas fire, its tangerine glow on our bodies shading to white before sloping into the darkness of the room. I lay there in a state of abstraction, thinking this was the opposite of punishment, it was like a reward for being stupid. Sex was so much better than I had imagined it would be. It was the answer to a question our bodies had been asking for some years, and although this answer was astonishingly specific, it was also surprisingly hard to remember. So much so, indeed, that we had to remind ourselves what it was like, by doing it again.

The world was never so drab, the next day, and the people in it all amazing. I looked at them from the top deck of the bus: that woman pushing her bicycle with the shopping bags; the man in his brown cotton coat, taking bread out on trays from the back of his van. They knew this thing – and yet they still went about their business, as though they had nothing better to be doing with their time.

As soon as the bus pulled away outside UCD, I felt a backwash of emotion, standing in the rain. Something in me failed and dropped, I don't know why. It might have been shame, though I did not feel ashamed. Perhaps it was guilt because I did not love Shay Vincent, at least not the way I loved you.

I dodged around college all week, waiting for the shock of seeing you sitting against a breeze-block wall, smoking a roll-up, or queuing in the restaurant with an empty tray in your hands. When we finally bumped into each other outside the library, I knew immediately. You had heard about myself and Shay.

I looked you in the eye. And it is a foolish thing to say, but it is nonetheless true, that the person who looked back at me in that moment is the person I live with now. Thirty years has not proved me wrong on this, or forty, or however many damn years there have been since then, through all the changes. There you were.

It is hard to recover from a look like that.

Your irises are speckled now and more faded, there are hints, in the brown, of amber and green, at least I think there are. I don't notice the colour any more. I drop you a quick text.

—When home?

Because the gate has not yet creaked, I am no longer sure what I actually see, these days, when I look at you.

EXACTLY ONE WEEK after I had sex for the first time, my mother went a bit crazy. I crawled out of bed on Saturday afternoon.

'What time do you call this?' she said and there was a sudden fight, as sometimes happened in my teenage years. Most of these spats ended in tears and reconciliation; this one ended, less typically, with my mother clearing my wardrobe in one frantic armload, which she brought over to the bedroom window, poking herself in the face, as she did so, with the wire hangers. She was trying to throw the clothes down into the garden.

'Do you want a hand with that?'

The window had been painted shut for years.

'Get out if you want to talk to me like that. If that's how you want to conduct yourself, you can get out of here, you can find yourself a different hotel.'

She had caught the jauntiness of my tone, not to mention the swagger in my step as I sashayed down the stairs.

The clothes came flying down after me and snarled into a heap which she then had to kick and stumble through in order to give my face a wallop. And this was considerably less than wonderful, it was a ringing blow and I felt the world expand in the echo of it. I stood a moment, then turned and walked straight out of the house. Of course, as soon as I hit cold air, I realised I had no coat and nowhere to go, so I went over to the little park and sat on a bench, appealing skywards to stop the tears.

I had spent an amount of time under these trees as a child, playing my chatty, solitary games. This is where I arranged my toys and told everyone to behave themselves; the dolly and the fluffy rabbit, the teapot and the fossil stone.

'Now be nice!'

I bashed them together and separated them briskly, and gave them what for.

And here I was again, sorting it out, alone. My mother felt threatened by the change in me, I knew that. She felt abandoned or outdone. She felt old.

And I was perfectly happy, that was the joke of it, because I had a secret life now and it was none of her concern. This new delight dragged something monstrous in its shadow, that loomed and was gone.

The day was very still. The winter grass was sharp in each blade, and the surrounding windows pewter with the reflection of a grey sky. I waited for the world to settle down, then I got up and walked back over to the house. It was silent, now, with no sign of Kitty, though lamps had been switched on in the empty rooms, waiting for night to fall.

My mother was up in her room with the curtains closed and, after an hour or so, I tapped on the door and went in. It was dark. She reached up her arms when she knew it was me, and I leaned down to gather her close, tucking in beside her to sit on the bed. My mother was tiny; I was, at nineteen, many years taller than her. I rocked her little body for a while, humming forgiveness, and released her back down to the pillows. Later, I had to support her upright, to help her sip from a cup of tea.

It was a disaster. We never fought about mother–daughter things. Neither of us threw tantrums about my hair or my lipstick or the way I was dressed on my way out the door. This unlike other girls I knew, who were such a problem to their mothers, they were a permanent source of exasperation. Every single thing they did was wrong, in a way that only marriage could cure. (My friend Melanie had to go to America to escape it: she came back every Christmas for the annual complaint about her hair.) But my mother was Katherine O'Dell, a woman who left condoms in the bathroom cabinet for her daughter's safety and convenience. This was my marvellous mother, who told me that I was marvellous too.

It passed, whatever it was. She put on a cream kimono, in wafting silk, and I found her in the kitchen, back on the phone and smoking up a storm. She had decided to learn how to drive, we would both do it. She found a nice man to torment, 'What do you mean, "turn left"? Is that left?' We sat in his learner car, with the funny, second set of pedals on the passenger side. And he certainly got to use them.

'Easy up, now. Easy up.' A thickset man with a soft, Donegal accent, his eyes were small and shiny with fear. We imitated him afterwards for a week.

'Easy up, now. Easy up.'

It was coming up to Christmas and, after we had wrangled the tree, she poured me a very grown-up sherry. 'So who is this young man?' Does he have a name?'

And I burst into tears.

'Oh dear,' she said. 'Oh, never mind. There'll be more, darling. There will be another one along in a while.'

*

I met him in the street. Maybe ten days after the event, I saw my lovely deflorist Shay Vincent on Anne Street and he looked at me as though we had never slept together, and never would. I asked him if he was going down to The Duke and he didn't exactly blank me, he said, 'Bit skint.'

'Ah sure,' I said. Meaning that there was always the chance someone might stand him a drink.

'You haven't seen Barry?' he said, for something to say. 'Not today.'

'Right,' he said, and swung past me. He might have said, 'Good luck, so.' He probably did the upward chin toss, before he fisted his hands into both pockets and walked on.

I stood looking after him. As I turned to continue on my way, I felt the echo of a word in the air, as though someone had shouted an insult – one which I realised too late had been intended for me. My clothes were all wrong and I felt enormously fat, suddenly. I waddled on towards The Duke, where no one was drinking, apart from the woman with a black eye-patch, then down to O'Dwyer's, which was also empty. And for the next few weeks I walked about in that strange, clattering world of a woman who is waiting for a man to call.

In the New Year my mother was gone again, working in America, and I was sorting through the post on the hall table when I saw an envelope with my name on it. Shay Vincent had written to me – a proper letter, as used to happen, on thick blue paper and in his unfamiliar writing, which was neat and small. He said he treasured the memory of our meeting and that he would always hold me in the deepest respect, but he did not think it possible he could love me in a way that I deserved. I went round to his bedsit and he did not let me in the door; we went instead to the Coffee Inn, where he slid his hands across the sticky tabletop to say, with much difficulty, 'It was my first time, too.' Then he talked himself into an awful state, his eyes rolled up at me, his hands sometimes grasping mine. He did not love me, he said.

'That's all right,' I said. But it wasn't all right, apparently, it was a disaster. And we could not do what we had done, ever again.

We were all half-mad in those days. The men were beside themselves, the women were always crying. Every time you got drunk, someone tried to bang their head off a wall, or they flung the window open and roared out into the night. Or am I just imagining it? Our house was near the canal, where couples often walked, and my memories of winter evenings was always of women weeping, men's voices pushing against them in the darkness saying, 'Come *on*. Come *on*.'

That was the winter of Bloody Sunday. At the end of January, British soldiers shot up a civil rights march in Northern Ireland and, down in Dublin, people gathered outside the British embassy to protest. The news came through slowly – ten were dead, then thirteen. They had been shot in the chest or in the back, and one was shot with his hands in the air. On the Tuesday all the students marched from college to join the crowd at the embassy, shouting, 'Brits Out, Brits Out.' And though it felt right to make that particular noise, I did not go the next day, because the stones turned to petrol bombs as darkness fell, and I am afraid of fire.

There were more protest marches on the Wednesday. Some more students I knew joined in and others gave it a miss, because everything felt more serious now. I sat in with Kitty the night we burned the British embassy down. It was just a mile away from us in Dartmouth Square and the crowd made the same noise as a distant rugby match, except the songs were different and the game went on all night.

I switched on the small telly in the living room, and Kitty stood beside me to watch with a duster in her hand. When the news came on, there was an account of the previous day's fun. Two guys I did not recognise burned a Union Jack on the steps of the embassy, and a cardboard coffin with the number 13 painted on the side was carried through the crowd. I remembered the coffin and tried to spot familiar faces, including my own. I wanted to say to Kitty that I was there, or I had been there, that the guy with the megaphone was a student at Trinity College, not UCD, which meant that he was just a kind of tourist – or maybe they said Maoist – in any case he was not, as the lads would say, 'sound'. But Kitty was not listening to the news, she was tuned in to some inner weather. The faint smell of burnt paper had entered the room.

I had the strangest feeling, as I watched the footage, that the events on screen were happening right now, that I was on the telly and sitting on the sofa at the same time.

Later, I turned the thing off and Kitty went downstairs to start her round for bed. I went through the darkened house, to the front door to test the air, and then upstairs, from where I could see the glow of the fire from our top back window. I checked that everything was closed and locked, that the phone line still worked. My mother was in the States at the time, not working, or nearly working, she would come back soon afterwards frantic, almost famished, as though the marching and the shootings were a child she had abandoned, and not a whole country. Meanwhile the bakelite phone on the hall table, which was a glamorous cream, remained fat and silent, as did the beige plastic version on the kitchen wall.

Kitty, who enjoyed being a little miserable, said, 'With a bit of luck I'll be gone before it gets much worse,' and she creaked off towards bed and another twenty years of fretful good health while I sat, first in the warmth of the kitchen and then in my bed upstairs, wondering what would happen to us all now.

I dreamed, some night around that time, that you handed me a fish. It was a rainbow trout, you said, or perhaps you said it was a rainbow salmon. The fish was heavy, curved and gleaming, very like the one on the Irish florin, a coin that had recently gone out of circulation. I remember this dream because of the fish-money (we never, in fact, became rich) and because I did not dream of you again, not even when you were sleeping by my side. And I remember the weighty beauty of the fish, how unexpected that was.

I went down to see the damage the next day. The burned-out embassy was dank and empty, the roof just a few blackened beams against a wet sky. A few other people stopped to watch it, and then they walked on. Now that the building was gutted, some other mood settled in. The conversations at college skewed into irrelevance, or politics. The boys especially began to bluster and fall silent. It was like a smell. As though people were making quiet decisions; ones they did not want to share.

A funny thing happens when the world turns, as it turned for us on the night we burned the British embassy down. You wake up the next morning and carry on.

Into this changed national mood my mother flew, like a bird into a windowpane.

She was home before the end of March. I walked in one afternoon and she was asleep upstairs. In the middle of the night, I heard her talking on the kitchen phone. I came down to her in my dressing gown and she took me in her arms.

'How are you, my darling, how have you been getting on?'

She was hazy with jetlag. The table was already scattered with books and newspapers. There were a couple of scripts in brown envelopes worn to a fuzz along the seams.

'I was so worried about you,' she said.

'I was fine.'

'How has it all been?'

By then there was no 'it'. There were no more marches, and certainly no more petrol bombs, there were just a lot of rumours doing the rounds. A few guys were said to carry black berets in their canvas bags. Brendan McSorley from Walkinstown had an IRA balaclava, he took it out in Toners and put it on, becoming instantly transformed into something terrifying and ancient. He looked around the table and laughed, his teeth filling the mean, burned-out mouth hole.

The barman was out from behind the taps so fast he might have leapt over the counter. He pulled the thing off Brendan's head and hustled him out into the street, throwing the balaclava out after him, then he walked back in, twitching for a fight, his fingers fluttering by his thighs.

By the time my mother got back, the real balaclava boys in the North had let off a bomb in England, another in Belfast. There was a man bleeding into the pavement on the front page of the *Irish Times*, with his arm outstretched, in his office suit and tie. He was just a man. The boring man ahead of you in the bank queue was dying on the ground, and it was, already, not my bomb. Though, back in Toners, some of the guys evinced a kind of satisfaction, the way men get pleased with a football result, even if they never kick a ball.

'Everything's been fine, here,' I said to my mother. 'How are you?'

She had been staying in New York in a boxy little hotel room, working on a mini-series from NBC that didn't make it past the pilot (called, I think, *Slow Day in Kilfinoola*). Doomed, the whole thing, from the get-go, and she was just destroyed by it all, it was just too cold. She could not watch the news from home, and then there was no news. She went out to Amagansett and stayed for a week in a house belonging to Bob and Laura, completely alone. But it was wonderful, she wanted to get a dog and watch it run along those beaches, you know, the tail wagging in the dune grass, a little cafe still doing crayfish and oysters, but she felt so far away.

'Look at you.'

She held me by the waist – she took great pleasure in the size of my waist – and cupped my cheek with her palm. She leaned in to hug and inhale, and take in the smell of my hair.

She pulled back and gave a quizzical eyebrow.

'What?' I said.

'Oh, nothing.'

'What?' I said again, annoyed because she was making some insinuation about my goddamn sex life.

'Just. You look so grown-up, is all.'

'Well, you've been gone a while,' I said. Not without bitterness. Three phone calls on crackling lines, the cost in those days prohibitive, but it was not the cost that stopped her. She did not like speaking to me on the phone, it made her feel so disembodied, she said. As though she was already dead.

(Or perhaps she did not say this, perhaps I just imagine she did. When I was a small child, I famously stamped my foot and refused to speak to my mother on the telephone.)

In any case, we forgave each other and walked back to the stairs with our arms entwined, both in our sateen dressing gowns, she in lilac, me in powder blue. She hauled herself up by the banister rail, saying, 'I'm sorry I didn't get home last week, had to stay for the parade.' She was on a float going down Fifth Avenue for St Patrick's Day, pretending to play an enormous golden harp: a reception afterwards at the Irish consulate, where the talk was 'muted' to say the least, it put her in such a rage.

She went into her bedroom, where I helped her to clear the bed of notebooks and papers, a new American electric typewriter that might or might not run on Irish current, a rattling bag of strong American drugs: supercharged pain-killers, antibiotics, creams dense with cortisone, the dreaded packs of Trojans, which I eyed with more interest now – because she was quite right, I was seeing someone, I was out every Saturday night.

I was with that medical student you hated so particularly. And indeed, there was much about him to dislike. It was like one of those relationships that teenagers have, for practice. We had sharp, pistoning sex and not a single decent conversation from one end of the week to the next, but he was My Boyfriend and I was His Girl. Perfectly good-looking. He wanted to go into orthopaedics, he said, because it was carpentry, basically. Emmet Mahon from Monkstown: best reason in Ireland not to break your leg.

I could not figure out why sex, which had been such an amazing discovery, was no longer amazing. I thought it was just a question of putting in the time. Meanwhile, back in Belfield, I was spending all day with you. We had decided to launch a magazine but we did not know what kind of magazine it should be. We had long discussions about this. It had to contain real ideas. We drank a lot of tea.

(Actually, you and your guy friends decided to launch a magazine and I elbowed my way in as typist. That new IBM Selectric my mother brought back from the States rattled out words the way a machine-gun did bullets, and

I loved its marvellous noise. Melanie from school was my wingman. She flicked her hair during editorial meetings and handed around Polo Mints.)

When the thing was done we had a real fight – one that wasn't just about French Cinema. It was late in the evening, in the Students' Union, where there was a Gestetner printer we were allowed to use. We had finally rolled off a batch of *Comment* which was the new magazine: cartoons by your mate Noel, words mostly by you, a brilliant piece from your mate Barry that, sadly, turned out to be lifted entire from Paulo Freire, and to finish up, half a page of Knock Knock jokes from your mate Jim.

I said it was OK.

It wasn't really OK. I had to type it on to crackling sheets of stencil paper, that was extra fine and hard to manage. Everything stank of solvent and the final product blotched here and there to white. Which was not the problem, according to you. The problem was the little satirical piece I had delivered, written from the point of view of a 'skip' or cleaner in Trinity College, where the posh students were said to go. You found it a bit winsome. You said I was not engaging with the real issues at stake here, by which you meant (as we drilled down through the subtext) that yes, I might indeed be too middle-class for *Comment* magazine, and by middle-class perhaps you were saying morally as well as financially autonomous, which might or might not be code for sexually promiscuous. Or that was certainly not what you were saying. Actually, the fact that I thought it was a problem was the real problem, because the last thing this magazine needed was a woman going on about herself, when we could be focused on the actual mechanisms of change.

So it was all my fault, whatever way you looked at it. But I also heard the compliment your anger contained.

What you really meant was that you wanted – or you certainly did *not* want – to sleep with me too.

Jesus.

Sometimes I don't know why I married you.

I grew up surrounded by mad people and I think I enjoy them in a way, but this was too foolish and cutting, even for me. I walked away. I strode off in my new leather clogs, ker-klopp ker-klopp, as you followed, saying, That's not what I meant. And I cried, and you comforted me for hurting me, there on the path out to the bus stop, and that is the way we continued for forty more years.

No, that was a joke.

But it continues true that you are fine if you 'have' me, and hurtful when you don't 'have' me, and this sense of possession can shift in your mind, without me speaking or smiling or moving from the room.

We kissed on the path that night in April 1972 and continued kissing throughout May in various locations in Dublin town: against some railings on Northumberland Road, with your two hands holding the ornamental spikes on either side of my head; on a bench in Herbert Park, the whack and thock of a tennis game echoing our kissing's back and forth; in the secret garden at the back of Earlsfort Terrace; at the bus stop for the 14A which was your bus, the engine idling massively behind its screen of orange mesh. We kissed poetically on a bench above Baggot Street bridge, endlessly on a window ledge on the corner of Suffolk Street, where I left my bag behind, so drunk was I with kissing, the memory of it lingering for years, even as the window was knocked into a doorway through which people now walk, right through the ghost of our kissing. We kissed near my house, against a canal-bank tree, and I did not weep and you did not push against me, lowing like a sick calf, 'Come *on*, Come *on*.' We kissed sitting on the front steps in Dartmouth Square, by which time you had figured out how to get me into bed.

'Let's go to bed,' you said. And that is what we did.

By the beginning of June we were seeing each other all the time – much sneaking around in Dartmouth Square so as not to upset Kitty, or indeed your mother out in Rathfarnham, who would be upset too. We were lovers. We were not doomed lovers, I think there is a difference. The sex was frequent and heartfelt but we lacked expertise and almost preferred to talk – we were incredibly good at talking – we did so, naked and dressed, for long days at a time. And we got much better in bed, despite Duggan's slander on the housewives of the world, or his slander on men and women both – that sex is a route to dissatisfaction and can only go off, over time. It really did not go off. And I don't know why this is.

I don't know why he thought that, or why he was wrong.

It is very real. It's not a performance, I mean. There are no masks, no costumes or cruelty. No one gets hurt or pretends to be hurt.

Well, maybe a bit.

Or I am wrong, and it is all cruelty – it is such a serious thing for two bodies to do. There may be, at the heart of it, some mutual destruction. There is certainly a kind of undoing, that leaves us remade.

Thinking about which is a great distraction. I pick up the phone and call you, and hear the cricket chirp of your mobile downstairs.

'You there?' I shout, down through the floor.

No answer. I close the laptop on the slew of papers, push away from our daughter's school desk, and stick my head round the door.

'You home?'

And the house around me is a puzzle of absences, room by room.

My mother sailed out of her bedroom one morning in July, said, 'Oh hello,' when she saw you going into the bathroom, large and hairy and stuffed into my blue sateen dressing gown. And you, to be honest, were a disaster. You ran back in to me and hid under the covers like a character in a French farce.

It wouldn't happen like that in Rathfarnham, you said. And indeed it would not. If I had been 'caught' in your bedroom at home, which you, in any case, shared with your brothers Tom and Andy, your Mass-going mother would have had a nervous collapse, your stoical father fallen silent and disappointed, and you might, in time, have married some other girl.

You might.

Instead of which there was a sweet and mocking query as to how you liked your tea – or would you prefer coffee? – she had a new Italian espresso pot, you just popped it on the stove. You got her famous toast and marmalade and, a little later, a formal introduction, which involved the use of my mother's reading glasses, over which she looked at me to say, 'Darling, you haven't introduced us.' Then the offer of a newspaper supplement – it must have been the weekend – which she passed over without looking, as though to an old friend.

And then, after many years of loving us both, or at least of putting up with it all, you shouted, 'You and your fucking posh fucking mother,' and I remembered the ticking mortification of that morning, how you resented sitting there, you who became, over the years, a reader of news-papers, a lover of long breakfasts, a coffee fiend. You threw it back at me, when the children were small.

You and your fucking posh fucking mother.
And I said, 'Oh there it is. There you go.'

What is it about heterosexual men? I have seen it so many times. That pang they get when a good-looking woman smiles at them, as though she has just humiliated them in some way.

Six months after Bloody Sunday, Katherine was photographed on a protest march in Derry on the first anniversary of internment without trial. She linked arms in the front row with local women and civil rights activists. She had a kind of housewife scarf knotted under her chin, though it was actually Hermès, and as she passed the camera lens, she threw her head back and smiled.

The route was blocked by British soldiers and the protest later turned into a stone-throwing riot, which is all that made it on to the news. I missed it on TV – the flaming bottles and the skinny men with white handkerchiefs over their faces lobbing half-bricks – I did not even know she was there. Then a photograph appeared. It wasn't even in the national newspapers, it was in a local publication that she folded open on the kitchen table and left out for me to see.

I didn't discuss it. I am not even sure I saw it properly. I should have been worried she would get herself shot but all I remember feeling was irritation. I had my own life to lead. I was twenty-one years old, and in love all day.

This was our first year as a couple and we spent it looking into each other's eyes, walking around in a soulful daze, asking, 'Where do you want to go?' and, 'Where are you going?' and, 'Where were you? I was waiting right here.' We held hands, and had small skirmishes about whether you really fancied me as much as you fancied some other woman you looked at from under your long lashes, as she passed by. You said you didn't. Really. How could I get all that so wrong? You said I was a cool customer, you found that sexy. You liked my analytical gaze, my ability to speak so intently and then just ignore you, the way I rose from the sheets and walked clean out the door. Because you were marked by our love, you said, it was indelible, while I was just an Etch-A-Sketch kind of girl.

Whatever that meant.

You said it was like I forgot you, each time I turned away.

'No, I don't,' I said. 'I don't forget you.'

I had enough going on, is what I mean. I had enough problems, practising facial expressions in the mirror, trying to look less of a cool customer for an overly intelligent boy from Rathfarnham. I have a still face. I always look the same in photographs. I think you could cut my image out of all the pictures in an album, and swap them around, and there would be no difference. Here she is at a birthday, here she is alone beside the sea. And this makes me feel invisible, as though the birthday did not happen, or it happened without me. You also said – it started as an accusation, but it is not an accusation any more – that I take things into myself, and seldom gave anything away.

So I tried to look less mousy and more interesting for you, because you were outlandishly interesting. Your eyebrows moved together, regretfully high, and you used your hands when you talked. Long, white, expressive hands. We spent our time in the restaurant discussing the future of art under capitalism as the spent trays circled back into the kitchen on their automated carousels. Nietzsche was a real subject for us, in those days. Various betrayals were mulled over, romantic or ideological. Who was fake and who was real: whether Barry actually meant it, or was he just *pretending* to like Artaud.

Your corduroy jacket and leather waistcoat were covered, that autumn, by a long salt-and-pepper overcoat with big curving lapels and a trailing belt, that always hung open, for me to warm my hands under, or slide over your skinny ass, while we stood in out of the rain. I bought an Afghan gilet: down to the ankle, ratty trim. I gave in to the blank face problem by accessorising it with a floppy felt hat and slim little Hamlet cigars. Perhaps that is why I did not take my mother's politics too seriously. It was just a scarf thing for her, I thought. It was just another change of costume.

My mother is long dead, and I want to think that nothing between us two ever went wrong. Katherine – as I began to call her in my college days – was too often away, and when she was home we wanted to be happy. We sat for whole evenings on the same sofa. She put a cushion on her lap for my head, and we smoked from the same pack, as though smoking were some kind of occupation.

I always had a book on the go. She would drink her rotgut Chianti, and read a script or throw it aside. If I offered an opinion about my place in the world, she would immediately agree – then add some small qualification that turned, over the next hour or two, into the opposite of what I had intended. It was hard to see where this happened, exactly. We pivoted about each other. We loved to agree.

I was, for example, quite keen to get married. She said that was a lovely idea.

'Oh, yes,' she said.

As though she did not know what you were like, that you were completely confusing and impossible to love. An hour later I was determined to stay single, or at least child-free, and she thought that this was a good plan, too. And we lolled and smoked, two women tranced by each other still.

We left the TV on with the sound turned down, and turned it up for the news, which was, in those days, mostly news from Northern Ireland. Shootings, reprisals, raids and bombings. When I look it up online, I find one bad day when they all happened together: an IRA man was shot by British soldiers, a British soldier was shot by the IRA, a random Catholic was shot by Protestant paramilitaries, and two men were shot in West Belfast for reasons unknown. All through 1973 people were bombed to bits in pubs and chip shops, they were shot by accident or in a panic, they were killed for no reason or in a highly targeted way. We heard all this, day in and day out, and the silence between us became increasingly sad.

We did not fight about politics. I said nothing about the foolish trip to Derry. I did not complain about the nationalist songs she played on the record player, or the dirges and the doggerel the moustachioed boys sang in the kitchen late at night (and then, out of nowhere, a song that split your heart in two). I remained tight-lipped when she went to wave the old shillelagh for a fundraiser in Boston, billed 'for prisoners' wives'. But it was hard to be in the same room with her sometimes – a silent, preening satisfaction when something brutal came on the news. There was pleasure there, and a kind of drift that infuriated me beyond measure.

At Easter of our final college year, you left me for reasons I could not understand. Then we got back together and spent two days in bed, before breaking up again to focus on our exams. After the exams, you sent me a poem by Patrick Kavanagh. Then you went off Interrailing with your English Olivia, who had never read a poem in her life. You missed my birthday party.

Sorry, I had forgotten that: You missed my twenty-first birthday. You rang the next day from a phone box in Padua, your voice made frantic by managing coins into the slot.

After which, you came back for three or four weeks of autumn, and we had poetry coming out our ears.

Then you left me for good.

Then, actually, I left *you* for good, because I couldn't put up with your nonsense a day longer, your boot of a mother, your poky Catholic hole of a suburban family nightmare out in Rathfarnham, complete with fucking horrible carpets, your overly intelligent, entirely stupid obsession with Artaud.

After which, we had a lot of break-up sex, because our love was so hopeless and it was coming up to Christmas. And in January you got on the boat to London, because there was nothing in Ireland for an overly intelligent boy from Rathfarnham to do.

I had completed the bedraggled look, by then. My hair was long and my clothes drippy. I used a lot of eyeliner and liked to jingle when I moved. You said I looked as though I had just got out of some other man's bed, and this pleased me no end. At least, it pleased me at the time. Afterwards, when you were gone, I wondered why you would think such a thing, when the only man's bed I had wanted was yours.

I got a job that first winter out of college, putting the social listings together for a newspaper and later, writing copy for the entertainment section. I was a hackette. I put my platform boots on and tottered out into the winter darkness to an opening at the Gate Theatre, to the Spring Show at the RDS. I got the work through my mother's contacts and was lucky to have it – there were no jobs, back then – but I wasn't happy. My life felt like an imitation, and I was terrified it might become the real thing.

I was already jaded, with my clinky-clanky earrings and my bored look. In the years after you left, I became young and tired. I was out every night. I came home to a dark house, when she was gone, or to my mother's night-walking when she was home. I avoided her friends: the clapped-out bohemians in the drawing room and the young Republicans in the kitchen, tuning up for a song. I walked past them and up the stairs to bed.

They were a nervous bunch, the guys who hung their heads when the music played. White-bodied, quick-smoking; they had bad haircuts, and the narrow shoulders of men who had grown up poor. Most of them were not 'involved', which was the euphemism that we used for those active in the business of shooting and maiming, but perhaps some of them were 'involved'. The lines were not clear.

It was not a great time in my life. In the early seventies, as anyone will tell you, the whole of Dublin smelt like the top deck of the bus on a wet morning. I filed copy in Abbey Street and drank afterwards with the weathered journos in the Oval or the Batch on Bachelors Walk with its view of the night-lit river below. I was trying to break out of the entertainment section and into the real pages of the newspaper and the men who drank in these bars were on the inside track. They knew what was going on. They liked to predict what was going to happen, and when they were wrong – which was exactly half the time – they explained how we had all been misled. So now they were twice as right, they were right all over again.

'Go on down to Buswells, keep your nose to the ground.' The editor would send me off to the hotel bar frequented by politicians where my job was to flirt with old men, which I did, and find out things, which I really did not. I found things out about army pension bills and defeated family planning bills, but you could write that stuff up a hundred times over and no one would give a damn. The papers were full of letter bombs and shootings up North, and down in peaceful Dublin, everyone was obsessed with secret money and secret mistresses – everyone went around being *in the know.*

Flirting in Buswells was not the worst way to spend your Thursday evening and it did not make me feel especially soiled. I avoided sleeping with most of them, though there were nights I stumbled out of there, dusting myself down. It was a game we played; some old fucker ordered up champagne and you said, 'Get away out of that,' then you drank it anyway, and left.

I did not always leave, of course. There was the thing with Duggan – though that came later, and it certainly did not involve champagne. But I can't properly describe how fond I was of these men, the ones in the Oval who looked after me and the ones in Buswells who did me so little harm. I liked their sad and guarded eyes, the way they turned me into that gallant object, the Girl About Town.

And one night, it is true, I bumped into Duggan and I let him flirt with me, and I did not run away.

Duggan was one of my lecturers from college, though I did not take his seminars, if I could avoid them, because there was no point having Duggan the Fucker marking your essays, if you were a girl – that would be a sign of great stupidity. I did sometimes glance into Theatre L where he packed them to the door, lecturing on D.H. Lawrence in his baggy suit of dark green corduroy. He said the word 'genital' an amount – he did it in his Monaghan accent – and that was a huge draw in a university where the toilets were segregated into 'male', 'female' and 'nuns'. He admired Bellow and Mailer, was ferociously, invigoratingly anti-Irish – that was his calling card – and this stance made him an outsider and a great rebel altogether.

But I liked our complicity. He made me feel not just smart, but better than all the smart people, who were – let's face it – actually useless. Not like us.

'Look at you,' he liked to say. 'You could pull the whole house down. You could pull it down around their ears.'

I did not know if he was praising me or taunting me. I was a quiet student and watchful. I thought if I pulled anything down, I would do it like a thickening vine: I would creep on unnoticed and wreak, over decades, my vegetable destruction. But how did he know? That if I wanted a man, I could just walk over and get him – did he know that? Even though I was a lovely Irish girl. He used to sort of growl it at me. You're a lovely Irish gurrrl. Later I wondered how many women it worked on. I mean how many lovely Irish gurrrls he eventually got into bed.

Four years out of college, I bumped into him in Grogan's, after a poetry launch, and I was all grown-up, as he said to me, 'Look at you, all grown-up,' though I just felt hardened, and sad. He picked up on my new cynicism and threw it back at me, and we blathered and argued through three pubs, all the way back to his kitchen in Ranelagh. This last invitation made me feel grown-up too – in all the time I had known him, I had never been to his home. And it is not as if I did not know what we were about to do.

There had been so much of Duggan, so much from him over the years, all of it provocative, hard to catch. But whatever impulse I had to contain him, or even to shut him up, went away as soon as we hit bare skin. Duggan was big in the belly, and his arms were thin by comparison, also very white and hairy. You don't see them any more, or not so much, these men pregnant with porter, and they were powerful-looking men, in their day. Even so, his erection seemed at odds with the rest of him. I was, as I recall, surprised all that still worked, he seemed so old (he was, I calculate it now, fifty-one).

So there I was, in the arrogance of my youth. And there was Duggan, supine on his dodgy back: me on top, feeling all lithe and disappointed. He was just not like Duggan – a man who was about badness, and the things people got up to if only you knew it; the lesbians up the road and the priest down the road, and Jonathan Swift's obsession with shit. He was surprisingly withheld. Having sex with Duggan's body was like having sex with the least interesting aspect of the man, and that, I suppose, was the revenge I had been looking for.

I lay in his arms afterwards, planning my escape, delayed by the warm sound of his voice in the gristle of his chest, the unexpected sensation of his hand at my head, sorting through the unfeeling strands of my hair.

We were in the little house on Rugby Road that his wife had abandoned some years before. Nothing was clean. The sheets were starting to introduce themselves, so I pushed them away, showing, as I did so, the pure line of my own body's profile, the curve of hip and waist. Duggan was talking about the year he spent in a TB hospital when he was a child, and what happened when a boy wet the bed. He did it in a sudden shriek, 'Sister Margaret!' he said. 'Sister Margaret!' And I wished I could tell someone about this. How Duggan complained about wetting the bed, five minutes after he had come.

No one visited him in this place, the whole year he was there. Not one person made the trip down from Monaghan to see if he was alive or dead; not his mother or his father or the local priest. He was eight years old. The next day, I felt a swoop of sorrow and regret, as though, by sleeping with the man, I had done him further harm. It was a little punch of emotion I often got in those days, thinking, Christ, the TB ward, how hard was that? One of those small, dark holes that opened in your morning, into which the whole of Catholic Ireland fell.

But at the time, lying in his unwashed sheets in Ranelagh, I thought it was almost hilarious. Professor Niall Duggan, the man who stormed out of a dinner with Frank Kermode and once refused to sleep with Pinter's first wife, was talking about wetting the bed.

Sister Margaret! He's after doing it again. Sister Margaret!

One bright evening in 1974, I was walking home along Merrion Square and I heard the sound of something falling, not very disastrously, in the distance and this was followed by a sharp crack.

'Did you hear that?' I said to a passing man, as though we had known each other for years.

'I think I did,' he said.

Dubliners talk to each other very easily. We talk as though getting back to it, after some interruption.

'Mind how you go,' he said, and we both hurried up a little, trying to get away from the centre of town.

At the corner of Holles Street, I felt a huge sound. I thought it had happened under my feet but, when I looked down, nothing beneath me had changed. I glanced back the way I had come and saw a woman on her hands and knees up by the Mont Clare Hotel. I knew she was a woman by the handbag still attached to her wrist, flat on the ground, and also by her hat which was hanging on by its hatpin, about to fall. I had an impulse to catch it. I don't remember running back to her – those forty seconds or so dropped out of my mind, never to be regained – but by the time I arrived, a man had pulled her upright. There were two matching holes in the knees of her tan stockings and grit marks on the heel of her hand. She ignored all this as she fumbled with her hair, patting and tucking stray bits back under the hat.

'Oh God,' she said. 'I am due tomorrow,' meaning the hairdresser's.

'You're grand,' I said. The odd mortification about her hair was enough to keep me distracted from the stopped traffic and the smoke rising up by Trinity College. A few yards away, a man with a bloodied face came to a standstill, and wiped the liquid out of his eye.

Later, people described the injuries they had seen, or they declined to describe them. There was a woman decapitated on the Dublin street three hundred yards away from me, but it was another twenty years before I saw a photograph of her horribly shortened body lying on the ground, her high-fashion platform boots sticking out beyond a stranger's overcoat. It was a man's coat and the thought of it stayed with me for a long time: the idea of taking it off and laying it on a girl's body with nothing above the collar line, then walking home without. Your wife saying, 'What happened your good coat?' And I remembered looking away from the bloodied man in order to give him a moment's privacy, he seemed so exposed.

I could hear sirens now, but they were somewhere else. The street was very quiet apart from the whisper on the footpaths of people walking quickly away.

I was trying to bring the woman with the hat across the road, so she could catch a bus. But no, she said, there might be worse up by government buildings. A man came walking down the central painted line between the stopped traffic, he said it was a car bomb, it had been in a parked car. Hard to describe the conviction I felt, as we walked back towards Holles Street, that every bonnet and boot we passed would blow us to hell, every polished or dirty Fiat or Volkswagen, in black or green or tan, would turn to shrieking, ripping metal, we would be showered by windscreen glass, impaled by a bent wiper, we were about to die. The cars stayed, in the circumstances, astonishingly mute. The hat woman was trying to get away from me. She said she would go down to the flats, where she had a cousin. I left her on the corner of the maternity hospital, where nurses were gathering on the steps, pinning on their capes and leaving at a run for the site of the bomb.

I was also wearing stupid heels that day, and I stumbled in them the mile or so to Dartmouth Square. There were people standing at the door to Larry Murphy's pub, they said the buses were all stopped, there was more than one bomb, there had been three so far. At the corner of Fitzwilliam Street, a car exploded with the sound of a yapping dog hurling himself against the side window. Someone had left a Jack Russell in there and, as I told everyone later, it was *going ballistic*.

When I got back home, the hall smelt of old lilac in the vase, gone over in the unexpected warmth of May. I arrived upstairs to find my mother listening to the radio in the living room. She saw me walk in and did not smile.

'Have you heard?' I said. 'Did you hear it?'

She looked at me and looked at me.

'Not us,' she said.

Two words.

'What do you mean, "us"?'

There was a thing her green eyes did at moments of – it seemed to me – great irrationality. They became a thicker green, the pigment muddied and opaque. She became masked, somehow, in her own gaze.

'*Us?*'

Who did she think she was?

She wasn't even Irish.

I lost my temper that night. I went from room to room in a state of agitation. I dragged out a suitcase from the cupboard under the stairs and went up to my bedroom, the thing bumping emptily against the banisters. Then I did not know what clothes to put in it, or where I might go. I was in shock. I sat on the edge of the bed and stared.

There is a psychological test you take for certain jobs – pages and pages of questions about your personality style ('Are you an arrow or a boat?') And the second-last question is: 'Is or was your mother a good person?' Apparently if you answer 'no', that is taken as a sign that you are unhinged, because no one's mother is a bad person. There is no such thing.

They never found out who was responsible for the bombings in Dublin that day, though it is probable the British secret service was involved. I am also aware of the rumour that, in the early seventies, Katherine O'Dell had a lover who later rose to become an important member of the IRA. I don't know what to say to that. Firstly, I don't think it is true. And if it were true – which it is not – I can understand how such a man might have, in the days after Bloody Sunday, been regarded as a hero. My mother was not a snob, she had a keen sense of injustice, and also, if you ask me, she could sleep with any man she liked. But I think the cause was just a dalliance for her, and this makes it worse, somehow. My mother flirted with violence. She may have slept with violence – I neither know nor care. The sexual act seems, to me, beside the point.

And, by the way, we all consider sleeping with the bad man – we want to fix his hurt, or we want him to hurt us – one way or another, we are all attracted to the shadow.

It was just, in this instance, too real for me.

ALTHOUGH IT WAS all so maddening for my mother, in the mid seventies – although success was maddening and failure was maddening and injustice was maddening and English people were especially maddening – I did not consider her to be clinically mad, in those days. The uncertainties of her profession were starting to take their toll, of course. She was hard to work with. That was well known.

Or no. She was *wonderful* to work with. My mother was *fantastic*. She worked *all the hours* and was *incredibly gracious*. She was an *absolute perfectionist*. All of which became a way of saying that Katherine O'Dell was more or less furious, most of the time.

She had long and disruptive opinions about the business of dying in a play – she was against it. She was also against monologues, which she said belonged on the radio, and children, of course. Not because they stole the limelight but because they broke the fiction. They were too real. Children are like dead bodies, no one believes them – with the exception of the boy in *Godot* because no one is asked to believe anything in *Godot*. Or if the child is there to sing, because when you sing, then all bets are off.

'Oh Christ, don't get me started about children,' she said.

She even hated the ones who never made it on to the stage. I was her baby. I was her one-hundred-per-cent success rate when it came to reproduction, and maybe we were just lucky, but if she got another script with a dead child in it, or a long-ago dead baby, or the ghost of a child, or an adopted child returned again, she would scream. What is all that about? Women actors fiddling with their hair, letting an absent-minded hand graze the place where life had once been. Why were you always asked to clutch at your forlorn womb?

Her rage towards critics was legendary, especially Irish ones. It was all envy, apparently.

'Who criticised him?' she said. 'Who whispered into his young ear that he was no good, or not good enough, or just plain wrong?'

Some days, she even took against the audience. Vampires the lot of them, out there in the darkness, licking it off you. They just want to see you suffer, she said. They want to see you cry.

And indeed, she could cry out of one eye or both, Hollywood style. I will always remember – or think that I remember – sitting in a movie theatre watching *Mulligan*, my mother's face twenty feet high. Her cheek was a white cliff, a sweet wall, and a single tear – that first swelling bulb of water, trembling and light-filled, as it brimmed over. It would fill your outstretched arms. It was the size of a chandelier up there, waiting to fall.

On stage, she could howl like a Greek tragedy, or put a knuckle to her mouth and then tear it away. She could also do beautiful, realistic full crying, whether in sympathy or anguish. Hers were, for the most part, noble tears, though she could also snotter like a serving-maid, especially if someone was hitting her, which they also really did. They hit her quite a lot. Usually across the face. Biff, bash, boff.

Slap.

Hard to say how that felt, when you were watching it. It was like an out-of-body experience for me. The world stopped. This was back in the day, when women asked for it – sometimes literally. They asked to be hurt, not because they wanted to be hurt, but because they wanted strong, pure men to feel bad about themselves. There was one ageless bit of dialogue in a play called *Emotional Blackmail* that opened in Manchester in the autumn of 1974. I helped her with the lines. We used to go around chanting them from room to room.

'Hit me, go on, hit me, you know you want to.'

'Oh you'd like that, wouldn't you.'

'Go on. It's as low as you are.'

'Don't tempt me, woman.'

'Go on.'

'Don't tempt me.'

'Hit me. With the baby in my belly. With your baby in my belly. Go on.'

'Stop screaming at me, woman. Stop screaming at me now.'

Manchester was not a high point, but it was becoming typical of the choices she made in those days. She wanted to make it real, she said, by which she meant political, or harsh.

Work on the main stages had dried up, by then, or was unsatisfactory, and she moved towards the fringe. This was the cause of alarm and delight in the smaller theatres: the idea of slapping Katherine O'Dell had the actor in Manchester in a state of nervous decline, so it wasn't the impact so much as the sweat, she said: 'Talk about a wet kipper.'

She was, by then, beyond her childbearing years so the line about the baby was a bit of a stretch. ('A mature performance,' said Michael Billington in the *Guardian*.) After Manchester, she took stock, or was obliged to take stock and, when she next walked out on stage, she was old. No one can know how much this cost her – the hours she had spent in front of the fan-shaped mirror in her bedroom, the sound of her wardrobe door opening and shutting, opening and shutting, the diets of grapefruit and boiled eggs, the mud packs and mud baths, the injections and enemas, the work, the work, the work. In 1975, Katherine O'Dell finally gave in. At the age of forty-seven, she moved from her unconvincing twenties to her mid sixties – there was nothing for her to play in between. And though this was painful beyond all reckoning, she did it in style, with a production of *Mother Courage* at the Edinburgh Festival in August of that year.

The role was huge, she had never worked so hard. On the opening night, a nest of baby spiders hatched out in her new grey wig – many hundreds of tiny dots, already secreting a fine spider silk, which they used to abseil down over her forehead and eyes. She twitched a bit, but no one noticed because my mother was *a complete professional*. She sang 'The Great Song of Capitulation' that night in Brecht's third act and poor, raped Katrin, her stage daughter, said afterwards that the chill of recognition swept all the way to the back of the hall.

An Irish critic, who had travelled over specially for the production, reported that his emotions had not been sufficiently engaged ('By Brecht!' she shouted. 'That is the point of Brecht!') and he declared the production to be a failure. The London press was appreciative, the Scots more circumspect. She was happy enough. During the day, she walked the streets of Edinburgh, went to matinees and met wonderful young people. She dyed the hair under the ghastly grey wig a more thrilling shade of red.

This was the beginning of a relationship with the emerging director Denis Malone, who adored her, at least for a while. Together they staged a little-seen, iconic production of Beckett's *Not I*, which she performed in the Ailwee cave in County Clare and then in cave complexes in Yugoslavia and Mallorca. They also planned a film version of *In the Shadow of the Glen* that failed to make it into production, despite the interest of Boyd O'Neill, the man she would come to shoot, and not in a filmic way, in his office in Dublin a few years later.

Katherine adapted the script from the play by J.M. Synge, and reconceived the central character as a mature woman, or at least not a May bride.

'A normal woman. What's wrong with normal?'

'Absolutely,' I said.

The big American typewriter was moved from her bedroom to the spare room, where it was surrounded by a proper desk and shelves. I would come home late at night to find her still there, unwilling to let the work go. It was hard to fall asleep through the fitful noise of her inspiration: the brief runs and long, tugging silences of the big electric typewriter, that we called Monica for the way it thrummed with relentless anticipation as soon as you switched it on. One night, I shuffled in at four in the morning to put a folded blanket under the thing and we were a picture: me bleary and half-asleep, Katherine wild-haired and dreaming.

She startled and did not recognise me.

'It's only me,' I said, and it took a while before she was reassured.

The script was done quickly and badly, then slowly and well. She did not think to check the copyright, and that would prove an issue with Boyd, who just tsked at her, she said.

'He just tsked!'

He said there was no point his reading it, if the thing would not run.

J.M. Synge was very long dead, so I have no idea what the copyright problem could be, but I do know that Boyd's irritability magnetised my mother. She was already a little obsessed by the man, or perhaps 'taken' is a better word. He occupied her thoughts and hopes. 'I'll just get this down to Boyd,' she might say. Or, 'I don't think he'll like it. Do you think he will like it?' He was often inaccessible to her by phone.

If I had to date it, I would say her interest in Boyd had been caught on the day he turned her down. The audition for *My Dark Rosaleen* must have happened some time in the winter of 1970. It was not a day I noticed much at the time, although she later turned it into a song of complaint. One ordinary day in winter, she went off to audition at Ardmore Studios ('He didn't even send a car!') for a part she was too old to play – because, although she was still getting away with it on stage, film, as everyone knows, is forensic.

She sat on a plastic chair outside the soundstage until she was called in, and the producers were delighted to see her. The wild American director was a huge, powerful man, with a beard and a bawneen sweater. He took her hand in his big paw and would not let it go.

'Just. What a blast. It is such an honour to meet you, Miss O'Dell.'

He was a fan.

Boyd, who had been hanging back from all this, gave her a quiet nod, so she settled herself in front of the big camera as the surrounding lights dimmed. She took her cue, lifted her face and said the few lines perfectly. You could hear it in the darkness afterwards, how well she had delivered them – that after-silence when they don't know what to do with you, now.

There was a small consultation. Boyd's voice came from behind the camera asking her not to act so much, or 'emote' so much. Or perhaps he just asked her for 'less'.

She gave him 'less'.

He asked her to 'do it blank' and she went, for him, as blank as the sky at noon. She was a field of untrodden snow as she said the lines, which were awful, and she still made them sing.

He did not want the lines to sing.

'Just nothing. Just completely nothing.'

She did nothing. She did it so the broken sentences stuck out like a bone beneath the skin and when she was finished, Boyd O'Neill leaned over to the wild American director and, *sotto voce*, he said, 'You see what I mean?'

There was a small silence. The big American was ashamed, now, because he had liked her, it made him feel all wrong.

'Thank you, Miss O'Dell. Can you show Miss O'Dell the way, please? Mind the cables on the floor.'

What had he seen?

Boyd obliged her to say the lines badly and then he claimed that she was no good at saying the lines. But I really don't think it was a question of the lines.

She was never going to be right. Maura Herlihy, who was born and reared in New Jersey (*She isn't even Irish!*) had the kind of face the producers finally required. She wore pale lipstick and the indifferent look of a woman who might have sex in various different positions, just because she is bored. She was modern. She was also nineteen. What such a creature was doing in the virginal neverland of the Irish countryside was anyone's guess. Katherine O'Dell would have been perfect for the part because Katherine O'Dell was from another time. Which also meant, sadly, that she was far too old.

And there was something more humiliating again about this audition. Boring old Boyd O'Neill overstepped her. He did it in one move.

'You see what I mean?'

Boyd made himself a success by turning her into a failure, one all these men could agree on. He was no longer the least important person in the room.

'You see what I mean?'

And everything she had ever possessed was taken away.

Katherine came home and cried. She knelt on the sofa, holding a cushion to her belly, and she *keened*.

'Oh God. Oh God.'

I found her there when I came home from college and I wasn't all that sympathetic. I was getting a little tired of the whole merry-go-round that was Katherine O'Dell's career.

'Come on,' I might have said. 'Come on. Up you get.'

And so she did.

She wiped her face in the cushion, requested a dry, dirty martini, rearranged herself on the sofa and waited the two or three years it would take for Maura Herlihy's star to fizzle out and die (in fact, it took six, and each one of them was long).

She might have avoided Boyd after that but, being my mother, she did the opposite. He was at my twenty-first birthday party in August, sparring with Duggan, and after the movie came out in September (Maura Herlihy was terrible in the role, it was very satisfying, the way she dragged the whole thing down) she began to court Boyd in earnest, with small suppers of poached salmon followed by pineapple fool, during the course of which I never saw him do anything but flinch away.

I think she even flirted. In fact, I have no doubt that she flirted with Boyd O'Neill, a man who would prefer not to be flirted with, if at all possible, by my mother.

She really thought he was important. She put Boyd in charge of something in her head – and if this was a bit of a fantasy, it was was also a fantasy he did nothing to deny. In the years after *My Dark Rosaleen*, Boyd styled himself as the man in charge of film in Ireland – although there were no films in Ireland. Or else he was in charge of something else that was hard to define.

He was the kind of man who always knew better than the person he was speaking to. Boyd loved an inaccuracy, for example, because an inaccuracy could render everything else you said void. It was just a trick. And the copyright query was another *trick*. As his authority begins to fall apart for me, I see him as a series of half-lies and, perhaps frightened, manipulations. He was always ahead of you, Boyd. As Hughie Snell liked to point out, the man was happy to win an argument by agreeing with you, so when he walked away, it was hard not to feel robbed.

And Katherine O'Dell was an artist. She was all about sincerity, courage, self-sacrifice. That was the whole point. With each iteration or draft or performance she gave it everything she had. Everything!! Boyd, in response, saying – not unreasonably – that perhaps the pages could do with a number at the bottom. Boyd saying the market was thin for such things. Boyd never saying that it was some years since he had secured finance from anyone for anything, or that he was simply not interested in this kind of stuff. It became important to both of them, I think, that my mother should always be slightly in the wrong and Boyd always be in charge.

It was to prove a dangerous dynamic, but it did not seem unusual or unhealthy at the time. Nor was it immoral, though shooting the man certainly was immoral. This is what I thought about in the long days of her incarceration. I thought about how Boyd 'drove her mad'.

Of course I blame myself, though I am not sure it is a child's job to keep a parent sane – this seems the wrong way around to me. And actually, my mother had a shrink for these self-devised problems and paradoxes. From very early on, all through the seventies: she went over to see him every Thursday at half past nine.

Father Des Folan was the kind of man who divided opinion in Dublin. For every person who could not stand him, there was another who said it was Father Des who had saved him (usually) when the going got bad. He was also, of course, a priest, so he was the only shrink in town with absolution on the menu and the clients were queuing out the door.

He had been, for years, a frequent visitor to Dartmouth Square. When I was a child, he was my mother's spiritual advisor. He used to lend her books with prayer cards slipped between the pages and, on at least one occasion, he said Mass in the living room. Kitty came up from the kitchen specially, and we all had to kneel in a line for communion. My mother tilted her head so the white mantilla touched her shoulders, and I did not like the way she stuck her tongue out for him; the tiny muscular heavings under the nubby pink skin of it, the blankness of his face, after, as he moved on to me.

Des Folan was a young man, a decade or more younger than my mother, and handsome in a generic way. He was not tall. After some years spent mitching from the Jesuits in my mother's living room, he went to London to sort himself out and, when he came back to Dublin, five years later, he looked like a pocket version of God. His smile was entirely benign, his hair prematurely white. He was the future of the liberal Catholic Church, Father Des. He wasn't even gay.

With the exclaustratory blessing of his Father Superior, he started to lecture seminarians on existential psycho-analysis and he became, over time, a Jesuit at large. He did not call himself an analyst, although he had trained while in London under a student of Lacan. 'Once a priest always a priest,' he said, with a rueful glance at his beautiful small hands. His vocation had not gone away, it was just that, now, he liked to save people one at a time.

Inevitably, this loving impulse towards mankind involved helping my mother once a week in his rooms on Ely Place. She took a taxi over there and the same taxi back (an hour on the meter), every Thursday morning, all through my college years. Afterwards, she came home and slept. Father Des was her secret weapon – that is what she called him. He was her lifeline.

I could see the attraction of having a Father Des in your life. My mother spoke to this man once a week because no one liked her for herself, she said, which was a little bit paranoid and a little bit true.

She had an odd effect on people. It was worth going around with her once in a while to watch it happen. Strangers sometimes garbled their first lines to her, she had to wait for them to settle down. They might approach her with something very specific to say: 'I don't think you should wear yellow,' they really needed her to know this. Or it could be somehow soul destroying: 'You must have had a very tragic life,' a woman said to her once. 'I feel so sorry for you, when I see you perform.'

Occasionally, they said she wasn't as good as some other actress. This opinion always came from a woman, and there was a faint preening to it: she pawed her necklace, perhaps, and looked off into a high corner of the room.

'Oh, Liz Taylor's the one for me.'

Or they looked right at her, their eyes glittering with intent: 'Yes. I saw Billie Whitelaw in that part. Just incomparable.'

People told my mother how they felt about her. It was a favour, she liked to opine, that she rarely had the chance to return. And though she was sustained all her life, by the love of those who watched her from the darkness, it took just one of these barbs to send her running back home.

The problem reached a peak in the late seventies, when she did a commercial which was shown constantly in Ireland, but also in cinemas worldwide. You could say she did it for the money – she really needed the money – but she actually did because the role was intended for Maura Herlihy. Also, there would be a helicopter. Herlihy had a calendar clash and my mother did not hesitate. She picked up – not for the first time – the old plaid shawl.

It was an ad for Irish butter. In it, Katherine O'Dell stands on a wild island headland, the shawl wrapped about her, and the wind at her hair, while a curragh – the beautiful black row-boat from the West of Ireland – makes its way towards shore. The boat dips behind one huge wave after another, the rowers strain at their oars, and Katherine O'Dell says, 'Sure, 'tis only butter,' in a melancholy way, as though the cargo might not be worth the effort or the risk. There is a forward flash to golden butter gleaming in the dish, and we realise that it might be worth any risk, that she is saying this too, by the yearning lilt in her voice, and the lean in her stance. The sea surges, the men battle another wave, we flash forward again to the turf fire, a loaf of soda bread turned out warm from the tin. Another wave. A golden curl of butter pulled away from the slab. There is a swirling aerial view of Katherine on her high cliff top (helicopter shot), as the butter is smeared, with a slow flourish, on to the bread. She turns to the thatched cottage as the exhausted men pull the boat up on to the beach below, and there is a faint ruthlessness in the way she finally bites into the damn slice of bread, laden as it is with its prize of glowing, hard-won butter.

The ad became instantly iconic. There was a surge in the electricity grid any time it was shown, as half the population went to the kitchen for immediate tea and toast. Katherine could not have foreseen the consequences. The refrain, 'Sure, 'tis only butter,' became part of the national conversation, it followed her wherever she went. Whenever the result was not worth the effort – or sometimes when it was – any time people witnessed foolish feats of endurance, or efforts that turned foolish by being too long pursued, you would say, 'Sure, 'tis only butter.' It seemed to sum up something about futility and pleasure. Children said it to her in the street. Waiters said it to her in restaurants, as they put the plate down. She was described in a newspaper as 'Ireland's best-loved granny (Sure, 'tis only butter), Katherine O'Dell,' and although she managed a laugh, I think it became a true low point for my mother, one that ground ever lower, as the stupid catchphrase refused to go away.

The days preceding a public appearance were now punctuated by crying jags and general hopelessness. She could not do it, the script was wrong, there was no taxi, no one told her how she would get there, or how she would get home, there was, astonishingly, astonishingly, astonishingly, no fee. What did they want of her? What?

They were eating her alive, she said.

Everything went missing – the right blouse, the right shoes, lipstick, Pan-stik, curling tongs. She blundered from room to room and wailed. I had learned, from a very young age, to go very still while my mother got herself ready for the world. I always knew where to find her keys. Out of her bedroom, back into the bedroom for some forgotten thing, patting herself down as she clattered down the stairs. Finally, at the hall door, she turned to the mirror to put herself together and this was a wonderful thing to witness – the way she locked eyes with her own reflection and fixed, by some imperceptible shift, into her public self. A tiny realignment of the shoulders, neck, chin; each element lifted and balanced, as though on hidden weights and wires, around the taut line of her gaze.

Hello you.

Then she walked out the door and was famous all day.

But if fame was part of the problem, then Father Des may not have been the perfect answer, because Des Folan really liked famous people, and he liked being famous himself, and sometimes he appeared on television chat shows, talking about matters psycho-spiritual. He also, some time in the late seventies, gave my mother LSD in order to enhance, or release, her creativity or her hurt, I can't remember which. I heard this as part of the evidence given in court, after my mother went fully mad, and it was all news to me. The 'treatment' happened some time after the butter ad, apparently, but rack my brains though I might, I can not say it made any difference to her level of eccentricity at the time.

I am not entirely sure what she did all day when she was 'resting' – which was most of the time. She never drank before five, except on a Friday, when she had lunch in The Unicorn. Some mornings there were beauty treatments, vocal exercises, a feeble stretching routine that seemed most advanced at the time. She did the crossword, despaired, got on the phone, despaired, avoided the typewriter, attacked the typewriter. The thing gathered dust for months at a time, and then, suddenly, I would hear it going all night, in clattering runs and horrible, hour-long silences. There were piles of paper, most of which ended up on the floor.

She wrote a couple of monologues, a form she claimed to despise. I think one was from the point of view of Hazel Lavery, the woman who was depicted as 'Erin' on Irish banknotes. Another was about a woman called Asenath Nicholson, who came from America and travelled around Ireland during the Great Famine. She got Hughie Snell in to read them aloud with her, and she roped in Duggan, the literary man.

The script of which she was most proud was the story of Dorcas Kelly, the murdering madame of Copper Alley who was burned up the road from us, in 1761. Or, 'Half-hanged, half-burned,' as she liked to clarify. 'They called it Gallows Lane.'

I did not see the full finished result, nor did I want to. The bits and scraps that caught my eye were written in mock-ee-ah Restoration dialogue with a Hibernian twist. It was a bit, as Hughie Snell put it, 'Prithee Sirrah and Begorrah.'

''Zooks, Madame, is that a knife you wield?'

'Sure why would the likes of me be wielding anything at all, when you be so much the gentleman, Your Honour, sir. Let me help you with that.'

Duggan seemed as embarrassed as I did by the quality of the writing – his eyes flickered up at me when I crossed the open doorway of the spare room. But I was not interested in conspiring with him on this one. In fact, I was not interested in conspiring with Duggan on anything, any more.

'What's this bit again?'

He was at the desk, surrounded by my mother's writing mess, one ordinary Saturday afternoon. Katherine sat in an easy chair, with her feet together, eyes panicked and unblinking, a rabbity twitch in her upper lip. She leaned towards him.

'Sorry. Where are you now?'

Duggan the Fucker was the wrong man to ask for help, I thought. He picked up the page as though it was delicate, or soiled. He made a mark, from a distance, with his pen.

Duggan was a lecturer in English literature, and it was well known that he hated fiction of all kinds. He was too old for it. The books he taught were those he had read between the ages of seventeen and twenty-five, after which it was all downhill for Duggan. And this would be fine if he lived in any other town, but in Dublin every fool had a novel on the go, so he was, as Hughie Snell liked to endlessly repeat, 'a eunuch in the great harem of Irish literature'.

Despite knowing everything, he did not know how to write, or more accurately, he did not know how to make things up. In this he was like Boyd O'Neill: they could be in charge of it all, but they could not do it themselves. Something stopped them or blocked them, some looming, castrating fact or event.

'Sorry, is this a continuation here, or is it a new scene?'

Nothing was right. Perhaps he had been pushed so impossibly low, in his young life, that art had to stay impossibly high.

'Ah. I see.'

I was doubly embarrassed to find Duggan in the room beside my bedroom – not just because I had slept with him some weeks before, but because it had happened again. And not because I wanted it to. It just did.

A week or so after I ended up in his bedroom on Rugby Road, the phone rang and my mother picked up the hall receiver to hear a silence at the other end. This was common enough in those days. We had a whistle to deter such callers and she rooted around in the console drawer and left it out on the tabletop. I think it even got used once or twice, a fact that cheers me up now, in hindsight.

It was not until I answered the phone myself, that it became clear who had been on the line.

'Where were you?' he said.

It was Duggan.

'Sorry?'

'Would you not pick up?'

I did not know what to say to that.

'Would you come down to The Hill?'

The Hill was a pub that lay halfway between us, with a little snug for old women to drink in and a bar full of men.

'I would not,' I said.

'Smyths then.'

As if the choice of pub was the problem.

I met him the next evening, as you might meet a black-mailer (that great, old-fashioned word) although there was nothing wrong with meeting Duggan. There was nothing wrong with any of it. I was twenty-five at the time. He was fifty-one – which was not exactly love's young dream, but it was very far from illegal. Even so, he held me somehow hostage by the knowledge of what we had done.

Or what I had done. As his smile of greeting seemed to indicate, it was as though he had, himself, not done anything. I was the one who had taken off my clothes.

He had just watched, perhaps.

Duggan put my glass of Harp down on the low table and threw a packet of cheese-and-onion crisps beside it. Then he sat in beside me on the stitched vinyl banquette, and my heart sank.

He opened the crisps and nudged them around towards me.

'Would you look at that.'

It was still bright. Duggan had a great fondness for drinking in natural light. It made him feel he was getting away with something, he said. He scooped the over-spilling cream of his pint with a square-topped finger, then flicked the excess on to the floor.

'So.'

Then he lifted the thing and poured it into himself – quite simply – you could hear the liquid flow inside the meat of his neck. His throat moved mightily, once, twice. He slapped the pint back down, half empty, and gave a tiny, upward nod to the barman, who reached under the counter for a fresh glass. Then he used his lower lip to drag the upper clear of foam, and sat back.

He did not belch.

He looked at me and said, 'I'm a bad bitch.' He used a thick Monaghan accent. It was one of his sayings.

Exactly three quarters of the way through my own second drink, I decided that the only way to get out of this situation was to go through with it.

'You'll have another.'

'I won't, Niall.'

'You what? You will.'

I told myself I would let him down gently, that I was drinking to give myself courage to do just that. But I also knew that I might have to pay for sleeping with Duggan by sleeping with him again, and it seemed wise to be, in advance, a little reckless, a little bit numb.

Also, I really wanted that third drink. You could say that I drank to escape the wretched drinking, which was a funny way to think and very hard to justify. But I was well drunk by the time Duggan pushed his worn key into the door of Rugby Road.

('You'll come back for one.'

'No, I won't, Niall, I won't.')

I was drunk as he kicked the door closed behind us. Drunk as he pushed me backwards up the stairs with his hands inside my jacket, so the path away from his embrace was also the path to the side of his bed.

But I just could not go through with it, drunk as I was. I told him to give over, and swatted at him, a little ineffectually.

'Give over,' I said.

'You're lovely,' he said.

There were two moments that evening when something loosed in me, or gave way. The first was three quarters of the way down my second glass of Harp, the second was at the side of his bed, with the edge of the mattress pressing into the hinge of my knee, when my protestations had continued to fail.

(In Ireland, as I sometimes explain to foreign-born friends, you always refuse a cup of tea.

'You will have a cup of tea.'

'I won't, thanks.'

You each do this three times and it means nothing. There is always tea.)

Perhaps this is why I helped Niall Duggan with my underwear. The need to sort men's incompetencies, perhaps. *Here, let me get that.* Even though I was at the time saying no and he was not taking no for an answer. The inevitability of what was to occur made me pull out a single leg from the entanglement of tights and pants, as he reached down my back and hauled my jumper up over my head. I was helping him in order to make it less awkward, or even painful for me. This was a late thought, but curiously – I do not know if this is a common experience, but it was my experience – apart from the horrible preparatory rub between my legs, apart from that, or despite that, my body opened easy enough for him, so easily I thought of it, later, as an evolutionary advantage perhaps, the ability to be entered without damage.

Maybe it was the drink. That jolt of aversion or arousal you get sometimes, when you are scared, that did not happen. I was not scared. So there was no excuse, really, for my lying there.

The room was the same, the same crooks in the fall of the net, the pinkish curtains still stuck at the same point along their plastic rail, with a deep hem, dirty along the seam. It is possible the same clothes were on the floor as two weeks ago, when I had been on this bed before, the same book on the nightstand. I can't remember the title, though I remember contemplating the spine of it, as he finished fucking me – though it did not feel like he was fucking *me*, he was just trying to find and catch his own pleasure. Which took quite a while. He wore a condom, I knew by the smell and by the interior drag of latex. He propped himself up on one arm, so I was spared the weight of him – he did it to protect his bad back (I had, as I recall, a flicker of concern for his bad back.) He did not try to kiss me, much.

And I think I said it clearly. The 'no', I mean. Not the way they say it in the movies, in a voice muddled by desire. But I also did it the way an Irish girl says it, with a wretched squirm in the word. Sweetly, I said it. Then, I stopped saying anything and I thought, *This is happening*.

When he was finished, he hoisted himself back and shut my knees together, which brought me, in a roll, on to my side. He slapped my haunch, and said, 'Now.'

I stayed like that, curled up and unmoving. Slightly too long.

He went to the bathroom and I heard the sound of the tap going a moment, then he came back in, his shirt half buttoned, and looked for his pants on the floor by the bed.

'Are you right, so?' he said.

And I didn't want to make a thing of it, so I dragged my clothes towards me and put them on, and after some desultory conversation he walked me down to The Triangle – the local intersection where you might get a taxi – where he leaned in the front window to chat to the driver, and have a small laugh about something, and give the man money to take me home.

It did not occur to me to consider what had happened there was wrong. Duggan had been so inward, so inert in his pleasure, it was hard to know what he had been thinking. Perhaps he was right, this was just the way sex usually happened: women said, No, and men said, You're lovely. It was the nature of the act. This is the way sex was supposed to be.

But it was not like Duggan to walk me down to the rank like that. It was not like him to be so chivalrous, and this made me dislike him, somehow. I resented the little laugh he had with the taxi man. And I really hated the half-smile on his face, after I got into the thing and he closed the door.

He knew that he had won.

I woke with a hangover and heart-sore, and I don't know how I felt for the next few days, I suppose I felt fine. The old fucker had done his business between my legs and that was that. I felt as you might feel after a burglary, when all the stupid things are taken – the hi-fi, the cassette player – and they leave the things you love most, because those things can not be seen and have no price. The little photograph, the faded flower. What did they get? people say and you say, Oh, just stuff.

But I found it hard to weather the storm of anger that came blowing through me, briefly, a week later. I had been so stupid – by going to the pub, by going to the house – I had brought it on myself (Duggan collapsing on top of me, unloosed). My life was so lonely now.

This is what you get for chasing Daddy, I thought. You get more than you had bargained for.

It came back at me at odd moments, for the next while – spikes of self-hatred that impaled me, it seemed, from the inside. And though the event itself was merely drab, I did not know if I could survive the shadow of it, that repeated in my body any time it wanted to.

So I dumped it.

I don't know how else to describe it. I just threw the hurt away.

I cycled out to Seapoint for a swim, and the chill of the water was fabulous. The sun was low over Dublin, the sky a watery yellow, the sea flat and silent. I was halfway through drying myself before I remembered the reason I had come. When I got home to Dartmouth Square, I found the whistle again and put it back by the phone.

And now there he was again. Duggan the Fucker was in the house, a little grey about the gills from last night's Guinness, and he was discussing bad historical dialogue with my mother. There was no getting rid of him, clearly.

He was quite massive, sitting at the desk in the spare room, and she looked very small in the easy chair, the way old people are small – this was a woman who could look any size she wanted to, under the lights.

'Hello,' I said.

I thought about this a lot afterwards, how sweetly I said it.

'Hello.'

So polite. Just in case he was worried he might have done something wrong.

Also because Duggan was not the kind of man who ever said hello first. He never crossed a room to speak to anyone, he never started a conversation, except in a mocking or

186

difficult way. And that was another reason he had been so fussed when he rang to order me down to the pub. It was all about weight, orbit, heft. Duggan the Fucker did not make the first move.

'Is it yourself?' he said.

I did not answer that. I went down to the kitchen, where Kitty was making tea. She had a thing wrong with her leg and she could not manage the stairs. So it was I who brought the tray up, not Kitty. It was I who called up from the first landing, 'Will you have it down here?' My mother said, 'Bring it all the way up,' even as Duggan said, 'Yes,' and after a moment they both came down to the middle floor.

I carried the tray through to the dining-room table and they arrived beside me and it was all done like a play on the Abbey stage. I fumbled the milk. The little jug leapt out of my hand and it was spilt on to the mahogany tabletop, very white on the dark wood. I was more upset by this than I might have been, and Duggan more excited. He did his sudden TB-ward shriek.

'Sister Margaret! Sister Margaret!'

But, despite the great noise he was making, there was an odd flatness to his expression, and I forgot myself so much as to look him in the eye. When I did, I saw it flare: the gleam he had hidden from me in his own bed.

Yeah. Here I am.

He knew exactly what he had done to me. He thought, if he could twist my wanting hard enough, he might get to do it again.

'Get a cloth sure, girl,' he said, smiling. 'Off you go.'

And I went.

I did not come back with the cloth. I put my coat on, and went out the front door. I walked the canal, eastwards towards the sea, and stopped at the bench by Baggot Street Bridge. I did not feel well. I got up again and walked all the way to Boland's Mill, and then I don't know where. I found myself back at the bridge and I sat down again on the bench where we used to kiss. I stared at the canal, and at the sky reflected there.

This is where I could die, I thought. Beneath that stalled tumult of white cloud. I could just roll into the black water under it, and inhale. I did this many times, feeling the split between air and cold water move across my cheek and mouth. I did it over and over, in my mind. And when I tried to surface from these thoughts, I found myself coated in the slick horror of Duggan's intent.

You know you want it.

That is what he was saying, that I wanted to be broken from the inside. And I did want it. As I sank or rose from black water to anguish and abjection, I wanted to be devastated, finished, named.

But not by Duggan.

One evening as we stood to go home, we fell into a long embrace at just this spot. We held on so tight, we wanted so fiercely to pull each other apart – I did not think we could survive it. You can also be destroyed by love, I thought. You can be unbearably named by the person you love.

Norah.

It passed in a shiver, a drag of wind across the water. A pair of swans above the lock, the waters pouring down into the pool below: the rightness of things restored me to my own proper desiring. I got up and walked back home very slowly, putting the right motives back in the right bodies. This is what Duggan did, this is what I did. This is what he wanted and knew, this is what I wanted. This is what I did not want. This is what I did not know. Also, the difference between what happens in your head and what happens in the room. The big difference.

When I got back, the milk was wiped up. There was perhaps a faint loss of sheen on the wood, that Kitty's cloth would soon buff away.

I never saw Duggan in the house again.

We did not speak about my abrupt departure, or the time I had spent outside, but if you ask me when it was my mother went mad, I would say it happened just then. Because when I came back into the house, I found her sitting at the dining-room table as though she had not moved since the time I had left. Her fingers were touching the tabletop, quite lightly, and when she looked up at me, her eyes were fully green.

WE HAVE SLEPT together in various rooms, over the years, sometimes I wonder which one we are sleeping in now. I wake in the night and locate the dark oblong of the door, if it is to the left or the right. I leave for the bathroom over carpet, or rug, or bare wooden floor, and come back, when I am done, to the warmth of you asleep beside me. And although my eyes are by now used to the darkness, I don't look at your head on the pillow – eyelids sunk, chin collapsed, the disaster of the body when it does not know itself, or realise that someone else is there.

You are not handsome, asleep. The muscles that make your mood are gone slack. You have, in your sleep, no personality. So although I am happy for your sleeping – it must be restful – I am not happy outside of it, looking on.

In the morning, I can tell without opening my eyes where the window is, and if it faces the dawn. I sweep my hand in an arc across the sheet to find you recently gone, a thermal ghost in the cotton. Or the bed is cold. Or I bump against you, a slight shock of skin roughened by hair and you do not stir. I leave my hand there until you wake. There is a moment of silence. Of silent wakefulness. And then you turn.

It always amazes me. Even though I have dragged you from your dream, you are pleased to see me there. It feels like forgiveness, every time.

There was a week or two, maybe thirty years ago, when I woke every morning to see you standing over a plant on a little side table. It was a little morning glory, sprouted from seed. Perhaps it had a cane to support it, those vines really race along. So you were standing there, as though you might catch it in the act, the little trumpet flower like a twist of paper, unfurling to show its interior blue. The light came down from the dormer window above, you were not yet dressed, and though the scene, as I remember it, is beautifully still and your body young and amazing, that was, actually, one of the times when we were most sad.

We were always coming to the end of things, always leaving or being left. But you know, if I could appear, like Princess Leia, in a little hologram beside the plant pot to plead or reassure, 'Don't worry, in thirty years' time you will still be together,' I don't know if it would lift the mood. Our love has always carried its freight of dread.

This morning we wake in our staggered fashion to Bray, County Wicklow, and it is raining. I know where the door is, and where the window is, and I know where you sleep, because it is always the same side, no matter what bed we are in. But I do not know if you are there or not. And, though I fell asleep on my front, I can't remember what way I was facing when I woke. How can it escape me?

Our daughter Pamela had endless games and rituals around her sleep. We did not put her to bed so much as abandon her in it and try to go to sleep ourselves, listening to the sound of her tossing and turning next door.

'Why is it,' she said, 'that bed is the most uncomfortable place in the world when you are trying to fall asleep, and the most comfortable place in the world when you wake up?'

Why indeed. The light comes in from my left, the silence of the house is through the doorway on my right. This is the moment before my life starts up again. You are between me and the window, where rain scatters against the glass. The weather is still grim. It is already May and the stretch into summer has gone on too long. The year has not yet snapped into itself. I know some of this (but not all of it) as I decide to meet the day.

There were times – whole years, perhaps – when you annoyed me, in one way or another, but you don't annoy me any more.

These days I am happy that you are alive in the bed beside me, though there were mornings when I woke to the thought that you were dead, and somewhere in the realisation – oh no! – was a flick of joy. He is so still. He must be dead. He is dead! The body beside mine was no longer doing the body thing, it was no longer inhaling, exhaling, being alive, the body beside me was turning into an ex-body, it was cooling down. This was the image that frightened me awake, so I wasn't thinking it as much as dreaming it, and the jolt of alarm dragged a tiny pleasure after it that was quickly wiped away. No. What a terrible way to think. He is alive. This body. This man's body. The body of my husband is alive.

My guilt turns just as quickly to gratitude – and this too a little fake (oh Darling!) – I roll towards you, and find the puzzle of your body moving towards mine, forearm, belly, a question that is so easily answered. My goodness, yes. Reaching up for a closed-mouth kiss, because of what is held in your dents and cavities: old breath, last night's wine, pockets of dissent in the body's republic. I lay my head in the crook of arm and chest, my ear pressed to the heartbeat of the human being I sleep beside.

I don't count the years. Some time, a long time ago, you said we had known each other longer than not. Countless turns between sheet and duvet, our morning bodies so warm.

I think about gratitude a lot these days and I also think about sadism – the dark streak in Niall Duggan and the high disdain of Boyd O'Neill, both of them, by their own lights, important men. Of course they were sometimes horrible to each other, that goes without saying, but when I think of how they treated my mother, under the elaborate courtesy I saw something truly unpleasant. Envy, perhaps. A need to possess or stain, not her sexuality but her talent, her life's beautiful, foolish flame.

Which is something I became interested in, much later. I became interested in my own cruelty. That moment of tenderness as the pen touches the page, the possibility for sadism in the place where words are born. To name the thing. To have it and to finish it. I recognise the temptation that Duggan offered me once: 'Who are you going to kill?' Myself as writer-murderer, full of fake power.

But I wake in the morning and the body beside me is not dead. I have killed no one, except, perhaps, in my dreams. I never will.

WHEN I WAS six or seven, a boy pushed me at some party or occasion and my mother, in full make-up and with her taffeta skirt swaying behind her, bent down to hiss, 'If you touch my daughter again I will bite you.' Her response was so much worse than the offence – I learned very early not to tell my mother about the cruel teacher or the mean girl in the playground. She found my hurts unbearable and this made them twice as bad, because they were not unbearable to me. They happened when she was not there to protect me, that was all.

After the incident with Duggan, the curtains were drawn for weeks, there were whole days when she did not get out of bed. I checked in with her in the morning and again in the evening, and I got on with things, the way I do. I might have been more concerned, but I was too busy being helpless, wondering how to fix her.

'Really,' I said. 'Really, Mother, you should get up and get some air, it will do you good.'

As the weeks turned to months, I think we both realised this was more than a passing mood. And still I could not break whatever taboo was in the room to say Duggan's name. I could not tell her that I was fine.

Hughie Snell pattered up the stairs, now and then, to gossip and make her laugh. And she still had Father Des, the man who once declared that her acting brought us all closer to God. I was grateful for Des in those months, because she dressed to her heels once a week for him. She rose early on a Thursday morning to wash and sort herself into her therapy clothes and she got into the waiting taxi in one or other printed dress, cheerful and chic, in stretch silk jersey or forward-looking Crimplene. Always the same taxi driver.

'Ah, Manus, good to see you, how are you this morning?'

She came back later and slept.

I sometimes wonder why he did not save her.

Spring came in. She looked out at the wisteria in the park and the tears poured down. She walked around the room shaking her forearms – an odd puppet-like gesture that reminded me of myself, after my bad night with The Fucker, when I wrung my hands, briefly, like a character on the Victorian stage. After a few days she stopped with the hand-shaking and scrabbled about the room.

'What's this doing here?'

She started throwing stuff in the bin, then spent a frantic afternoon looking for things she had just thrown out. She cried again, slept, woke, had a large opinion about an article in the newspaper (she was reading the newspaper!) and then, in the middle of the night, the typewriter began its ghastly, spasming runs and silences. She was working again. And suddenly she was furious with it, she was starting this and starting that. Father Des encouraged her in this – apparently, he thought it was a good thing.

At least that is what she said.

I rang him once from the office, at lunchtime. I thought he might be able to help me in some way.

In those days the phones were heavy things, and your breath left condensation on the receiver rose, which

195

sometimes made it feel dirty or warm. I remember bringing the thing close to my mouth even though there was no one to overhear, and how odd it was to speak to him at this intimate remove. Actually Father Des had the kind of voice that seemed to come from a distance even when he was right there in the room. Yes, he said, in his floating way, Yes indeed. These matters were, by definition, confidential.

'Once you open the box, it stops working,' he said, or something like. He mentioned Schrödinger's Cat, and we both thought that was apposite and funny. But I was her daughter, he said. I knew her better than anyone, much better than he did, really.

'Yes,' I said.

And that love he said, was very real. It was indestructible. Whatever I felt just there. That was the truth of it.

I felt so much better when I put down the phone, it took a while to realise I was no further on.

His rooms intrigued me for all the years she went to see him. Did he have carved African masks in there, a chaise longue? Was there a crucifix along with an incense burner or a Buddha? Perhaps the walls were white and clear.

I tried to imagine what it was she told him, and before I knew it, I was telling him everything myself, in my mind. And he was wonderfully reassuring, this fantasy shrink, who was almost Des Folan. He understood me better than I understood myself.

I said I felt guilty about sleeping with Duggan in the first place. I felt I might have stolen him from my mother. As though we were rivals for the Old Fucker, when we were the opposite of rivals.

'The opposite of rivals,' he said.

I said that Duggan surely stole me from her, because he was such a horrible man. He wanted the thing that my mother loved most. And that was me.

The Fucker.

The things I told Father Des, in my head, felt truly significant though some of them were also very small. I told him I wanted to study chemistry but there was no way for me to do such a thing because I was a girl, so I ended up doing English instead. And I don't know what Father Des could do about all that, it was just the way the world was. I told him that I went to the pub. I was the only woman in the pub. I was the only woman in Smyths that evening with Duggan, because women did not really go into pubs, not really, unless they were old and wore an eyepatch, it was not done. And I was in pubs all the time. I told him many of my girlfriends were still virgins. At twenty-five.

'And how does that make you feel?' said Father Des.

It made me feel as though there was something wrong with me, I said, because I really enjoyed having sex with different people, I thought it was a great thing to do. I loved their various bodies, and the way they paced their touching, how they did all that, each in a different language of kisses and coaxing. But I didn't know any other women who were like me, I told Father Des, because the ones I knew went giddy and stupid at the mention of sex and I was not giddy. Sometimes, between the chemistry obsession and the promiscuity, I thought that maybe I was a man. My mother had turned me into a man. Which could not be a good thing.

'No?'

Not in the long run. No. Because girls who slept around did not end well.

'And what about your mother?' he might say.

'Oh, don't get me started.'

I would tell him all the things I was not allowed to say to anyone, ever, because no one must ever know. I betrayed her freely. I described her in hair curlers, the state of her drunk, the way she called Olivier 'that old queen', the mess of the bathroom when she was done.

Especially, I told him about the man I saw on the landing having sex with my mother, or trying to have sex with her, the man I saw kissing my mother on the landing when I was around six years old. I came out of my room half asleep with a full bladder and there they were. The fact that I needed to pee was significant in this conversation I had with Father Des – my own arousal (if you could call it that) a sign of complicity in the tangle happening against her bedroom door. It took a moment for them to see me there. Though I just woke in the night, I said. It was dark and I needed the bathroom. I explained this to him many times.

'And how did you feel about that?' said my imaginary Father Des.

'Well,' I said.

After that there were no more men on the landing, certainly, so that was a good thing.

'Yes,' said Father Des.

When I asked my mother about her time with Father Des, and what his rooms looked like, she said, 'It's like nothing, really. You know, high ceiling, shutters. There's a. There's a.' She could not finish. 'There's a very thick rug on the floor, like a foot rug. A sheepskin. For my feet. Or anyone's feet. The horny sons of toil.'

This is an approximation. It is difficult to reproduce the shifts and fractures in my mother's speech, when it started to break down. She was neither logical nor illogical. Every sentence turned a blind corner to end up somewhere unexpected. And if she was obscene, it was in an oddly ordinary way. She could not pass a dog without discussing erections, for example, but in the kind of tone people use to talk about bus routes, or the weather. She was also quite funny.

'Oh, there goes the lipstick. *Pink Passion* by L'Oréal.'

And though Father Des seemed so kind and so present for her, I got a lot further with the local doctor, an absolutely monosyllabic man who refused to consider any illness below the waist – this is simply true, he would sit on the side of the bed and look at my mother, and if she offered any part of herself to examine he would mutter, in his Cork accent, 'There's no need for that.' But he was an excellent diagnostician, despite or because of this reluctance; all his brilliance was eaten up in observation. This boulder of a man gave her tablets – though she was already on tablets – and her syntax seemed to straighten out soon after. She became more calm.

No one noticed, or seemed to notice, her time of duress, the purdah of the drawn curtains, the way she wore sunglasses, even when it rained. In a way it was expected of her. She was a star. But it was also hellishly lonely. As April stretched into May she sat up for longer and, with the help of Kitty, established some kind of routine.

This episode, as I came to call it, made sense of other times in the past when things had been impossible and the curtains remained closed. It passed as the previous ones had done but, this time, she came out dulled. She had lost half a year.

Over the course of the difficult winter of 1977 and all through the year that followed, Katherine did no work onstage. Her days were quiet. She smoked constantly, tried to write and failed to write. She hated her medication which Kitty insisted on, standing beside her bed in the morning like Patience on a Monument, with the capsules in her hand.

She went down to the National Library to work on the Dorcas Kelly play, and they loved to see her there. She carried a slim manuscript bag, wore leather gloves and a hat.

'I see your mother often,' a poet said to me once. 'She sits, gazing off into the middle distance, like *this*.'

Her drinking became more effortful. Alcohol did not have the same effect – perhaps it was the pills – but she put the work in, nonetheless. I found her asleep on the sofa in a stink of acetone, and the boulderous doctor said she must take water constantly and tea constantly and alcohol not at all.

Yes of course she would. She said this made sense.

She encouraged me to leave, and really, I had to leave. We were both agreed, it was important that I had a life of my own. I had moved from newspapers into a women's magazine and was doing quite well, by then. I looked for a flat but nothing was right. I told myself that I wanted to move to London, instead. I spent nearly a year trying to establish connections there, none of which came good.

Slowly, she got back to work.

If she was more prone to difficulty offstage, onstage she grew, I thought, extraordinary in these last years. Katherine O'Dell weathered very beautifully. The fictions got some-how thinner, the actress behind them more acutely, pain-fully there. It was an elaborate, slow peeling of the self, hard to watch.

Six months before the attack on Boyd, she took up an offer from the Polish director Aleksy Wójcik to do a piece with him in France, called *La Bête* and the only good thing I can say about this production was that it happened in a foreign language. I am one of the few people who have seen their mother naked, in the company of three hundred and fifty other people who are viewing her mother naked. It was, as an experience, very pure (to use that word). I mean, I did see the point of it, at the time.

Wójcik had a reputation as an edgy director, and my mother wanted that now. Otherwise what was the point?

She wanted him to reduce her to some essence of herself, or that was what she said.

The scenes of degradation all took place in the first half of the play, when her character lost, one piece at a time, her beige trench coat, her beige turtlenecked jumper, her A-line skirt and her shoes. Underneath, she was wearing ordinary underwear: flesh-coloured tights, cotton pants, a cheap bra. I forget the plot, if there was a plot. I was rigid in my seat, conscious above all else of the smell of cigarettes from my fingers and clothes. I was afraid it might gross out the man sitting beside me, who I suspected to be a critic.

The rape was done, the way you might expect, on a blackout. My mother, in her underwear, is dragged yowling about the stage by her hair by an actor called Bernard DuBois. He slams her down on a table, rips off the horrible 30-denier Dynamite tights, wriggles about with the undoing of his fly, after which there is an interminable – and cleverly directed, I thought – pause, as he manages the unseen business of his and her anatomy, after which, head still yanked back – blackout – into which darkness she gives that distinctive, animal sound of the penetrated human being. At least in fiction. The fictively penetrated human body. Though it sounded damn real, I have to say.

The house lights up, the stage is empty, my hands are pressed down on the armrests on either side. I am literally 'out of my seat', there are inches of air between me and the red plush. The man beside me gives a little thrill of admiration before the series of courtesies and rearrangements that allows me out to the bar, where I drink, against my usual practice, a glass of Johnnie Walker Scotch, neat.

She asked me not to go. And then she told me not to bring anyone. And I could see why. I never got a free ticket from my mother – I think that is an interesting fact – although she welcomed me, very happily, into her dressing room any time I turned up at a show.

In the second act, then, she is naked. There are about twenty more minutes of Bernard DuBois doing this and that (he is a butcher, they have a real set of cleavers and half a cow to dismember – he got so good at it by the end of the run, the crew took the chops and cutlets home). He speaks to a young female customer who is wearing a summer dress and they have a sweet-seeming romance. And then there is Katherine again, she walks on naked. She has beautiful feet. Each footfall very cleverly releases a hidden spring, and a rush of clear water follows her as she walks across the stage. My mother is fifty-one years old. And there is no doubting her lived-in flesh, the story her body tells. The stage is dark, the few lights are not exactly flattering and, after a while, her nakedness does something to the air around her. The sight of her occupies more space than her body occupies. She glows.

This woman, who is too real, almost, to look at, stoops to lift some water in her hands and uses it to clean the streaks of muck from her arms and thighs. The rest of the water has run downstage to fill a shallow pool. She lies down in this pool and seems to float, her arms cruciform, while Bernard DuBois stumbles and splashes towards her in his everyday clothes.

I can't recall the end of the piece, after this dream-like scene of my mother floating there. I do recall making my way backstage to her, the urgency of my search for her dressing room. The theatre in Lyon was a terrible warren, smelling of old costumes and bad plumbing, it was full of unexpected corners and steps going nowhere. And although my mother is dead some years I still dream that she is trapped in a place like this: there is a fire and she is searching desperately for an exit, running along the back wall, up ladders and across gantries. In real life I found her door easily enough, and the sight that greeted me when I walked in through it was Katherine in her towelling dressing gown and a pair of smart black slacks, bending over to put on her street shoes. Her room had a few things, not many. The card I sent for opening night was stuck on the mirror, there was a white orchid – in those days a rarity – in a simple glass vase. A scattering of papers, scrawled in her favourite green ink. Her dressing gown was white. The turban around her wet hair was white.

She said, 'I think that damn water is giving me a gippy tummy, they won't put chlorine in because of the smell, you have to love the French. How are you darling, you look a little tired.'

Tired was only one word for how I felt. I was outraged by the sheer normality of her sitting there. She angled her foot to slide it into the shoe, before straightening back up to say, 'Oh darling, you should have said you were coming.'

Because that is what she always said when I turned up, despite all her warnings and embargoes.

'I have this wretched dinner, I'd love you to come but it might as well be the local county council. Self-important old men, such a bore.'

As though I didn't know she went back to her rooms every night, hollowed out by it all, that she ended her evening with more water, a bath this time, and even though she was careful when working, a bottle (no more!) of wine. Hard not to drink wine when you're in France.

We arranged to meet the next morning, before she pretended to hail a cab and slipped away from me to walk the streets, a middle-aged woman in conservative clothes who looked as though she knew the area, though not where her life was going. Some nights she walked for a long time, before finding her way back to her room.

The next day we did breakfast, very late. I rang up from the foyer so often to get her out of bed, we just gave in and called it lunch.

We were always good at restaurants. We liked being that thing, a mother and her adult daughter with a menu to be discussed, a request for news. What news do you give your mother? This and that. The fact of a relationship, but never the truth of it. A selection of small successes to make her happy for her daughter. Some difficulties at work, so that she can sympathise.

I have a boyfriend, I tell her. A nice guy called Mark, I describe him a little.

'Lovely,' says my mother. 'He sounds just lovely.'

'Yes.'

'What does he do again?'

'He's with the IDA.'

'The what?'

'Just business stuff.'

'Don't tell me he has money.'

'Not really. '

'Clever you.'

And I am clever. Mark is a good guy, he is broad and strong, he follows the rugby and is surprisingly giddy. There is nothing wrong with Mark O'Donohue who is somehow blessed. His anger is a private matter, rare and slow (and incredibly surly). He sorts himself out, Mark, he doesn't throw it back at me.

'He's very steady,' I say.

'Oh, I am glad,' reaching anxiously for her bag for tissues, her wallet, her keys.

I am not allowed to ask how she is. Or what is next up. It is only proper, when you are with your mother, to talk about yourself, or about an agreed version of yourself, a person for whom you can both be pleased.

Six weeks later, I come home to Dartmouth Square and see her on the sofa in the living room, sipping wine. The ashtray is overflowing, she is in her dressing gown, her naked feet tucked up beside her. I sit and stroke her heel below the ankle bone, where the skin has a faint blue lustre. I try to think of her on stage in Lyon, with her feet wet. I have not yet been able to describe, to my boyfriend Mark, the play she has just done. I feel he would not understand.

And Father Des comes in, then. He is wearing chinos and a button-down blue Oxford shirt that makes his white hair glow. He has a cup of tea in his hand and he is smoothly startled to see me there. He does not falter.

I just dropped in, I tell him, to pick up my tennis gear.

Then I wonder why I am excusing my presence to this man, in my own home.

As I get up to leave, I notice that he is not wearing any shoes.

Father Des was the man I saw on the landing, when I was six years old – that's what I think now. I tell him this in his consulting room, the one I attend in my head. I sit and face Father Des or I lie down on his inevitable couch and I tell him how, when I was young, I oversaw this primal scene, or imagined I did.

He asks me how was all that for me.

'I thought she was being murdered.'

'Did you?'

'I thought I would be left all alone.'

And, as I tell him this, I turn his room into a cube, checking one corner of the ceiling after another with my eyes. And I do not tell him about this secret shape, how important it is to me to make this space that will contain these things. The pair of them in the middle of it, like something materialised, in the throes.

And he says, 'You felt excluded?'

And I say, 'Up to a point, Father Des. Up to a point.'

As soon as I knew they were intimate, which was when I saw his bare feet in our living room, I knew that it had been happening all along. It started shortly after Lillian MacVeigh died, bless her, when my mother was sore-hearted and in need of solace. Father Des came to pray with her. He tried to ease her sorrow with the touch of his sacramentally healing hands, and once he touched her it was done. They fucked. He fled. (I am guessing here, but you know already the way this story goes.) He begged God to release him from desire and lust and agony and desperation but God did not seem to mind about all that and the situation lurched on, impossibly, for some years. Father Des was disastrously in love with her. He came to declare his love every Thursday afternoon.

The noise of their fighting then, in the middle of the night, rage and blame and humping silence. I got pretty sick of him – if it was, in fact, Father Des who was wrestling with his conscience in my mother's bedroom. The whole thing left me with a contempt for men, or some struggling sense of the arses of men, straining upwards as she leaned back, exposing her throat, against a wall. The grappling need he had to get this leaky tip of himself into her. That is what I must have seen.

Father Des went to London to figure himself out, and he came back five years later to figure everyone else out, including my mother. It is possible they did not sleep together for the first while, and then they did. They kept trying not to. It was wrong in every way you might imagine, and it suited my mother well enough. Father Des was discreet, he was regular. He tended to her, as best he could. Which was not – believe me – well enough. But, you know, she could not exactly sleep with the postman. Dublin is a small town.

And he did not leave her.

I WOULD LOVE to say that, after my mother winged Boyd O'Neill, we were surrounded by kindness and support, that calls were received, flowers sent, debts forgiven and food left on the doorstep of Dartmouth Square, but that is not the way it worked. What happened in the wake of my mother's madness and arrest was a silence. Followed by the slight sound of many pairs of feet scurrying away.

She was taken from the house to Pearse Street Garda Station, and remanded the next day to the female wing of Mountjoy. Two days later, she was sent over to the Central Mental Hospital in Dundrum, and nothing happened for a very long time.

They took her away.

It was surprisingly simple. Back in Dartmouth Square, the silence of the house was the silence after a door slams shut. Those days were, each of them, long. There were many hours of time in which the phone did not ring, unless it was a stranger on the line.

One bright Irish evening around this time, I opened the door to a man who walked into the hall and handed me a letter. He stood waiting for me to read this letter and I opened it, wondering how bad the contents could be. I saw trees outside in the late sunshine and the movement of children running in the park. There was a taxi beached on the footpath, blocking our gate. The letter was hard to read. It was from a newspaper. It seemed to say that this newspaper would interview me whether I wanted to be interviewed or not. The man was a taxi driver, this person who walked through the front door as though legally obliged to enter our home and ensure I read this stupid letter all the way to the end. He kept his sunglasses on indoors and I could tell by his stance that he was profoundly excited by the power he had over me. I don't think he was sexually excited, but perhaps he was also that. My mother's degradation – my own possible degradation – had him in thrall.

Then he snapped out of it and made for the door. He did it quickly, as though I disgusted him too much to stay.

This incident with the taxi driver, it seemed so small, hardly worth mentioning – and it took me a while to realise that there was no one to mention it to. I spoke to my girlfriends, but the, 'Oh dear, oh no' of female consolation did not really do it for me any more (why did I have such helpless friends?). I needed a lawyer. Mark was in Chicago at a trade fair, which was a blessing, though he did ring.

Mark rang.

He did not know a good lawyer.

The phone was otherwise silent in Dartmouth Square, though phones were, at a guess, ringing all over Dublin. The gang of people my mother called friends were now busy being a gang without her. The difference between inside and outside was so swift, it was almost the same thing. She was, from that moment, more spoken about than to. She was the talk of the town.

In all of this there were a few exceptions. The boulderous doctor arrived with his bag and disappeared into Kitty's room to tend to her bad leg. Afterwards, he came out to the kitchen and looked at me a good moment. He twitched to leave – a little like the taxi driver, indeed – then he turned back to say, 'You know where I am.'

Hughie Snell was in regular attendance at the mental hospital, he wore his best tan crombie, with a yellow buttonhole rose, and he walked in there with his head held high. Hughie carried a great burden – or it was a burden to him at least, because the whole world knew that he was gay, even as Hughie lived in fear of being found out – so they were in something together now; the dreadful business of being disgraced.

And there was Father Des – so well known to the nurses, 'Hello Father, how are you today?' He sat holding her hand in both his hands, his head bent in silent prayer, then he turned to greet me with a smile.

She always knew who I was, but in this, the most florid stage of my mother's illness, she pretended not to like me. A sneery thing set in. She turned away when I came into the room, as though her nose was filling up with something, and she gave a high sniff. I asked how she was and got no answer. Nothing I brought her was right: the wrong pyjamas, the wrong book, her worst lipstick, horrible chocolates. She crooned, 'Oh thank you, oh how lovely,' not bothering to hide her sarcasm, because there was no fooling her: I was the enemy now. One time, she tossed a bouquet of pink carnations back over her shoulder, even as I sat there. She did it right in front of my eyes.

So it was, literally, a thankless journey I made every Saturday afternoon, as soon as visits were allowed. We sat in her little cell, or we sat in the communal day-room, a clapped-out institutional space, quite normal apart from the cage around the television set, which was high up on the wall and always on. There were a few mild-looking, fretful women in this room: Brenda, Mary, Mary, Siobháin. Their clothes weren't great, their posture was poor, and their crimes surely pathetic, though one of them had sucked a stranger's eyeball out, at the top of O'Connell Street, apparently (at least that is what I was told, on my mother's release, from the orderly who walked us down the avenue). These women sat about and watched me being ignored by my mother. I could see they had various opinions about that. I could also see that they liked my presents.

The only thing my mother wanted was the carton of cigarettes I brought every other week, containing twenty packets of John Player Blue. She had always run out, was always desperate by the time I arrived. But she could not let me know she was desperate, in case I snatched them away again. And so we played (I played it too) a wretched game. I laid the carton on the table, very casually, and she pretended, very casually, that they were not there. I am ashamed to say that I enjoyed it a little. Two hundred fags sitting between us, a blue oblong of desire. Me chatting away while she cast about for some distraction. It could be anything:

'You look terrible. Maybe it's the hair.'

'What I would really like in here is a bird.'

'Do you see that woman over there? She had a baby once, it came out of her dead.'

By the time I had looked back, she was scrabbling the cellophane off the carton, tucking one pack and then another in under her clothes. She cracked a box open and smoked four in a row. My goodness, she dragged those lads down. My mother was suspicious of everything, from the taps in the toilet to the tea in her cup, she said the nurses were trying to kill her and refused to wear a pair of 'poisoned' shoes. But the cigarettes never turned against her. I sometimes wondered at it. Her madness was never so mad it interfered with her smoking. Her madness was, in this respect, a sensible beast.

I sat there while she got on with it, watching the flesh of my mother's face rearrange itself into patterns I did not recognise.

She was in there, somewhere. She was hiding a mile behind her mad green eyes. *Come out, come out!* I sat there in a state of silent imploring. She pulled in the smoke, pushed me away with every felt exhale. One week she had lost a tooth.

'What happened your tooth?' I said.

'Oh that,' she said. 'That's been false for years.'

I learned not to ask questions, not to oblige or manage her in any way. I echoed what she said back to her. And, if I did this for long enough, if I was entirely neutral, then she might come close to the surface of herself. I would catch a glimmer of the person I knew. Most of the time, she was – I don't know how to explain it – only incidentally my mother. But if I got that little glimpse, then I was, piercingly, her child once more.

There were many Saturdays I got nowhere, and I learned to smile and let her be. She had to stay hidden for a while, I understood that. Things were so impossible for her now.

She was not herself. This is what she said to the orderlies, the nurses and the very occasional doctor.

'I am not myself, today.'

'Are you not yourself?'

'No, I am not myself, today.'

Or sometimes it was, 'I am not feeling myself today.'

Which produced the strange, slightly indecent-sounding, 'You're not feeling yourself today.'

'No.'

Or, in a final variation, 'I don't feel like myself, today.'

'You don't feel like yourself, today.'

And this last begged so many questions about who she did feel like (Napoleon, Garbo, Joan of Arc, Sister Mary Felicitas), it made me smile.

As the months passed, the catatonia and the sneering were replaced by her 'loving look'. This was a profoundly adoring gaze that spooked the hell out of me, and made me sad. She shook her head in wonder at the wonder of me. Everything I did and said was precious. It made her so lonely, the fact that no one else saw how marvellous I was. Her only daughter. Who was. And here she stalled. Who was.

Something had happened to her daughter, she leaned in to whisper it. She was the sweetest girl.

'It was a man,' she said. A man had stolen her. He had taken her only delight and her best thing.

I came back home at the end of these unspeakable days to Kitty, who sighed and slapped about the house in her old leather slippers. She failed to buy toilet paper, cooked lamb chops to a crisp and managed to be irritating in a way that was, in the circumstances, altogether heroic.

WHEN I GOT home from my pilgrimage to my mother's birthplace in Herne Hill, I decided to take one of her rings down to the jeweller's – something I had put off doing for years. I had worn the ring faithfully after she died, but when the children came, my fingers swelled so much I had to use soap to prise it off. Then I did nothing. I suppose I imagined my hands would change back again, that they would become once more slender and young, but I gave in, after Herne Hill, to Time's obdurate thickening and I decided to get the thing sized up, once and for all.

The ring was a last remnant of her Hollywood days. She liked to call it her black emerald, and maybe that is what it was. The stone was dark green with three baguette-cut diamonds on either shoulder and I loved to trace the facets with my fingertip as she sat by the fire. It was a kind of fascination: being jealous of the ring, wanting the ring, wanting to hear her say, 'Some day it will be yours.'

Not wanting her to die.

I had put the ring away somewhere safe, but I could not picture where it was, exactly. It wasn't in the obvious places:

the bedside locker, or the jewellery case I keep on the chest of drawers. It wasn't in the box at the back of the sideboard or among the bags and suitcases under the stairs. I went into Max's room and checked his drawers for no possible reason, finding along the way a single balled-up football sock, many years unwashed, three derelict phones, a favourite old T-shirt at least six sizes too small, that I held to my cheek for a moment. A plastic axe. I took a photo and sent it with the word:

–Bin?

It took a moment.

–Axe, he texted back.

This was followed, a few minutes later, by a picture of a bat, a little flying cartoon in pink and grey.

–When home? I say, and there is no reply.

Pamela is away on rotation in Waterford hospital. Her room is, as ever, pristine. I always feel a little guilty in here. As though I might be found out.

Were you in my room?

I searched it silently and with great precision, convincing myself as I went that she had taken the ring, of course she had – the same way she used to take my nail scissors, or tape measure, or hall door key. Actually both of them were addicted, as children, to things that were vital and very small. There was a spark of fury as I remembered all this – a single shoelace from their father's dress shoes, the necessary cable, the gizmo that plugged into the gadget. 'I am just,' she would say. 'I am just going …' off on some dreamy mission to disaster. I used to think it was the catastrophe they wanted – that ruckus when you try to leave the house and find some child has undone the path that leads to the front door.

But, *Maybe they just wanted to keep us at home*, I thought now as I opened Pamela's wardrobe, scooped a hand uselessly into one after another of her coat pockets, all empty, except for a camera card I take out and put safely on a shelf, wondering what pictures it contains.

I have an office space in the attic loft with a Velux window and a view of sky and of passing birds, but it gets warm up under the roof and there are too many papers, so sometimes I sneak in here to work instead. It feels slightly criminal. Pamela's is the most ordered room in the house, with a cool north-facing light. I like to think of her growing up in here, with infinite slowness, filling the length of the bed.

There must have been a day when she stopped taking my stuff. Some ordinary Saturday when she used my eye pencil and put it back again in my make-up bag. When she was out of the trance of childhood and her adult self came good. My beautiful girl. She had not taken the ring because this is something she would never do.

Nice as this was, to sit on her bed and think about how well she had turned out, and then to text her:
–Yibble
–Bib
I knew it would bring me no further on.
–Where grandmothers ring???
–<Eye roll emoji>
–Seriously.
–<Heart emoji> <Heart emoji>
This made me miss her so much I had to sit on the bed, to let my love for her settle back down.

The children's rooms ransacked, I decided to go through the house in an orderly fashion; back to front, top to bottom. But it was impossible to stay in one place, seized and distracted as I was by sudden convictions: it must be here, it must be here. Some places were rifled many times over, not because the ring was there but because it clearly and unbelievably was not there. The bedside locker for the fifth time, all the underwear taken out of the underwear drawer. It was not in the sideboard, it was not in a forgotten china cup, it was not in that damn suitcase under the stairs.

I had hidden it. I had lost my mother's ring by making sure I would never lose my mother's ring. So I was angry now, not at the ring but at my own stupidity, the fact that I was losing my marbles along with everything else. And suddenly I was raging against all the losses I had ever suffered or endured and all the losses lurking up ahead. I emptied out a pair of boots from the bottom of my wardrobe, felt desperately along the tops of books on the shelves, pulled some out. I scattered my life all over the floor.

It was gone. Up in our bedroom, I sat on the edge of the bed and put my head in my hands. If I could just stop looking, I knew, I might remember where it was. You must let the thing go, in order to find it.

First, you must mourn.

But I did not feel like mourning, I felt like kicking something. I decided to give up for a while, go down and make a cup of tea. On the way out of the room, I gave the bag on top of the wardrobe a resentful poke with a clenched wire clothes-hanger and, when it fell into my arms, there was an old tin inside it. And rattling inside the tin were four safety pins.

I shouted your name, but you were not yet home.

IN THE YEAR before she died, my mother donated some papers to the National Library. When I went there to enquire, I was told they had three boxes of ephemera, mostly theatre programmes and posters, but also also a script of *Mulligan's Holy War* marked up for production in the hand of Laslo Molnár. I ordered it up and spent a sad, ecstatic few days taking notes, turning it into information I might use.

I rang seven different church and state institutions looking for Des Folan. I was told by one that he was in Buenos Aires now, another said Ecuador. I suffered a recurring dream of a storage unit – a box-room with a roll-up shutter that contained my mother's 'performance', whatever that might mean. This room also contained her stuff. The pair of white kid gloves signed by Charles Laughton. A chair Alec Guinness liked to sit in, whenever he was in town. Her awards! Big lumps of glass or metal, heavy and often pointed, one of them so vicious we put it out in the shed for fear someone might get themselves impaled. In the dream, these things were not lost, I had just forgotten where they were. And one night, sitting in the corner (I am embarrassed to say) was Kitty, her duster in her hand.

I woke to the sad truth that we had cleared the house in such a hurry, I hardly remember doing it. There was no storage unit. We packed it all up or threw it out. We distributed some bits and sold others for so little, it was barely worth the price of the van. And Kitty was also long gone. She had been dead for fifteen years.

I met a Frenchman once who had lived in Dublin. He said, 'You Irish are so wonderful. We had a cleaning lady there who sang as she worked.'

'Really,' I said.

Kitty did not sing. Our Kitty sighed. She had a string of round plastic pearls, a Sunday dress of navy crêpe. She wore a housecoat of bright professional blue that swished nylon as she walked and her scent was a sweet, turpentine mix of rags, carbolic and sweat. When I was very small, I would climb into her lap at lunchtime, with the radio playing and her *Sacred Heart Messenger* on the tabletop. I played with the underhang of her jowls and the round, spongy mass of what was probably a goitre. At the time – I must have been very young – it was all about the big pearls that I tried to spin along their plastic seams. And when she put a defending hand to her neck, I wriggled and was set down.

Her full name was Kitty McGrane. A Dublin woman, she told me the same three stories about her childhood as though she did not deserve to have four. Her brothers were all married – a fact that was somehow mysterious to her – and her sisters lived together in a small house on Warren Street. When I was five or six, Kitty brought me up there on Saturday mornings, for showing off and biscuits. She also brought me to the public library and she brought me to Mass.

'I'm just bringing the child to Mass.' She would tap on my mother's door and put her head inside to discreetly mention some forgotten feast day, and off we went down to the huge church in Rathmines. Sometimes also to the library for a new book, then a bus back up to the canal because it was a long way to go for my short legs.

Kitty occasionally went to the theatre, but it was only to see Jimmy O'Dea who did comic turns and panto. She never, to our knowledge, saw my mother act. I think she would find such a thing slightly indecent.

Hughie Snell spread a rumour, once, that they shared the same bed.

After the house was sold, she moved in with her surviving sisters in Warren Street. I brought the babies to her there, for showing off and biscuits, and she sent a card every subsequent birthday with a five-euro note enclosed. But it wasn't an easy journey in from Bray and when she died, I felt very guilty. I thought I had been busy loving people, but of course I had also been busy running away.

The funeral was in Rathmines. The church was still vast, and it made the mourners seem very few. A pair of tiny old women – the last of Kitty's sisters – sat up front, and the descendants organised themselves behind. You could see the difference in height from one row to the next, a foot or more taller with each succeeding generation. The youngest were a clutch of rangy teenagers and there was a kind of fond embarrassment to the way they stooped over the old people outside the church, receiving instructions too vague or inconsequential to carry through.

I shook a few hands and worked my way in to the sisters, who wore differently styled coats in the same lilac-coloured polyester. They nodded and were delighted, and knew exactly who I was – it was so good to see everyone again. They took my hand with both frail hands, fidgeting the inside of my wrist with dry fingers, their faded irises gleaming. Such an ardent business, being alive.

I had Max with me that day, he must have been about three. He was not impressed by the funeral. He was, in fact, outraged by the whole business of mortality – surely it did not apply to *everyone*.

'Yes, everyone,' I said.

Max refused to believe me, which solved something for us both, I think. I took him on my hip and let him pull and pat the flesh of my face, 'Gently, now.' But he was already gentle. Max was born mild. Not that the labour was gentle, it was the opposite of gentle, but from the centre of that storm came an easy baby, who opened his eyes and considered me, in a way that was almost amused.

When I brought him to Warren Street, Kitty peeked into the baby carrier and put a hand to her chest.

'Well, that's a relief.' Then she looked up at me and said, 'It's Mr FitzMaurice all over again.'

Kitty was of a generation to believe in bad blood. Not my blood of course, she was tactful enough to think that malevolent DNA – as she assumed my father's to have been – was only ever expressed in the male line. Once I got over my affront, I saw that she was right. Max had my grandfather's eyes of periwinkle blue. He looked like Fitz: a man genetically incapable of doing harm.

So that is one thing that has not been lost, I suppose.

After I woke to find myself still bereft of a storage unit, I decided to look up Kitty's niece – the one who did the catering for my mother's salmon suppers in Dartmouth Square. I rang an address I thought was hers on Sweetmount Road and the call was answered by one of those rangy teenagers from the funeral; her son, Ned, now fully grown. He said she would love to see me. He also said there might be a couple of things in the attic, all right. He would go up to check.

I arrived the next Saturday afternoon, and he looked at me as though at some fictional character made manifest on his Mammy's front doorstep. Then he sorted himself out to say,

'Come in, come in. You'll say hello to Mam. Will you have a cup of tea?'

His mother was in the living room, sitting in a huge, orthopaedic armchair, with a drop in the right half of her face and a gleam in the other eye. There was a table beside her containing an open box of Milk Tray and she jabbed at them impatiently for me to partake. I went over to kiss her, though we had never been kissing friends.

'Hello, Detta.'

She was someone I liked very much.

Ned indicated a seat and took one himself. He was full of chat.

'I will always remember, I saw your mother one day by the tulip fountain in Stephen's Green. She shook my hand and I must have been about seven years old. I said to my own mother, didn't I, Mam? I said, "That is the most beautiful lady I have ever seen."'

I don't think there is a tulip fountain in St Stephen's Green, it is some other flower, but I didn't say this to Ned. People always remembered my mother in iconic or imagined places, as though she never went down an ordinary street. So it was the usual guff, but it sounded good, coming from him.

'I'll bring that down for you now.'

He left me with his mother.

'It's good to see you, Detta,' I said.

She indicated the chocolates again, with the same jabbing enthusiasm. I think she knew me, it was just my words she could not understand.

It was a good, sunny room. There was Waterford glass in a display sideboard that also held some family photographs, and a few pictures on the wall, two of them oils. I thought I recognised one of them from Dartmouth Square, and quickly looked away. It would be rude to check – unthinkable, really. I thought of the woman I loved as a child; the way Kitty ducked her head down as she crossed a room.

'You know, I still miss Kitty.'

And I looked at the carpet in a surge of self-pity, thinking there were times when I had no one, when I would have died, if it hadn't been for Kitty McGrane.

Ned had the things assembled in the hall; two suitcases, a large one made of soft blue vinyl and a small brown thing that looked like a prop in one of those films about evacuated children during the Second World War. But it was not a prop, it was real.

'Will I do the honours?' he said.

And it was with something like a flourish that he went down on one knee, to squeeze the metal catch on the little brown case and make it snap to. A cheap thing made of cardboard, the inside was printed in a gingham pattern, and there was a label in the middle of the lid that said, 'Made in England.' A bit like my mother, I thought, as I glanced at the contents: a silk flower on a safety pin, a large card that contained other smaller cards, nested into each other. There was an unlikely blue garter. I lifted a small collection of religious pictures; memorial cards of the Catholic dead. I shuffled through them, and then, in a row, there they all were: the Cassins and the McCormicks, Anna Manahan's poor husband Colm who died on the honeymoon that year in Egypt. One asked me to 'Pray for the soul of Niall Duggan.'

The Fucker.

I might. And then again, I might not bother.

'Oh my God,' I said.

I closed the lid and pressed the rusted catches home. I had started to cry and I felt Ned's pity as I did so, kneeling there in the hall. This is what remains. Magical objects with the magic gone out of them. A few cassettes and no tape machine on which they can be played.

AS SOON AS I get it home, I go through the personal debris in the little brown case. I find a couple of notebooks. One has 'Memoranda' in gold script on a pliable green cover and inside, in a schoolgirl's hand, 'Please return to Kitty FitzMaurice, c/o Pleasance McNamara, Bailey View, Howth.'

A diary.

I stroke the cool underside of the paper as I turn the pages, feeling the intimacy of my hand slipping between leaves that are about to be seen for the first time in many decades.

'Easter Monday, 1942'

But when it comes to the point of putting my eyes to the words, of letting those words make sense in my mind, I find it hard to do.

'I wore my Orange Beads of Bohemian Glass and played with Floss. I did not think of him at all.'

There is a difference, I discover, in the awe we feel at touching such objects and the effort it takes to absorb them. There is some mention of Pleasance, some mention of a boy she call 'T.M.' and a dog, I think, called 'Floss'. This book has exactly sixteen pages filled, and the rest are blank. On the last, she has written out a poem:

> 'The desire of the moth for the star,
> Of the night for the morrow,
> The devotion to something afar,
> From the sphere of our sorrow.'

She was fourteen years old. I have no idea why she saved this book from the wreckage of her life. She must have given it, quite carefully, to Kitty. Or Kitty may have taken it into safe keeping for some reason that is now lost. But the book is not lost. The book is still here.

The second notebook is black and expensive and it looks as though it should contain poetry, but it is in fact dense with notation that is hard to read. 'Sat 9th, noB, mlk x 120, grpft x1 26, L Dobbins, <u>wine</u>????' After a few pages, I realise Katherine was detailing her calorie intake for the day. This seems to consist of grapefruit, cups of tea and a long boozy lunch or dinner. Pages and pages of closely written lists detail her food, drink and calorie intake from the age of thirty-nine, with some breaks, to the age of forty-five when her weight is recorded at eight stone thirteen pounds. Everything she ate, every day for seven years – except for the uncountable calories in a bottle of red wine, clearly. And I never noticed her doing any of this.

How mad is that?

To cheer myself up, I turn to the blue suitcase which is light and full of clothes. The first I pull out is a great treasure: a cream kimono in thin silk – I think it is called pongée silk – with a design of chrysanthemums, in teal and apricot, thickening towards the hem. She loved this thing; I almost believe it belonged to my grandmother. There is a gala dress fumbled into a ball and, under this snarl of tulle and spangles, a fox-fur stole; an ordinary bit of Irish roadkill, looking unhappy. I always hated this guy. She used to wear him to the hairdresser's, to get her colour right. I drape it over the back of a chair, so he can bare those tiny dead teeth at the floor.

A yellowed pillowcase yields another fur, this time a hat: very soft and huge, it rises in the open air, like a fluffing cat. In the bowl of it is a slim rosewood box, with a clasp on the side – and this must be the relic of Padre Pio, I think, with some excitement, remembering the dot of blood behind its bubble of plastic, the serious words 'ex sanguine' intoned along the top. But when I open the box, I find a different kind of medal; a white enamel cross pinned to blue watermarked taffeta. On the facing side is a photograph of the soldier who won it, my mother's grandfather, Captain John FitzMaurice.

I have not seen this thing for sixty years.

Captain FitzMaurice was the most handsome man born. My great-grandfather had large, dark eyes, a lush moustache swagged about a playful mouth. In the photograph, his uniform is impeccable: round imperial collar, white piping, leather gloves slapped into his left hand. He is so careless and fine. The photographer's mark reads, *Fermoy, County Cork, 1899.*

Behind the photograph is a folded paper: 'Captain John FitzMaurice was mentioned in dispatches by Major-General R.A.P. Clements and posthumously awarded the DSO, the citation for which reads: 'For conspicuous gallantry and devotion to duty at the head of his platoon in an assault on the mountain pass called Slabberts Nek, and consolidation afterwards under a heavy barrage. When he came opposite an enemy artillery gun, he and another man dashed at it, killed two of the team, and captured the gun.'

Under this, in a woman's copperplate: 'He was seen to ascend the hill, although the air was full of molten lead, and walk as if he were out for an airing.'

Later, because I can not sleep, I drag the laptop into the bed and look up Slabbert's Nek on the internet and I find a bare settlement in the middle of nowhere in South Africa – a few buildings at an intersection of long straight roads that extend outwards into the veldt for hundreds of miles. I am astounded that this place exists, and that I can see it as soon as I type the name. I drag a little swinging figure down to street level and land at a crossroads where a woman is walking along a dirt road in heavy boots and a grey shift dress. She has a white sheet under her arm and carries a large furled umbrella in the other hand and she looks at the camera as it passes her by. The dress is possibly a maid's uniform, but it takes me a moment to realise this, as I tilt the angle up and look around for the mountain pass. Vast plains everywhere this woman looks, as she walks, unless she turns north towards Bethlehem where there are some peaks, sheer and impressive, a trek away.

That is where he fell.

The dirt is a dull mauve, the bare rock on the summits scoured to white – or perhaps it is snow. It seems a long way to go to die, at the age of twenty-five. I want to show you the place, but you are asleep beside me in the bed, eyelids trembling slightly with the idea of waking to the blue light of the screen.

The next morning, I go through the rest of the detritus in the little brown case – used airline tickets, a pink smallpox vaccination certificate, an Irish driver's licence (although she never, to my knowledge, took a test), along with other hopelessly faded official and semi-official pieces of paper.

What did she keep these for? Invitations to one function or another, a meagre bundle of fan letters; I also find two drafts for a note, sent in 1951 from the Brentwood address:

'Thank you for dinner last night. Yes, I am ~~tough~~. Yes, I am a little fox,' 'Just a little note to thank you for dinner last night. I had a   I woke this morning bright eyed and bushy tailed, Your little Irish ~~vixen~~ fox.'

I look at these for a long time. They were sent – or not sent – the year before I was born. I wonder if the note was to a lover, perhaps even to my father, the ghost in my blood – a man who might have been any man at all, though he was not any man, he was a very specific man, I am sure. He is the person, I realise, that I am scrabbling through these papers for.

One afternoon at the hospital, she said, 'There isn't a thing of him in you. Except maybe your little ears.'

The comment came out of nowhere. I resisted the temptation to touch my small ears. I took my chance.

'Does he have a name?' I said.

'No.'

'No?'

'No, he does not have a name,' she said.

'Everyone has a name, Mama.'

She spread her hand in front of her face and spat into it. Then she slapped the palm on the tabletop and drew slow circles, as though erasing something there.

'No. Name.'

'No?'

'Doesn't deserve one,' she said, in a sane kind of voice, and when she looked up at me, her eyes were a bright, phlegm-green.

Something rose in me as I gazed back at her; the idea that I was, at times, a very cool individual. It occurred to me that I was watching her in a way not dissimilar to the way he might have watched her, this father man. I was watching her, or he was watching her, from a very calm place.

Perhaps the man was not just in my little lobe-free ears. Perhaps the man was in my thinking, he was in the wiring of my brain. I had a mind of glass, I wanted to tell her. And this was not a good thing or a bad thing – it was just something that kept me from harm.

Her insanity was rattling away, that day, like the lid of a boiling pot. But her syntax was good, she was making connections, and I was buoyed by that. I felt it was a good sign. When I went back the next week, I found her damped down again, stoned, gone.

When there is nothing else to be done, I go up into my office under the roof and crawl though a hatch into the attic proper, where I poke among the boxes to find the one that contains her manuscripts. These were, sadly, not accepted by the National Archive, and I could neither throw them out nor look at them, after she died. I have avoided these pages for decades; yellowed photocopies of *Copper Alley*, her play about the murdering madame Dorcas Kelly, with the staples rusting in the corner; three different versions of her Asenath Nicholson play, and no telling which version is better than another. Dead ends. Countless drafts. I always found my mother's writing unbearable. I wrestle the box down to the living room, because I can not be alone with these pages, and I start the business of going through it all, dust in my nostrils and some ancient, non-specific grease coating my hands.

This is where you find me, weeping, some time later, when I am no further on.

'Just leave it,' you say.

But I can't leave it. I go back to it every day. I read and I file and I take notes. There are mad things hidden here. Inserted between the pages are index cards, the lettering spiked and erratic.

'his yellow teeth laughing at me'

'bricks of babyshit yellow'

This is her psychotic handwriting. I recognise it from the time before the medication kicked in, when every line was pushed to the margins, or slopped unheeded over the side of the page.

'He does not feel heat or cold as I used to do'

'those vagina paintings that are in fact cathedrals'

But there are also production notes that are sane and almost interesting. One little spiral notebook, titled *Mother Courage*, contains jottings about the Thirty Years War, notes on Lotte Lenya and on dental hygiene, back in the seventeenth century. 'Mother C does not walk upright. She <u>leans</u> into it, she is always pulling the wagon in her mind.' There is a wonderful set of drawings marked 'Tatyana' with no sign of who sketched them, a postcard of Seán O'Casey in an embroidered cap. There is also a French school copybook marked *La Bête*, bought in Lyon. This was when she worked, naked, wet and violated, with Bernard DuBois, an actor who turned out to be a thug in real life too. And actually, the director, Aleksy Wójcik's, career also fizzled out in controversy, when he took his aesthetic of cruelty to the wrong part of America. Now, I wonder what working with these men was like, for her. And though she seemed, at the time, happy enough, the handwriting is not happy. The handwriting is entirely mad.

The copybook starts with a few ordinary pages detailing rehearsal times, followed by some jotted translations of stage terms from French into English. There is a clipping from a French magazine of a butcher's guide, showing, on a friendly cow, various joints of beef. I flick further along, flick back again. Then I walk slowly out to the kitchen, where you are waiting for the tea to brew. I say, 'Can you read something for me, would you mind?'

'In a minute.'

'Not in a minute. No. Not in a minute. Now.'

The writing is right to the edges, very disordered and large. She used a green marker and there are just a few words on each page.

when I was twenty-three years old

and an adult woman

I was

by a man called

and I

woke up with

I went away with

my baby my baby

because I wanted something to hold

He said that I had learned to be a good girl

He said I was a bad

He convinced me I

where do I go from here

I tried clenching my vagina shut, thinking I could just make it not exist there would not be an opening and he made his own opening he kept breaking through I still remember the blood crawling down my legs and my body shaking beyond my control I felt very cold

The worst part now is he laughs at me.

He was an important man. That's really funny. Pig.

He was so important making a movie that never got made. I THINK THAT'S FUNNY. Never made it off the cut cut cutting room floor.

Dead now anyway.

The first time it was in the restaurant and I wore my. I went to the restroom and IT at my neck. My body had a weakness. pushed my shoulders and I was crumpled me down so my knees were on tiles. It was a washroom. The attendant was not there. very sudden very sudden around my neck one hand pulling it one hand at his zipper THERE out pushed in stuck in again gagging and no air my lungs exploding. I saw the world for the last time the horrible toilet. dying-beingkilled.

I saw it from the ceiling

it was his belt around my neck very sudden and then MAN said, MAN said Help me out here, help me out and SAID Take this bit off please, Can you please do this for me? I was crawling around on the tiles coughing said Quiet. And was I don't know how he did it I must have helped. IT was When happened finished said God almighty, clean yourself up. I came out after and I sat down with my make-up nice The lady will have the ice cream, I think. put a hand on my back when we left

I went around my living room looking at everything. Then I went back in and I got my hat and gloves I went straight to Blessed Sacrament. I need to start this over again. I knelt in the church, feeling hot in my insides, warmth in my insides, it was a thickening warmth. I waited for the priest because I was frightened and I did not know what to do.

I need to start this over again. I was in the church of the Blessed Sacrament and it was a very low ebb in my life and I prayed so hard when I looked up I saw Our Saviour on a ray of gold. He came down and touched me. It was indescribable. I had love in the form of Our Saviour touch me just at the curve of my back. I was thinking of taking my own life at the time, it was such a low ebb. And His touch, I can't describe it. I felt His pity. I felt God's own and infinite pity. I looked up into the face of Our Saviour and I saw His tears. I have never stopped believing in God because He lifted me up. As soon as I said, 'Yes.' The moment I said, 'Yes,' He lifted me up. And when I say I saw Him on a ray of gold, it was like an old wooden sculpture painted gold, it was very solid, and Our Saviour's tears were real and wet. They were for me. He touched the curve of my back and I felt it move all through me. I was filled with melted gold.

WHEN MY MOTHER winged Boyd O'Neill – who was not a bad man, so far as I know – when all of this happened, I was with Mark, who was also not a bad man, and I was working on a magazine called *Irish Life* which did photo spreads on country houses, when we could get them, and articles about artisan pottery, or cheesemakers in West Cork, followed by pages and pages of social diary we called 'the frocks'. The magazine was understaffed but the result far from terrible. Most of the revenue came from advertising sales, which slowly slid away from us to more contemporary, shiny publications. We lost a respectable amount per month and the paper died very slowly, like one of those slightly uncomfortable and finally boiled frogs.

And although I lived at home, I was on my way in life. I had a proper job, which turned out to be the wrong job, and a decent man, who turned out to be the wrong man – if there is such a thing.

And I might have continued in all that, I might have remained cheerful, sane, loyal – what Duggan liked to call 'suburban' – for the rest of my days. Of course when Duggan said 'suburban' he meant 'female' and 'fake'; some woman in an apron, because all women are hypocrites when they make apple pie.

But I thought it was better to be nice than horrible – I mean, if there is no point to any of it. And I have no problem with pie.

I nearly bought a house with Mark – the prices were so low back then. I pass it sometimes, a handsome red brick I could not now, in three lifetimes, afford, and I think I should have married him instead, *Maybe it would have been worth it*. There was nothing wrong with Mark.

But she smashed it up. When she walked up the narrow stairs to Boyd's office and lifted the gun.

I might have had his children, I really would have had Mark's children, if my mother had not ridden in there, wielding chaos and destruction. I might have had two, at least, children by Mark O'Donoghue, when I was Mrs Mark O'Donoghue. I would look at them and be taken by how inevitable and right they were.

(Actually the thing about Mark was how athletic he was in bed, it was like sleeping with a football player while he was playing football. He looked so splendid you could put up with it all day, really. Though he didn't exactly make you come. But I digress. Or maybe I don't digress, maybe that was my point, all along.)

My mother walked up to Boyd O'Neill and she demanded her script back. This is what she said, apparently, before the gun discharged, she said, 'Give me back my Copper Alley!' and the life I had planned veered away from me. Three months later the ulcer I was ignoring decided to perforate and I spent many weeks in hospital, recovering from peritonitis. Mark sat by my bed. He had not expected any of this but he was doing his best. He brought in my toiletries. He kept forgetting my hairbrush. He took my nightclothes home to be washed.

He loved me, he said.

But I did not think he loved me, I thought he was just doing the right thing.

There are moments from that time I turn over in my mind, but I find it hard to remember the order in which they happened. The sequence doesn't make sense to me, and the things that do make sense are hard to share.

I woke one afternoon to see an elderly woman curled on the next bed. She was facing away from me and the blue hospital blanket was pushed down to her waist. Her gown was split open so I could see, gathered along her lower spine, a badly puckered seam of flesh, long healed. She lay there unmoving as I watched over her – and perhaps it was the morphine because everything about her seemed marvellous and sad; the thin white skin that had never seen the sun, the groove at the top of her backside silvered like abalone or the nacre of some other shell. And this did not seem an odd thought to have, about the beauty of her clefted lower back, as I guarded her silently, all afternoon. She was awake. At one point, she fumbled about with the blanket, throwing it back across her, and I waited to see if her legs would move as she did this, but her legs did not move. The nails on her hand, I saw, were painted firebox-red.

Or the next woman, wheezy and loquacious, whose face shifted about when she spoke, as though she was gobbling soft food. And there was something wrong about this food, it was the wrong kind of mush in her mouth – tapioca pudding with no sugar, or yoghurt that was unexpectedly plain, her tongue kept pushing it away. A husband and children sat around this big baba each evening, anxious to please, and she was never pleased, nothing was right. One morning she left, and her place was taken by a young woman, almost a girl, who sat upright all afternoon, as though she had just realised something, and it really was time to go.

All of this made distant by the pain; the sound of rubber wheels on a rubber floor, the slither of metal clipboards pulled away from the end of the bed. Mark came in every day at seven o'clock and said, 'How are you?', dragging the hospital armchair in under him as he sat down. And I would say, 'You see that woman over there? No, don't *look.*'

Later, then, there was the night to get through. There was no avoiding it. Each time I woke, someone else was turning between strange sheets, eyes open to the dark.

I am a loyal person, as I think I already said, and I would have stayed loyal to Mark and to the future we had agreed upon, but over the course of those days and long nights, some version of myself dried, cracked, fell to the floor. I stepped out of it, like a woman stepping out of a dress. I walked away from my appointed life, naked, freshly peeled. Back to you.

Well, not straight back. It took a while, as you know.

THE CASE TOOK nearly a year to come to court and it lasted just three days. There was no doubt that she shot Boyd, as his secretary Mary Bohan tearfully testified, there was no doubt that she was bonkers, as they all lined up to say; Martin Rice, a lovely man who said, on behalf of the defence, that she was as mad as a plant, Melody Ffrench, an equally nice woman, who said she was very mad indeed.

Father Des was called on the first day of evidence. His white hair was backlit and blazing as he walked up to take the stand and he did the bible thing so intimately, it was hard to watch. When he turned to face the room, I felt oddly hopeful. I think I expected him to say what was wrong with her, we would hear all her reasons and extenuations, we would finally learn the truth.

Des Folan agreed that yes, he had been seeing my mother in his capacity as psychoanalyst for twelve years. He said she had not consented to the release of her counselling notes to the court, but they had been seen by the forensic psychiatrists who were giving evidence on both sides.

He remained, as he said this, his usual smooth faced self.

The barrister said, 'Thank you, Father Folan, that is all.'

I looked over to my mother and found her racked, her beauty all undone.

As he stepped down, Des Folan held on to the edge of the box a moment. He turned to face her in the dock and inclined his young, white head.

She did not listen to anyone else, I think. For the rest of the trial she looked down at her hands, which were tightly clasped, or she glowered up from under her eyebrows, like a shrivelled, sad little girl.

Dr Tim Ryan, GP, said my mother had been on a low dose of lithium since the spring of 1977, when he had also prescribed an MAOI tricyclic anti-depressant, as well as Valium, a sleeping pill she had been taking for many years. He kept this prescription renewed for that purpose. After six months the antidepressant dosage was gradually lowered, and this was followed, at twelve months, by a lowering in her antipsychotic to a maintenance dose. She was a reluctant patient. She claimed the lithium interfered with her ability to work as an actress and that it made her gain weight. It is not impossible that she came off her medication suddenly, against medical advice, and that she suffered a rebound psychotic episode as a result. This was a well-known side effect of abandoning the drug, which had to be tapered with care.

The arresting officer said she was mild and quiet when he brought her down to the station but that the answers she provided were off-kilter. She stated herself to be a member of the IRA and would not acknowledge the jurisdiction. She would only provide answers in the Irish language, he said, but the language that came out of her was not Irish, though she had the feel of it all right. He was from Gweedore himself, he said, which anyone would tell you was the hardest Irish in the world to understand, and hers was nothing like, it was gibberish, though it was also very good gibberish, you might say. She continued to speak this pretend language for two hours, interspersed with some phrases and slogans used by Republican elements. Any attempt to speak to her in proper Irish was met with 'a strong silence', he said.

Boyd O'Neill said my mother had sent him a manuscript of some kind, some three months before the incident. This was an historical piece about a murdering prostitute called Dorcas Kelly and she was interested in turning it into a film, one in which she might also perform. These were not, in any way, realistic expectations. The 'script' was one of the many ideas that crossed his desk in any given month and he passed it on to an experienced writer to develop, with some money from European funds. There was never any question that Katherine O'Dell should write it for the screen. Mrs O'Dell may not have understood the process, but what she also did not understand, he said, through gritted teeth, was that this film would never get made, no matter who wrote it, and if it was made, which it would not be, she would not be the star, nor even the star's mother, because she was too old for either role. Also her name meant nothing, unfortunately, when it came to the business of raising funds, not any more.

All he was doing, he said. All he was *doing*, with my mother's idea, or synopsis, or whatever it was she had sent to him, was bouncing the ball. It was a way to keep his connections interested until the right idea came along.

The thing she wrote was terrible, by the way. It was, moreover, based on the historical character of Dorcas Kelly, whose life was in the public domain. And sometimes, yes, these things had a life of their own. Sometimes, to every-one's surprise, the damn film got made. Because of course, on some level, you were just throwing spaghetti against the wall, to see which strand would stick.

But a good idea has many fathers, he said. There is a great difference between an international feature film and an idea sketched out on a beer mat in a bar.

Boyd seemed genuinely puzzled. It was as though he could not quite hear what he was saying, so he had to keep saying it over again. He really thought he was doing my mother's idea a favour by having it himself. When you see this happen, as I did that day, you see it quite a lot, and it remains a very strange thing – the ability of a man like Boyd to assume that it is their interest which makes something interesting. As though, if he shut his eyes, the world would be really dull.

Anyway, she shot him for it. There was always that to consider.

After what was generally seen as an arrogant deposition, Boyd stood to leave the box. He fumbled his crutches and took his time, and this difficulty seemed to afford him some satisfaction. I remembered the man leaning against our living-room wall, looking at people as though he thought very little of them. Now, it seemed, he thought very little of himself. I wondered if he had taunted my mother in some way, if he had enjoyed condescending to her. Probably, he had.

As for the script: my mother was a clumsy writer, and that was the truth of it. Lord knows what Boyd would have done with the story of Dorcas Kelly, the serial murdering brothel madame of the 1750s. In those days, the past was all cleavage and foaming tankards; a few years later, everything looked like Vermeer. I sometimes wonder in which direction he would have taken it – the wrong way, at a guess, Boyd was more or less good on repression, but sex itself was not his thing.

Katherine O'Dell was not asked to take the stand so it was impossible to know what her intentions had been. The gun was an army-issue pistol from the 1950s, there was no identifiable link between it and any terrorist organisation. Hughie Snell said, later, it came from the old Pike Theatre, where the director, Alan Simpson, was an officer in the army reserve. It had been in Dartmouth Square for years.

My mother told me she shot Boyd because he stole her offering. She said this in Nerja, a little town in the South of Spain, where we went for an off-season fortnight the year after her release. It was an interesting word, I thought.

'Your offering?'

'I wanted to give it to him and he stole it anyway.'

Then she said she shot him because he was such a bore.

A COUPLE OF weeks ago, I got a beautiful piece of spam
– I mean, as pieces of spam go. It was addressed to a woman
called Honey Schwall, and I should not have opened it,
because I am certainly not called Honey Schwall, but there
were no attachments so I took the chance and clicked. It
was a piece of text. It read:

'and rough-voiced, deep-chested hymning of the fish-
erman congregation. Far ahead we saw the strait full
of ice. Not that the ice itself could be seen; but the
peculiar, blue-white, vertical striae, which stuccoed
the sky far along the horizon, told experienced eyes
that ice was there. Away to the right towered the long
heights of Newfoundland, intensely ...'

That was all.
That was enough.
Newfoundland, intensely *what*?
A small amount of searching told me it came from a
piece, published in the *Atlantic Monthly* in 1865, that
was called '*Ice and Esquimaux*'. The long heights of

Newfoundland were, in fact, 'intensely blue, save where, over large spaces, they shone white with snow'. This far sighting of ice spoke so directly to me, I could not shake the sense that these words were not randomly sent, but intended for me alone. Or for us. I had always wanted to go to Newfoundland.

I found myself looking up flights to St John's, until I remembered that we couldn't afford it. I went up to the bedroom, where you were reading in bed, with your whiskey beside you. A measured amount of Jameson – just exactly too much.

'You all right?'

'Fine.'

And I got in beside you, because it was so damn cold.

I can't remember when you sent me the postcard from London. My mother was in an asylum, waiting to stand trial, Kitty was more or less living with her niece, who had small babies out in Sweetmount Road. I was living alone. You sent me a postcard with a picture of Charles and Diana on the front of it and there was no mention of my mother in the message on the back, though she was, at the time, internationally notorious. The photograph was taken during the couple's engagement – Diana was wearing a pink Peruvian sweater and was blushing to match. On the back, you had written, 'God help us all.'

It must have been sometime in the spring of 1981. There would be a lot of fuss, later that summer, about the royal wedding, though really I had other things on my mind. It was typical of you – and very annoying I thought – to pick up a conversation we had never actually started, also to act as though nothing was wrong in my life.

'This is my new place,' you wrote (I had never known the old one), and you listed your address.

I went over some months after the trial was done. I was about to leave my job, but I did not know that yet, and nothing about that first meeting would tell me it might be a good idea. I took the boat train and we arranged to meet in a pub not far from Euston Station. I sat between the jukebox and the cigarette machine, looking at the yellow-brown carpet and glancing up each time the door opened. And, as one man after another walked through it, I wondered, very vividly, if this was someone I had slept with once. Anything was possible. I had no idea what you looked like now.

And indeed, you arrived as a different version of yourself: all gymed up, with gel in your hair. You were working in the City, you said, though it really was not the City, it was a printing business with a lot of blather and back-slapping, not to mention long nights in the pub, and I thought it was killing you.

You had moved from sideburns and socialism, to a man in a linen suit who insisted that London property was completely overpriced, the growth could not be sustained.

I kissed you, anyway. The inside of your mouth tasted the same.

We went back to your flat in Camden, two people with crap lives and each other to cling to, for one night at least, though in our case, it always seems to turn into eleven thousand and thirty-nine.

Later that year, you came to Dublin to see your family and stayed the night with me in Dartmouth Square. We kissed in the hall and on the stairs of that sad house. We could neither stop nor start. You stayed on, just for a while. You sort of moved in. We lived like orphans, until my mother died.

Later, in our big, old flat, we tried for a baby, and failed for a baby. We could not decide where to buy a house, then we bought at the wrong time. Or it seemed like the wrong time – now it seems like half nothing. But the property conversation should have been an indicator of other shifts and uncertainties to come. We never made up our minds about anything, I think. Except each other.

Coming back to Dublin was the right move but it made you feel a failure and you blamed me for that (you loved me, anyway). We fought a lot. Money always got you so fussed. You found it hard to have a mere job – even when I was pregnant – you always had to have a big theory about it.

I loved you, anyway.

After a long and provocative discussion about, for example, the future of international currency exchange, you decided to apply to the libraries. And for the next fifteen years you dressed as a librarian in a casual jacket and cords; coming home every day to a bigger music collection, a plan for a table quiz, a stack of bills, and a baby, about whose fine motor skills you also had a large opinion. Coming home to a growing daughter. A son. Coming home to two teenagers.

You were often late.

(I loved you, anyway.)

At forty-seven years of age, in spite of all my loving, you decided that you were old. You took up running and looked terrific again – in a way I had never expected. You looked like a different man. When Pamela left school, you decided to sell up and move to Italy, you planned this with some urgency. You were sick, suddenly – just a couple of years ago – and now here you are, healthy again. Every couple of years, you grow a bit of beard, and then you shave it off and get a buzzcut instead, you do not like the way it comes out grey.

I loved the beard. I loved the buzz cut. I loved the running man, the talking man, I loved your blather. Or I loved you, despite your blather. I was the constant one.

245

My job was to hold you, whoever you were being that day, and tell you that you would not die if, for a moment, you stayed still.

Now that you are nearly old, you read at night with a whiskey by the bed, and some nights, I climb in there a little early, to check who you are today. The thing is, I want to say, as I reach over and take away the book. The thing is, that I change too. Not just my body, which has, let's face it, gone to pot ('What? Never,' you say), two children, forty years on. I change all the time. It is just that I don't know what I am changing from. You were always so sure of yourself.

The only constant is this pivot, the crux where we join, me around you inside me. Your body, slightly more upholstered now, but still an excellent fit. It is always surprising, the way sex insists on the fact of the other person, the way it spins off somewhere else and then comes back again. And I remember, as we do just that, all the times we forgot as soon as they were done, the rooms and beds, the different bodies we have had, all our various and uncertain selves, joining here.

MY MOTHER TOLD me, once, that trees grow from the inside. We were in the park in Dartmouth Square. There was a rug on the grass, sandwiches, a flask of tea. I was enormously happy. She laid her hand on the smocking of my American cotton dress – I must have been about seven – and she said, 'If you think about it, the youngest part of the tree is in the very middle. It is the little dot that will widen into a ring, next year. The youngest part of any tree is the heart.'

HOLLY DEVANE HAS written to me to say she has decided my mother was a great Irish feminist. She was a great Irish disaster, I want to tell Holly. She was a great piece of anguish, madness and sorrow. And by the way, she was not Irish at all.

This interpretation is, besides, very unfair to Boyd O'Neill. He did, it might be argued, what men often do, and she responded the way women almost never respond. She turned him into a fantasy and then she attacked this fantasy, and this was very wrong because Boyd was a real person, made of flesh and blood. Or she took an old hurt and confused it with a new one (a theme I do not elaborate, to Holly Devane). She blamed him for everything, when he did just one thing, and even that was small.

Holly writes back to say that every man who kills a woman, or insults a woman, or defiles a woman, is attacking some fantasised version of a woman he has in his head. That is what men do.

Which I find so depressing. What about the ones they love? I want to ask. Or is that still allowed?

Dear Holly Devane,

I have written five novels since my mother died and they are still described as 'written by the daughter of Katherine O'Dell'. I can't complain, this is only true. They sit on a shelf in my study, five neat volumes about life and love. There is a lot of sky (I love a good sky) and an amount of water (I am addicted to large stretches of water). The characters are slightly nondescript. They rarely have sex and they certainly do not attack each other. They just realise things and feel a little sad.

I sit and I type. The days are dull enough, but the years are not dull, and the decades are a wonder. I have been so lucky in this writer's life. How did I get away with it? It feels, in its way, almost like a crime.

Bealtra in the Summer, The Realignment, Of Wood and Stone. My books have become, over the years, more simple and unassuming. I hear them each as a fading note (together they make a kind of chord), and this note, which is so fugitive and beautiful, is in my head – or it is nearly in my head – as I write them down.

People like them, even though they are not true. They are the lie I need to tell, *nothing happened, oh look! nothing happened again, there is nothing to see here, ladies and gentlemen, keep moving along.*

Each of these sane and lovely falsehoods is dedicated to my muse and my difficulty, Katherine O'Dell.

Hi, Ma.

But, you know, I am writing to you on my laptop, while sitting in my daughter's bed. I am actually sitting under her duvet, because it is so cold. We don't have enough money to heat the house all the way through and, as you know, it is not a big house. I should write a book about that, don't you think? That's much more real. The question of who is to blame for the cold.

At the moment, you blame your parents for things that go wrong. If you are lucky, you will find an intimate partner to blame instead. My husband blames me and I blame him and this arrangement has kept us both happy for a very long time.

Two years ago, he went to the doctor with a pain in his neck, which turned out to be a problem with his thyroid and I did not know who to blame for this. I heard the word 'butterfly' many times. I heard it more than the word 'cancer' which was very seldom used, except by the top doctor, who used it a lot. (I actually did blame this doctor, quite intensely, for a while.) Anyway, they took it away. They took away his butterfly and bow-tie, the spatchcocked gland splayed around his windpipe and all the cancer, which is now gone. So he is not going to die, any more. Until he does die. Because there are no exceptions to the final rule.

I don't blame him for anything now. Or not much.

All of this will, in some form, happen to you. You will wake some morning and pat yourself down. You will realise that you think too much and live too little and that most people, men and women both, are mostly fine. You will love more easily and relinquish blame. At least I hope you will.

With all best wishes

Norah FitzMaurice

I don't send it, of course I don't. I think about my mother, raped. I think about my father, who did not deserve a name. And I do not know how I can quell, in myself, the rage, the rage, the rage.

KATHERINE NEVER FAILED to recognise me, in the years after she got out of the asylum, but she did not always call me by my name. And though we had conversations that sounded normal, this had never been my mother's conversational style. She had no plans to work again.

We moved out into our big old flat by the Pepper Canister church and she lived on in Dartmouth Square. The house was, if only I knew it, remortgaged to the hilt. But she would not consider moving and we thought it best to leave her in her habitual round: milk left on the doorstep, a turn around the little park. She had Kitty, who had come back from her niece's house and who seemed to be getting paid; the pair of them increasingly like the pair of old lesbians that Hughie Snell had imputed them to be. She lived on eggs, so far as I could tell, and alcohol.

She also funded my writing with small injections of cash, and I did not question where she got this money, or I did not question it enough.

One week she asked me to drive her into RTÉ, and in those days all I had was a horrible little Mazda. I rolled down the window, humiliated by the crank handle that wobbled and stuck, and I announced my mother's name to the man in the security hut. He repeated it, in what may have been a Polish accent, and ran his pen carefully down a list on his clipboard. He asked me to spell it one more time.

'Oh. Apostrophe. Capital Dee. Eee. Ell. Ell.'

Her voice from the passenger seat was like a tired child, singing the letters out in a jaded rise and fall. Beyond the barrier was the TV centre where she had performed the night the national network went live, the studio where she went on the *Late Late Show* after 'killing it' at the Gate Theatre, when people said she was drunk on air, though she blamed fatigue and refused to apologise for upsetting a glass of water into the lap of her host, Gay Byrne.

'Oh. Apostrophe. Capital Dee. Eee. Ell. Ell.'

She sang it louder, and turned away to look out her side of the car, as the security man continued to trawl down his list. He reached the end of the page, started again from the top, and I am not proud to say it, but the fact that he was not Irish annoyed me suddenly. She was not part of his cultural DNA. He did not wrap an imaginary shawl about himself to say, 'Sure, 'tis only butter,' when the going got silly. He had never dreamed about her, turning up in his family kitchen for a cup of tea.

So I uttered them, the fatal words. I flung them out the car window, to land at the man's feet.

'Don't you *know* who she is?'

He dipped to look at her under the roof of the car, a tiny human bundle, her body lost and indistinguishable under the layers of clothes.

'Not so much,' he said.

She rolled him a resentful, mad eye and, to be fair, I hardly knew her myself.

There was a row of tablets every morning on her plate. She was back on the lithium, an antidepressant, a small dose of Librium, a beta-blocker, Brufen for her joint pain, Tagamet to protect her stomach from the pharmaceutical bomb that was delivered three times a day, a stool-softener to get it all out the other end, and Krystexxa for suspected gout. It might have been worse – she lived in fear of the hospital cosh, whatever that was, and would not take any capsules that were yellow and red. And of course there were sleeping tablets at night.

I was used to it.

I was instantly used to it. It took me no time to adjust after she came home from hospital. And I don't know what I loved, as I tended her fragile bones, but I thought I loved my mother. Because she was always the same person for me, no matter what her appearance, or her mental state, and some people seemed to find that surprising.

I had no problem, is what I am saying, recognising my mother in this small creature, whatever the name listed on the security man's clip board. Even though, sometimes, I am not sure she recognised herself. Perhaps she did not want to. When she looked into the mirror, she just looked. There was no surge in concentration as she morphed into her public persona, and I missed it; that slight tightening of the iris, before it widened again with the pleasure of meeting her reflection.

Hello, you.

She turned towards the security guard who was still peering in at her. The light, bouncing off the car ceiling, made the skin under her eyes look blue and so thin, you could see a pulse trembling there. Grievance set her eyeballs gleaming. She looked him bang in the eye. She gave him a good view of the disaster that was once Katherine O'Dell.

'Do you know me now?' she said.

The man reared back from the car window and quickly found, or pretended to find, our names on his list. The barrier clicked up to let us through and when I checked the rear mirror he was knocking back his cap like a cartoon cop, scratching his head.

She said, 'There's a rabbit we buried under there. Not a rabbit, a hare.'

We were passing the broadcasting mast, a huge pylon that stood by the wall of the complex, rearing up from four steel-girdered feet. The transmitter was nearly four hundred feet high, it soared over south Dublin, the source of all TV.

I remembered some escapade – herself and Hughie Snell when the site was still under construction as late, perhaps, as 1968. The only security in those days was two Special Branch men who hung about the canteen, which meant you couldn't smoke marijuana in there, and all the producers quoted Gramsci and wore plaid slacks.

They were sitting in the sunshine outside this canteen, herself and Hughie Snell, smoking and running their lines, when they heard a horrible keening from the long grass over by the construction site. A real banshee wail. When my mother went over to find the source, a brightness of fresh blood led her along a parting in the grass and there, at the end of it, was a wounded hare. And this was a terrible thing to find, because the hare was always special, and killing one tremendous bad luck. The animal was shivering all over, its powerful hind legs kicked out in a spasm, and the eye that looked up at her from the dent in the grass was entirely human. That is how she described it. She said a dying dog knows it is a dog, and a cat doesn't care, but the hare was brown-eyed, like a person you once knew, and it was also pure wild. She got a hand in under it, and felt a wetness there. When she lifted the poor thing up, the guts were falling out of it, and she had to run away to find a rock. She came back and hit the little skull, hard – once, twice – and the hare looked right into her, as it went.

In those days, Hughie was a bit of a trickster and handsome as the day is long. He charmed a spade from some burly builder, he went right up to the man and flirted. And he was so outrageous he might have got his own head bashed in but instead the builder – who knows for what reason – decided to lend a hand. The three of them marched under the mast and dug a hole. They buried the hare bang in the middle of those four buttressing legs, so when you looked up, the lines of the pylon girders converged to a point in the sky.

I had always known this story. The thought of the hare came to me whenever the telly was switched on, this magical fellow, the speed of him, 'the hare under the moon' she called him, or 'that gurrier'.

I got her into the radio centre where the receptionist knew her on sight, picked up the phone and said, 'We have Miss O'Dell for you now.' We were brought downstairs and I waited on a clapped-out sofa in the corridor as she went into Studio 7. After a moment, the researcher beckoned me inside, and I went in to sit behind the sound desk, and watch through a glass window as my tiny mother settled big earphones on her dyed red head. She squinted purposefully at the sponge cover of the mike, and 'Close your eyes,' that is what I told myself. 'Close your eyes,' as I sat waiting for the light to switch red and for the clear, sane tones of my mother to sail free of her old, mad mouth, saying, 'Oh, good morning, yes, it is a beautiful morning, and thank you for having me', after which, all I had to do was lean my head back and feel it land on my upturned face in a happy rain: Katherine O'Dell remembers the glory days.

When they were done, the heavy sound-proofed door opened and the researcher brought her out to me. She was very tired. She was shut in again behind her face, focused on something unsayable, her mouth pulled tight. But I caught her eye, and she peeked back out at me from behind all her difficulty – a child who knows she has done well, or an old woman who is not yet dead. I said, 'You were marvellous,' and she said, 'Was I? Was that all right?'

As we were leaving the Radio Centre, one of the older presenters passed us in the foyer and came back on a double-take to make a great fuss of her, taking her hand in both of his, and even making a kind of bow, that managed to be both playful and heartfelt.

'The wonderful Katherine O'Dell,' he said. 'You won't remember me. I was one of the young men in *Easter Rising*, do you remember that thing?'

'Oh, I do.'

'You were just …'

'I wish I didn't.'

'… wonderful.'

'The frocks!'

'Anyway, I just wanted to tell everyone that I met you again. You won't remember me, but.'

'Of course I remember you,' she said. 'I listen to you all the time.'

'Stop it.'

'On the radio. I do.'

'Stop it. You'll make me nervous. Oh my goodness, Katherine O'Dell.'

And I stood back and let them at it. The pair of them nellying away.

I THOUGHT, WHEN my mother was dying, that it would be too difficult, that her body, which I had known and also avoided all my life, would become impossible in her last illness. I rolled her hollow pelvis towards me, put the disposable liner on the mattress behind her, then I rolled her back on to it. Another roll over and back to straighten it, and rip the sticky tabs off and fix it to the sheet. She groaned the whole time, but she was not angry with me.

I realised I was doing something unbearable, which was also very ordinary.

'Good woman,' I said as though she was someone I did not know.

We kept her as long as possible in Dartmouth Square with a minder morning and evening and the promise of a hospice nurse, when the time came. I did not know how much time was left, and I wanted to remember it all. The wallpaper upset her and I promised to paint her room, as soon as I could. She scattered the bedspread with paint cards, for bone white, linen white, sail white. I wanted to say, 'It is just white!' She looked and looked. She ran her thumb along one or the other, she asked for samples, and she did not forget she had asked for them, because the next day she asked for them again. I painted up some cards and set them about the room. She was at peak white, the moment when every choice you make is tiny and utter. Bone white or sail white? The way the sunlight falls on to the carpet, and shifts slowly through the room. What could be more important?

Meanwhile there was the business of her body to attend to. I was amazed by how light and loose the stuff on her bones was. Everything yielded and gave way. I had a new respect for joints – the way they held her together just when you felt the whole fandangle might drop apart.

None of it was pleasant, so I was surprised by the gratitude I felt. The fact that I loved her was important, as I mopped and sorted and soothed, but some people do this for strangers, and they do it well. I expected aversion and found simplicity. When I tried to put a word on it, I settled, in some surprise, on 'piety'. As I put cream on her legs, or lifted her out and on to the commode, or worse, I felt at peace.

Meanwhile, it was a kind of anguish to leave the room to make a cup of tea, fumbling the kettle, and quickly throwing a bag into the cup. It was almost impossible to go out to the chemist's for new supplies of gloves and wipes, another packet of those little sponge lollipops they use to wet the lips of the dying, her tongue so greedy for the relief of water that her stomach could no longer hold. The doctor said, 'How are we today?' as he bent over her, and when she opened her eyes they were fervent with the wish for another hour, another day. Katherine O'Dell was going nowhere. She was all there. She was absolutely herself.

The aftermath was much easier. When she was gone, and there was no one left for me to cling to. I was alone in the house when it happened. She took a longer gap between each breath, and one of these gaps went on for ever.

I sat for a long time beside her, with no thoughts to distract me. The silence in my own mind was complete.

Suddenly, I was starving. I stood up and walked out the door – and that was an amazing thing to do, for some reason. I went to the kitchen with a new lightness, because I could, for the first time in weeks, be away from her bedside. I could move from room to room. I told no one she was gone – I did not know what word to use – and I rang no one except the number the hospice had left for me. Katherine died on the Sunday evening of a bank holiday weekend and it took a long time for a doctor to arrive in order to certify the body. She lay there for many hours, in a beautiful silence. I know it was sad. Dead bodies are a horror, maybe, or an affront, but there was, in my mother's dear remains, a comfort for knowing she was not in them. She was not there.

A WORD IN PASSING about my mother at a funeral. She was a frequent attender and had a great grasp of the form. She would have appreciated the turnout, on a spring day, the church decorated with cherry blossom in a way that looked, as the luvvies remarked, 'positively Japanese'. Everyone wore black. There were disappointingly few children in the hall, but a whole choir of them in the loft, and they sang in Irish for her, she would have liked that. A lot of doctors showed up, a number of men from the legal profession, a couple of nurses from the Central Mental Hospital, but all walks of life, really, and she would have liked that, too. In those days, which was only 1986, Dublin still did the big funeral. People who did not know her personally came to pay their respects and to mourn my mother as their own. She did not mind belonging to people in that way, especially to Dublin people, and we gave them a good show.

A theatrical funeral is, above all things, brave. People dressed well and looked terrible. There was an enormous amount of weeping, none of which was fake. Actors spend their lives stalking and catching their fugitive sorrows. They do this in all generosity, because no one cries alone. An appeal for your tears is also an appeal for justice: it releases the healing power of the crowd. My mother had a wonderful send-off. It was nuanced, it was true. Every actor in Dublin was there and a few who flew in. They were not afraid to sit towards the front, or to sing the hymns.

'Fay-haith OF our Fa-ha-the-errs, HOL-y Faith.'

And the readings were so perfectly done, you would think they believed every word: Ecclesiastes, to every thing there is a season. Corinthians, through a glass, darkly. Matthew 5, do not hide your light under a bushel. Not if you can help it, dear.

If you think the Irish do a good funeral, it is never so good as an actors' farewell. There was a standing ovation as the box was carried down the aisle, inevitable of course, but always unexpected. Roses were thrown, lilies. I felt I should, on her behalf, kiss my hand to them all. 'Up! up! up!' as she used to say – Katherine O'Dell who, according to Father Des (he was on the altar, of course he was) made the audience believe in God.

A FEW DAYS ago, I found a cassette player on the kitchen counter. The thing was huge and grimy. It was made of dark grey plastic with big, clunky buttons, and I had to admit I was not happy seeing more rubbish coming into the house.

'Where did this come from?' Then I saw the cassette beside it: *Poems at Twilight, as read by Katherine O'Dell.* It was one of the tapes I had found in the little brown case. The machine was a gift: you must have sourced it for me somewhere online and its neat little maw was open, waiting for something to play. I put the rattling cassette in the slot and squeezed the window shut, but I didn't know if I could press the button. I was convinced the tape would stretch and snap, as they sometimes used to. I was afraid of what I might hear.

My mother's voice.

'Are you home?'

There was no reply.

I looked at the playlist: Yeats, Pearse, James Clarence Mangan; her photograph on the paper insert, yearning and noble. Big hair, an actual cloak with a Celtic pin. It was not her. It could never be her. It was just the wonder of her voice, trapped on a shiny brown ribbon and waiting to be free.

I popped the eject, so the tape would not start rolling, somehow, without me and I left the house, shoving the front door key beneath a rock in the garden. I closed the small front gate and walked down the road towards the prom.

I took nothing with me. Even though the weather was on the turn. This is the way I like to walk – with no phone, no keys, no bag, no money. I love the air in my empty pockets and the wind along my back. I would wear no socks, but I have a rule about such things. It is important to be fully dressed when you are out in the world. Not that I would ever forget. But I have a dangerous dream of divesting, one piece of clothing after another, as I cross the stony beach to meet the waves. This is not a suicide, it is a swim, I must make that much clear. Even so, if you could put a dream into a pill, this is the tablet I would take in my last days, one that as you sucked released the sense of the sea.

We love living in Bray. A small town outside Dublin, it is a Victorian resort with a permanent off-season charm. There are amusement arcades and a bandstand, seagulls looking for dropped ice-cream. The seafront attracts off-season people: those who work odd hours, or not at all, and there is something desperate and joyous about us, as we walk along the prom, leaning into the wind.

I turned south towards Bray Head, a worried-looking hill at the end of the beach, that spends much of the day humped over its own shadow. Bray is a morning town, facing east. I rarely see the head in full sunshine and today was no different, the brow of the hill was furrowed, the rocks a velvet brown, as though considering moss.

The sea was on my left. The railings that run along the promenade stretched in a line, regular and familiar, for half a mile. It was wild enough. I could see the rain in a slicing, vertical haze heading towards the shore, and the water was already choppy. A squall was coming. The waves were busy and blurred over by flying points of spray, under which the water was sometimes jade, sometimes the colour of the dark stone on my mother's ring. But exactly. The sea was the colour of a black emerald, it held the light so deep in itself. And this fact flooded me with the memory of the days she spent dying, when my mother was so essentially herself, I could not consider turning to leave the room.

I realised I was gripping the top of the railing and this seemed a foolish thing to be doing, at my age. It was such a long time ago. Besides, there was no message for me in the colour of the waves – of course not. My mother was not 'there' for me in the coming storm. She had not sent her consolation.

But I had, as I turned for home, a great sense of the world's generosity. Even though it was just my own hopefulness in another guise. Even though the sea was just the sea – which was quite enough, really. The sea was certainly sufficient.

Enough to be getting on with, I thought, as I lifted my face to meet the rain.

ACKNOWLEDGEMENTS

Anew McMaster is a real figure, though he did not have a daughter called Pleasance. It goes without saying that the key characters in this book are completely fictional and are based on no person living or dead – this is especially true of Niall Duggan, Boyd O'Neill and Katherine O'Dell.

Much of the love in the novel is owed to my friends in Irish theatre. Special thanks to Hilary Fannin and to Pom Boyd, two Dublin writers who have given accounts of their actress mothers: Pom in *Shame* at the Abbey Theatre and Hilary in her memoir *Hopscotch*.

The soldier who 'was seen to ascend the hill, although the air was full of molten lead, and walk as if he were out for an airing' was 2nd Lieutenant George Dennis, as described in a letter to his family, after he was killed in action at Wagon Hill, Ladysmith, on 6 January 1900.

Thanks are due to Paul Greene S.C., Claire Bracken, James Ryan, Kathy Strachan, and to the many Irish academics who did not flinch at my need for urgent conversation about obscure matters over a conference glass of white wine.

Thanks also to my agent Peter Straus, editor Robin Robertson, Julia Reidhead, Marion Kohler, Beth Humphries, Mary Chamberlain, the wonderful team at RCW and all at Jonathan Cape.